*"You want to get into my pants."*

"Repeatedly." Jacob grinned.

"You're talking about having an affair." Melanie stared at him, not sure what to think.

"Is what we've done together so far nice?"

She glanced down, picked at a knotted thread on her linen top. "I'm not sure I'd call it nice."

"Then call it not-so-nice. But not-so-nice in a way that it's so hot, so tight, so—" Jacob clenched one hand into a solid fist "—so genuinely real that even if you do go back to the way things were before, nothing will seem the same."

Melanie looked into his eyes, listened to his voice, loving every second of what he was making her feel. Never in her life had she felt this sort of connection that went far beyond anything she'd ever thought of as sexual. This, this…untamed sense of being ruled by her body instead of the mind, the intellect she'd cultivated all her life. What was wrong with her?

He wanted to continue what they'd started. He wanted to call it an affair.

She said the only thing she could, a very simple "Yes."

**Blaze™**

Dear Reader,

I've had such a great time with the women of gIRL-gEAR, creating their stories and getting to know these heroines along with the rest of you. After reading the first three stories in early 2002, many of you wrote to ask the fate of the remaining gIRLS: Melanie Craine, Kinsey Gray and Annabel "Poe" Lee. So let's get started.

In *Striptease*, we find techno-wiz Melanie Craine dealing with her worst nightmare—a man who challenges her need for order and control while being guilty of the very same thing. Sparks definitely fly—and not only from the video equipment! *Striptease* defines the concept of high-tech romance!

I hope the wait for Melanie's story has been worth it. And I hope meeting Jacob Faulkner has you pulling that videocam out of storage to explore all the possibilities it offers! I'd love to hear what you think of *Striptease*.

Visit me on the Web at AlisonKent.com or gIRL-gEAR.com! And stay tuned for Kinsey's story, *Wicked Games*, coming in October, followed by *Indiscreet*, Poe's story, in January.

Enjoy!

*Alison Kent*

## Books by Alison Kent

**HARLEQUIN BLAZE**
24—ALL TIED UP*
32—NO STRINGS ATTACHED*
40—BOUND TO HAPPEN*
68—THE SWEETEST TABOO**

**HARLEQUIN TEMPTATION**
594—CALL ME
623—THE HEARTBREAK KID
664—THE GRINCH MAKES GOOD
741—THE BADGE AND THE BABY
750—FOUR MEN & A LADY

*www.girl-gear...
**Men To Do!

# STRIPTEASE

*Alison Kent*

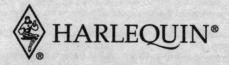

# HARLEQUIN®

TORONTO • NEW YORK • LONDON
AMSTERDAM • PARIS • SYDNEY • HAMBURG
STOCKHOLM • ATHENS • TOKYO • MILAN • MADRID
PRAGUE • WARSAW • BUDAPEST • AUCKLAND

ISBN 0-373-79103-8

STRIPTEASE

Visit us at www.eHarlequin.com

**Printed in U.S.A.**

For all the readers who continue to ask
after the rest of the gIRLS. This one's for you.

A big thank-you to Larissa Estell,
Jill Shalvis and Donna Kauffman for the daily whine fest.
That's what friends are for!

And to Jan Freed.
I owe you, bud, for fixing the parts I knew
were broken as much as for repairing what I couldn't see.
A girls' night at the movies to celebrate sounds like a plan!

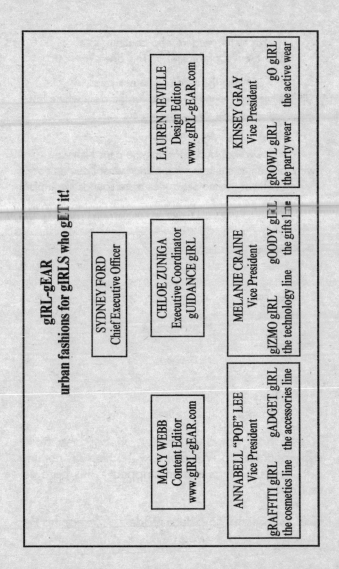

# gIRL-gEAR
## urban fashions for gIRLS who gET it!

**SYDNEY FORD**
Chief Executive Officer

**CHLOE ZUNIGA**
Executive Coordinator
gUIDANCE gIRL

**LAUREN NEVILLE**
Design Editor
www.gIRL-gEAR.com

**MACY WEBB**
Content Editor
www.gIRL-gEAR.com

**ANNABELL "POE" LEE**
Vice President

gRAFFITI gIRL   gADGET gIRL
the cosmetics line   the accessories line

**MELANIE CRAINE**
Vice President

gIZMO gIRL   gOODY gIRL
the technology line   the gifts line

**KINSEY GRAY**
Vice President

gROWL gIRL   gO gIRL
the party wear   the active wear

# The gIRLS of gIRL-gEAR
## by Samantha Venus for *Urban Attitude Magazine*

Samantha Venus, intrepid reporter, insatiable gossip, back at long last with news about our favorite fashion divas. They soon won't be only our hometown honeys, but national—dare I say international—treasures.

My favorite L.A. production company and my favorite television show hostess with more mostess than most, Ann Russell, will pry out secrets even my bloodhound nose has not been able to divine. And the prospect is just that. Divine.

Even better is this little tidbit Samantha has scooped for all you darlings. Ann and the gIRLS will be baring all, so to speak, for our local Avatare Productions' deliciously dishy videographer Jacob Faulkner.

This reporter, for one, can only hope for a bit of reciprocal baring. We all know that there is nothing quite as yummy as a man stripped to his bare essentials!

Until that blissful day, dear readers…Samantha Venus signing off for *Urban Attitude Magazine*.

# 1

MELANIE CRAINE ENTERED the sanctuary of the neighborhood church two blocks from the Hollisters' home. Three quick steps into the air-conditioned interior and she thudded to a stop.

"You've got to be kidding me," she muttered, knowing he wasn't kidding her at all.

What he was doing was ignoring every word of this morning's phone conversation during which she'd told him—yet again—where she wanted the cameras located for tonight's taping of Lauren and Anton's wedding.

Melanie jammed her pocket PC's stylus into its slot, then zipped the whole device into the pale yellow case at her waist. She was not about to let down the bride or the groom. Especially not after the honor of being asked to handle their wedding video details.

Setting her videographer on the straight and narrow had just become job one.

Her status as gIRL-gEAR's resident geek gave Melanie the inside scoop on the city's best in high-tech photographers and video firms. And Avatare Productions had been the obvious choice.

Or so she'd thought until she'd been stuck with the

company's hard-headed, opinionated and—yes, okay—
admittedly hunky crew chief.

No doubt about it.

Jacob Faulkner had been put on this earth to ruin
her life.

But she'd be damned if she'd let him ruin her day.

Marching down the aisle to the raised dais, she
stood on the first step, watching him tilt one of the
remote-controlled cameras he'd mounted on either end
of the choir box railing.

"Back up about three steps," he ordered her without looking up.

Melanie took three steps toward him instead. "What
are you doing?"

"The job I've been hired to do." Frowning at the
camera's LCD screen, he gestured to a point behind
where she stood. "Not forward. Back. About six
steps."

She shoved hands to hips and dug in her heels. She
*so* did not want to fight with this man. Not today. "I
thought we agreed the planter boxes were situated in
the best spot for filming the wedding party."

Jacob continued to check the LCD image. "You
suggested the planters." He shrugged. "I considered
the suggestion."

Obviously for about as long as it had taken him to
throw it away. She, on the other hand, had checked
out the angle at least a dozen times and knew she was
right. She tightened both hands into fists.

"Look, I know you're doing your job, but the bride
is one of my business partners and a very good friend.
She and the groom have put their trust in me to make
this work. I intend to see that it does."

"The very reason I'm here, sweetheart." Again he

waved her back before bending to check hidden wires and connections. "Six steps is all I need. Think of it as earning that trust."

Melanie pressed her lips together and held her tongue, an act that required more effort than she'd expected. Why were men so threatened by a strong woman's input, forget ever taking one's advice? No. They had to establish dominance and power and all other matters by penis size.

Frowning, Jacob straightened and resumed viewing the camera's display. "How tall are you?"

"Five-eight, but what my height has to do with anything—"

"Same as the bride. Heels look to be about the same, too. Once you're in place, I'll have a better idea of what I'm working with here."

Shoving a hand through hair that had to look like a mop by now, Melanie gritted her teeth. Compromises rubbed against her grain when it came to boys who thought they were the boss. But this wasn't about her. This was about Lauren.

So Melanie offered the only concession she was willing to make. "I know you can control the zoom remotely, but I'm worried the cameras are too far off center."

"They're not."

"So you say. I want to see exactly what you're seeing. Then I'll decide."

Blowing out an aggravated breath, Jacob glanced halfway in her direction. "Look. You've got control issues. That's cool. But could you save it for another guy? I'm not really into being whipped."

Melanie sputtered. Control issues? Whipped?

He straightened suddenly and met her eyes. "Hey, sorry. I shouldn't have said that."

Not "Hey, sorry, I didn't *mean* that." She crossed her arms and waited.

He gestured to his camera. "It's just that there's no way you can see what I'm seeing, even looking at the same view screen. We'd focus on different things."

"And how do you know that?"

"I've been at this for a lot of years. Time and experience have changed what I see, what I look for," he said. Then he added, "Besides, you're a girl. And I'm a guy—a very intuitive type, mind you, but still a guy."

"Intuitive. Really?"

"Really." He pressed his lips together in a cocky, bad boy sort of grin before adding, "Kind, considerate and sensitive, too."

She snorted.

He offered a modest shrug. "Hey, it's what all the women tell me."

*Bonehead.* "Right. You're not into being whipped."

Jacob's mouth quirked. A nice mouth, Melanie hated to notice. His burgeoning smile showed off great teeth and deep dimples, and hinted at a charming sense of humor. Just not enough of a hint to counter the black marks he'd racked up with his control issues remark.

Still…Lauren. *Think about Lauren.*

"Okay, here's an idea." Melanie uncrossed her arms. "Not an order, mind you. Simply a suggestion." She backed up three steps. "I'll stand in as the bride for you. You play the groom for me. How about it?"

"Hmm."

The unholy gleam in his eyes should've warned her.

"Sure *you* don't want to be the groom?" Jacob asked.

Melanie changed her mind. It was a smart mouth. A smart-*ass* mouth. There was nothing nice about it. "Yes or no?"

His smile widened. "Three more steps, sweetheart, and you've got yourself a groom."

This man was like no groom she would want, *sweetheart*. But she went ahead and stepped back to the spot where Lauren would be standing later that night. "Do you work this hard for all your comebacks, or am I just inordinately lucky?"

"I don't work hard at too much of anything," he said, making such a minor adjustment to the tilt of the camera that Melanie wasn't sure whether to believe what he'd just said or the contradiction of what he'd just done.

She preferred to believe her head and keep her distance from this one. His cavalier attitude, whether real or perceived, was totally beyond her ability to fathom—even as she recognized that her own obsessive and occasionally compulsive tendencies weren't the norm.

Detail-oriented, that's all she was. And right now, she was cranky. And considering that state of aggravation, she would have loved to believe that Jacob Faulkner was as lazy as he claimed. But she knew Avatare Productions hadn't come by their reputation employing bums.

And so she didn't. Believe it, that is. Especially since he hadn't stopped working long enough to pay attention to much of anything she'd said. "Well, maybe this once you'd make an exception and give it the ol' college try? I promise it won't go any further, you making an effort, cross my heart and all that.''

He finally stepped back from the camera and straightened to his full height, his full breadth, giving her his complete attention and the up-front impact of his grin, his focus and his deep, dark eyes.

*Whoa!* Melanie blinked, caught again between his actions and words. Not that he'd said anything that registered. Or was doing much of anything at all—at least nothing to merit the two-left-feet trip her heart had just taken.

All he was doing, in fact, was looking at her. Looking into her. Looking beyond her defenses with an intensity that chiseled out a great big chunk from between the bricks of the wall that protected her from bad boys.

''And what's a promise you make worth, Miss Craine?'' He shook his head. ''Never mind. With that control thing you've got going, you don't break promises, do you?''

''Of course not.'' Control? What control? And forget calling on her usual self-discipline.

She couldn't even think of a retort, what with flutters of pleasure flitting in and out of her belly. She was not the type of girl taken to mooning over a man's biceps and pecs and nice tight ass.

Sure, she appreciated beefcake as much as any of the women she worked with, but this…this was not simple appreciation. This was the sort of bone-jumping desire she'd always risen above.

For the life of her, she couldn't remember why.

Or how.

He started toward her, across the dais and down the first step, the second, his stride lazy and loose, his chest a broad landscape in a black cotton T-shirt, his dark indigo jeans slack on his legs but snug where the waistband rode low.

Nothing had changed from five minutes ago except now he wasn't looking at her pixilated image but at her flesh-and-bone body. Yet everything had changed for that very same reason, and Melanie could barely breathe.

He was seeing her both mentally and physically disheveled, not to mention at her absolute worst in terms of stress working her nerves. Her attitude was in the toilet. And her drive to mow down anyone in her way had no doubt made quite the unattractive impression.

And yet he still had that look in his eye. A look that spoke of all those unspeakable things that went on in cocky, bad boy minds.

Things she'd experienced only in her imagination since she avoided the type and stuck to men who were safe. Who presented no challenge. Who bored her to tears but shared her work ethic and professional drive.

She lifted her chin and retrieved her pride, then crossed her arms over her middle, hating how body language supposedly revealed one's state of mind. She felt vulnerable and exposed, and was angry at herself for the weakness. This reaction was not in her man-response repertoire and she did not like being put on the spot.

She especially did not like the sense of anticipation slipping between her clothing and her skin. Too aware, that's what she was, feeling the fabric against her body in a way that had nothing to do with comfort or fit but was all about sensation and sexual heat.

Jacob stepped from the dais into the aisle, his slow rolling stride bringing him closer, closer still, until he circled around and into her personal space. He moved to stand behind her, breathing, hovering, threatening, giving her cause to wrap her arms even tighter over newly budded nipples. *Ridiculous,* she thought, the warmth she felt sluicing over her at having him near.

He took another step and reached the groom's position. The thud of her heartbeat climbed to the base of her throat, and Melanie turned her head slowly. She lifted her gaze to meet his, which was even more disturbing from this distance—really no distance at all.

Oh, no. This wouldn't do. She was not going to stand here where she could smell a hint of the soap on his skin and the shampoo he'd used and the fragrance of the detergent with which he washed his clothes.

He was way too close, and his T-shirt revealed more than it covered. His stomach was flat, his chest sculpted and hard, his shoulders rounded with muscle, his biceps tightening the fit of his sleeves. He looked down at her from beneath a sweep of black lashes. She looked up and swore she was not going to take off her clothes.

He inclined his head, lifted a dark brow. "So?"

"So…what?"

With a tilt of his head, he gestured toward the dais and the choir box. "The cameras are all yours."

"The cameras. Right." Could she be any more of a moron?

And why weren't her legs longer so she could kick herself in the butt? Or steadier, at least, so she could make it up the two short steps of the dais without falling on her face?

As it was, she'd never been more aware of the swing to her walk, or the shape of her legs from the hem of her short, pale yellow skirt to her matching faux crocodile slides. Even her lemon-chiffon poet's shirt had become too revealingly sheer.

Her brainstorm to dress early for the ceremony, allowing more time to see to the video details, no longer seemed like the same stroke of preparatory genius. She'd much prefer to be wearing baggy khakis and a huge oversize camp shirt while under Jacob's scrutiny. What he made her feel was too...itchy and unfamiliar and...real.

But when she reached the choir box railing, she'd never in her life been so glad to be female, itchy or not. Because looking into the LCD screen, she saw things that a real man could never understand about another man's beauty and carnal appeal.

Hands at his hips, standing where Anton would stand to wed Lauren, Jacob Faulkner looked nothing like a groom, looked insolent and arrogant, looked like a model for DKNY or Calvin Klein. Or better yet, like a brooding hustler chalking a cue, waiting for a sucker to challenge his game.

It was an attitude, an aura, a sense of self more than it was the way he wore his dark wavy hair or the way he appeared to lounge like a lizard soaking in the sun. Melanie blinked, wet her lips and watched his other eyebrow lift in question.

If only she could remember the answer he was waiting for.

"Everything meets with your approval?"

*You have no idea.* Though, of course, she would never say anything so leading because she knew, any minute now, she'd get over this ridiculous and latent hormone attack. So she nodded, because he'd been right, after all.

The camera angle was perfect. And as hard as it was to admit after jumping to her earlier opinion, the man knew his business as well as she knew hers.

She moved to check the second camera, though really needn't have bothered. Where the first had shown Jacob from his left side, this one gave her the full treatment of his right. Both sides were equally devastating to her ability to disassociate her body's response from this man. She didn't want to react to him in any sort of physical way.

He was annoying and bossy and way too…observant for comfort. All he had to do was stand there and stare at her and he made her unbearably hot. And now, during tonight's wedding, she'd be sitting in the sanctuary, witnessing the ceremony, her attention drawn from the bride and groom to the cameras, with Jacob looking on.

He'd be sitting in the van in the parking lot. Studying the panel of monitors on which he could so easily watch her. And she would never know if he was looking at her or not.

Melanie ran a hand along the back of her bare neck and into the riot of spiky chunks she'd tamed into curls above her nape. Her gaze moved from the display screen to the floor, to the toe of her right shoe, where her skin, bare and only lightly tanned, contrasted with the yellow. Such a strange thing to notice in the midst of her meltdown.

''This will work,'' she finally admitted, because there was nothing else she could think of to say. Not when her thoughts had taken off in directions she didn't even recognize. Directions that were definitely not refined or genteel, or even logically intelligent. Directions that had her showing him the way to her bed.

She wondered what Jacob would think if he knew she'd undressed him a dozen times already, stripped him where he was standing and taken, uh, matters into her hands. That thought brought a grin; there was no need to wonder. He was a man, and the scenario she'd painted so typical of a male fantasy.

Guys were so simple, really. Wanting nothing more complicated than what it took to keep their urges satisfied. Discounting the fact that it had been a long time since she'd responded to any man the way she'd responded to Jacob, he was no different than the others. She refused to believe he was different.

Except he was. And understanding why would take more than their temporary working involvement. She just didn't have the time.

"What's so funny?" he asked, and she realized she still wore a smile.

Then she noticed he was now standing beside her on the dais. She looked at him over the narrow black rims of her funky rectangular glasses. She had to go. She really had to leave. This insanity had gone on far too long. "Funny? Nothing, really."

"Then why the smile?" He moved closer, forcing her to tilt her head back, making her feel uncharacteristically small and deliciously feminine. "Come on, sweetheart. Tell me. You don't want me to have to get rough, do you?"

She stepped back an arm's length. "Sorry. Intimidation doesn't work with me. But it does raise an interesting question."

"Shoot."

"Just who exactly is dealing with control issues here, Faulkner. Me?" She arched a cool brow. "Or you?"

*August...*

"OKAY, LADIES. Let's hurry this up. We need to get back to business."

CEO Sydney Ford's admonition to the gIRL-gEAR partners had become as much a part of their weekly meetings as had the gossip that precipitated the warning.

But with Lauren so recently back from her honeymoon to Ireland, the seven girls had much catching up to do, multiple trip photos to pass around and many souvenir gifts to unwrap.

Lauren had already given Melanie an extravagant thank-you gift of a bed-and-breakfast weekend for managing the details of the wedding video.

So being handed a tiny box wrapped in silver paper came as an unexpected surprise.

"Lauren, you are totally out of control," Melanie said, while pulling the tape from one end of the neatly wrapped package. "I didn't expect you to bring me back anything."

Sitting to Melanie's right, Lauren leaned back in the conference room chair like a blue-eyed, blond elf on a mission from Santa himself. A huge marquis diamond glittered from her platinum wedding band when she waved an encompassing hand over the rest of the women in the room. "Just spreading the joy of the season."

"What season? It's August. It's Houston. And I don't find the combination particularly joyous," Melanie said, cringing as Kinsey Gray, gIRL-gEAR's fashion authority, squealed from the other end of the table.

Lauren crossed her legs and admired her wedding set against the background of her cream linen slacks. "The bridal season, of course. A June bride. A July honeymoon. And now an August newlywed. A wife." Lauren sighed.

Her marriage-induced bliss had Melanie rolling her eyes as she pulled the gift box free from the tape and the paper. "Not trying to burst your euphoric bubble here, but the newlywed part will eventually wear off and you'll be a wife long past August. At least I hope that's the plan."

"Are you kidding? Anton is stuck with me for years and years to come."

Kinsey's squeals grew louder as she scurried to Lauren's end of the table to deliver a personal hug and thank-you for the delicate Celtic Claddagh pendant draped over her hand. "Lauren, you're the best. I can't believe you were shopping for us when you had Anton all to yourself. I never would've left the room. Shoot, I'd have kept Anton tied naked to the bed."

"Who said he went shopping with me? Or that I even let him borrow more than a corner of my suitcase?" Lauren's grin was as prurient as it was wide. "All he needed was room for a few nice strong silk ties."

"Don't listen to her." Macy Webb, content editor for the gIRL-gEAR Web site, showed off a toe ring and matching ankle bracelet with green stones in their Celtic knot centers. "Anton obviously did the shopping and only let Lauren borrow a corner of his suitcase for her battery supply."

"Batteries?" The newest partner and current vice president of cosmetics and accessories, Annabel "Poe" Lee, toyed with the white ribbon she'd yet to pull from her gift. "A month alone with Anton Neville and you packed batteries? What is wrong with this picture?''

Melanie worked the paper loose from her present, holding her breath and hoping no one would mention the fact that when Lauren and Anton split up last year, he'd spent those few weeks dating Poe.

And though Melanie hadn't been along on the group vacation where the two feuding lovers got their act back together, she'd heard through the grapevine that Poe had laid her intentions to pursue Anton on the line—the very wake-up call Lauren had needed.

"Poe, we really are going to have to find you a man.'' Still dealing with the initial craziness of launching the gUIDANCE gIRL mentoring program, Chloe Zuniga diffused the bomb. "You've clearly been too long without or you would remember how much fun you can have with a man *and* a vibrator at the same time.''

"Speaking from personal experience, Chloe dear?'' Poe's bow-shaped mouth remained unsmiling even as her dark, almond-shaped eyes glittered brightly.

"Yes, Eric and I have a great sex life, thanks for asking.'' Chloe gave her one-time nemesis, now very good friend, a withering look, then blew Lauren a thank-you kiss and fastened a pink quartz bracelet around her wrist. "But I'm talking about Lauren and Anton.''

"Hey, now.'' Lauren frowned. "I'm not sure everyone needs to know the details of my married sex life.''

"As if it's any different than your single sex life,'' Macy teased, looping the slender silver chain around her ankle.

"You might want to be careful there, Ms. Webb.'' Lauren leaned across the conference room table and arched both shapely brows. "I doubt there's a ladies' room in the city that hasn't witnessed your Mr. Redding dropping his pants."

From the head of the room, Sydney groaned. "Must we talk about Leo's...pants?"

"Or his lack thereof?" Melanie pushed her glasses up her nose and laughed. "You need to learn to knock, Syd. That'll save you from any future, uh, exposure should Macy and Leo decide they can't wait till they get home."

"Last year's open house incident was enough, Mel. I really didn't need the reminder." Sydney cringed while draping her new hand-painted silk scarf over one shoulder. "Now, I hate to be the bad guy here, but are we almost finished?"

"C'mon, Syd. How often do we get to marry off a partner?" Chloe asked.

"That's the first thing I want to talk about. These last few months have been insane with the never-ending showers and the bachelorette party and the wedding and Lauren out for a month-long honeymoon. So..." Sydney paused, made sure she had everyone's attention "...no more weddings allowed. With, of course, the exception of my marriage to Ray."

"Sydney!"

"Oh my gawd! Ray proposed!"

"When?"

Sydney waved off the burst of rapid-fire comments. "No date. No date. Just...eventually. But the rest of you can forget it. The company can't afford but one or two of these extended vacations."

"Hear, hear," Melanie seconded.

She pulled the last of the wrapping from her box as, with a twist of her mouth, Sydney went on to add,

"And now that Ray has popped the question, I'm calling dibs on the second—"

"Lauren! This is absolutely gorgeous! Oh, Syd, I'm sorry. But this…" Melanie really hadn't meant to shriek, or to cut off the boss, but she'd opened Lauren's gift and…and…*this was totally unreal!* "I can't believe it. I know this sculptor, and you spent way too much money."

"No, I didn't," Lauren stated, as Melanie turned the frosted-glass figurine over and around in her hands. "I found it in a tiny antique shop. A secondhand place. I don't think they knew what they had. But I knew you had to have it."

The female nude was sculpted in the style of Lalique. The piece was absolutely exquisite, the woman kneeling with her hands spread over her belly beneath her bare breasts, her head tossed back and her eyes closed.

Yet it fit in the palm of Melanie's hand. "You know I'm going to kill myself if I break this before I get it home."

Lauren grinned. "If it made it safely all the way from Ireland, I imagine you can make it from here to Midtown."

The rest of the women got up to see the delicate piece of glasswork, oohing and aahing in appreciation, though no one could possibly value the representation the way Melanie did. "This is going to look so good in my shadow box."

"Do you have nude men in your shadow box?" Poe pinned her black-marble-and-marcasite brooch to the collar of her jade-green silk blazer. "Or do you prefer women?"

Melanie refused to jump at Poe's bait. "I know this

may come as a shock, but I really do know what to do with a penis."

"I don't know, Mel." Chloe got in line behind Poe to give Lauren a hug. "Things might've changed since last time you had one. Evolution moves faster than you do when it comes to the mating process. You're putting in way too many hours at the office to have a love life."

"Chloe's right," Poe unexpectedly added. "All work and no foreplay leads to burnout."

"Very funny," Melanie said, though it wasn't funny at all because the conversation had brought Jacob Faulkner and his, uh, attributes to mind, and she'd thought about him too many times already since the wedding. "Don't worry about me. I'll wait for Sydney to get married before I go postal on all of you."

Her joke fell curiously flat. Looking at the serious faces all around, Melanie realized her friends were truly concerned. How ridiculous! She was fine, though a bit disillusioned.

Her partners seemed to have forgotten the percentages of perspiration and inspiration demanded by success. Besides, *someone* had to sweat out the declining e-tail market. She, for one, had financial obligations to meet.

Sydney broke the strained silence first. "All right, ladies." She glanced around the room. "Now that everyone has thanked Lauren properly and been brought up to date on Mel's familiarity with the male anatomy, I need to give you an update on the documentary in which we've been selected to participate. I've had the lawyers go over all the release forms, contracts, yadda, yadda, and the ball is finally in motion."

Kinsey groaned. "Please, Syd. Do we really have to go through with this? I'm not the least bit photogenic and would really prefer not to share that fact with all of America."

"All of America?" Chloe shook her head. "Sugar, you are way too optimistic. It's a series on female entrepreneurs, remember? We'll be lucky to show up on PBS."

Sydney waited for the silliness to subside. "The producers have contracted a local production company to work with the show's host, Ann Russell. She'll be meeting with each of us over the next few days and setting up her schedule for interviews in the office and for the at-home segments, as well. Any questions?"

*Sigh.* A local production company. Yes, there was more than one. But there was only one best. And even that one had more than one cameraman. But once again only one best. And Melanie knew that when it came to gIRL-gEAR, Sydney Ford never settled for less.

Melanie's good-mood balloon deflated. She'd known two months ago that the man was destined to cause her grief. She just hadn't thought the probability of working with Jacob Faulkner again would come so soon. And what had Sydney said? At-home segments?

She rubbed her thumb over the smooth, frosted glass in her hand. "Who's contracted to do the filming?"

"Avatare Productions."

Lauren jumped to the edge of her seat. "Hey, they did my wedding video. Excellent choice, Syd. Anton and I finally watched the tape Sunday afternoon and the edits were amazing. Brought tears to my eyes, seeing it all as if it was happening again."

"I didn't choose them but after witnessing the crew

in action at the wedding and reception, I did suggest to the producers that they request the same cameraman who ran the show." Sydney frowned. "I never did catch his name."

"Jacob Faulkner," Melanie said, and all eyes turned her way.

## 2

SITTING BEHIND THE DESK in her black-and-white office and feeling uncharacteristically frustrated, Melanie flipped through the catalog of gift items left by the sales rep who'd stopped by the office this morning. The list of possibilities she'd jotted on her legal pad was decidedly short.

She'd promised to get back to him within the week, but knew it wasn't going to happen. Just like last year, her gOODIE gIRL gift line wasn't hurting for product. What she was desperate to find was merchandise for gIZMO gIRL's electronic stock.

Affordable, practical and, yes, admittedly trendy items. So many of the gIRL-gEAR Web site visitors were teens with no source of income save for an allowance or baby-sitting money or, at the most, what they earned working after school for minimum wage.

And Melanie was having the worst time pinning down workable inventory. Her target price bracket meant sales reps offered her cutesy with no substance or functional with no style. She wanted it all. Her customers, no matter their age or earnings, deserved it all. And, she admitted, the challenge of providing it was one of her favorite parts of the job.

Not every girl was completely appearance or fashion conscious, yet plenty were—and were turned off by any design that hinted at boring practicality. And even if there was no consensus on what constituted cool, the pressure to conform was still hard to escape.

Melanie had been lucky in that her own early ventures into geekhood had met with moderate peer acceptance. Though she'd promised her two best friends that she was just as excited as they were about cheerleading, she'd ended up blowing off too many practices and had been kicked off the squad.

Her girlfriends had thought she was out of her mind, preferring to spend her time in the career center's computer lab, but the guys she'd hung with thought she was cool, if a little bit weird. Most were fairly weird themselves, outcasts and loners, but smart as hell. Ambitious, too. She'd liked that about them. Liked it a lot.

She'd enjoyed reaping the experience of their knowledge and sharing her own, as well as showing them up whenever possible—a good little feminist in the making. One as secure in her ability to write a batch file as her cheerleading buds had been in their tumbling skills.

And she owed that confidence to her mother and her grandmother, the two women who'd raised her. They'd taught her not to believe anyone who tried to convince her that it was a man's world, after all. Taught her that a smart woman never let on that she held the upper hand. Keeping the true balance of power under lock and key made for a much more…satisfying outcome.

Melanie leaned back in her office chair and used the eraser end of her pencil to push her glasses back into place. Grinning solely for her own benefit, she admitted to loving the idea of leading a guy around by the…nose and having him clueless that he wasn't in charge.

Then she grimaced. To accomplish that feat she'd need a major personality makeover, because she didn't have whatever that *thing* was that turned men into mindless mush. She was too *in-your-face,* and their face wasn't where most guys wanted a woman to be.

Swiveling her chair to the left, she studied the frosted-glass figurine that had yet to make it to the shadow box in her bedroom. For the moment, it sat on a shelf of the bookcase built into her office wall. The statuette epitomized what guys wanted.

The stylish elegance of Sydney Ford. The sweet femininity of Lauren Neville. The uninhibited nature of Macy Webb. The curvaceous sort of earth-mother figure with which Chloe Zuniga had been blessed.

The very same one Melanie would love to have had if genetics hadn't predetermined she be built like a board. Well, not a board, exactly. She did have all the requisite spheres and orbs. But where Chloe was lush, Melanie was simply…spare.

She supposed her boyish figure, her left-brain think-ing and her reputation for saying what needed to be said made a perfect combination. And if a certain ar-rogant cameramen had a problem with a woman who knew her own mind, that was too damn bad.

Stabbing the pencil's eraser at the tip of her nose, she swore she would not sign any of Sydney's release forms or contracts if Avatare honored her request and assigned the documentary shoot to that annoying Ja-cob Faulkner.

Uh-uh. No way. Melanie had no desire to spend the next few weeks working in close quarters with a man who had nothing more going for him than the fact that he revved her up, making her want to take his, uh, stick shift for a spin—

"Didn't your mother ever tell you not to play with sharp objects? Might poke your eye out, pierce your jugular, jam it up your nose and into your brain. Stuff like that."

*Well, well, well. Nightmares did come true.* She swiveled her chair around to face the doorway, where he was standing. No, not standing. Slouching. Lazy as a slug. Gorgeous as a summer afternoon with nothing to do.

Her chest grew tight as she struggled to breathe normally. He wore another black T-shirt today, this one more structured, designer quality, tucked into a pair of khakis that fit him even better than had the dark indigo jeans. His abs were absolutely incredible.

Oh, but life was unfair. He had his arms crossed over his chest, his shoulder against the doorjamb, one ankle over the other and the toe of that black biker boot braced on the floor. She wanted to slam the door in his face only slightly less than she wanted to run her tongue down the center of his torso.

"Don't move," she ordered, taking aim with one eye and throwing the pencil dartlike toward him. The point caught him on a downward arc and barely even grazed his chest. "Damn. I was hoping that would fly up your nose and into your brain."

A videotape held in one hand, Jacob bent to pick up the pencil, straightened and gave Melanie a look that was half smirk and half smile. "I wasn't sure you credited me with having a brain."

Slowly, she closed the useless gift catalog. Her concentration had been shot before he showed up. Now it lay gasping on the ground. Even so. He might have been put on this earth to ruin her life, but he was not going to ruin what was left of her day.

*Now, now. It's hardly his fault you can't get him out of your mind.* It wasn't even his fault for having gotten under her skin, and that was the crux of her problem. She was the one at fault here—a fact she hated facing, a weakness she wanted to deny. She knew better than to be taken in by a cocky, bad boy attitude and a body to make a woman weep.

What had they been talking about, anyway? His total lack of brains?

"Brains I can't speak to," she said. "But I can credit you with having a good eye. Perception, placement, nuances of lighting that most people miss. Stuff like that." She shrugged, figuring she'd just appeased his ego, though she'd only been speaking the truth.

"A rather backhanded compliment, but I'll take it." He crossed the office's trademark deep purple carpet to return the pencil. "Here. In case you want to give it another shot."

She twirled the pencil between her thumbs and index fingers while pretending to consider, then shook her head. "Bad idea. Might poke an eye out this time. And you need both, considering you've apparently been assigned to tape our documentary."

"I wondered how you'd feel about that." He balanced the video cassette on its side along the front edge of her desk. "You weren't too thrilled last time you came face-to-face with my camera. Guess I can't expect that to have changed."

"Except for one crucial thing." She nodded toward the cassette. "Now that I've seen Lauren's wedding video I can't argue with your skill." Which was a shame, really, since a verbal set down might get him out of her personal space so she could think. He was way too close, too masculine, too...everything that made him who he was.

Confident. Competent. In total control, she admitted, forcing herself not to sigh. If only he'd shown an inkling of respect for her opinion, her input. But no. Things had to go one hundred percent his way. She stared at him and his ridiculously beautiful eyes—a hazelnut sort of brown hiding behind that dark fringe of coffee-bean-colored lashes. She suddenly wanted a latte in a very bad way.

Melanie blinked, then stiffened her melting spine, noticing how strangely he was staring at her. As if she were an oddity to be studied, or a prospective subject for one of his documentary scenes. Any second he'd discount her skin-and-bones body as a waste of good videotape, her mouthiness as abuse of the audio....

She shoved back her chair, stood and headed for the bookcase, where she slipped the gift catalog into the first in a row of magazine holders. Nerves hummed beneath the nubby taupe sweater she wore bunched at the waist over slim black pants. Nerves solely related to the strain of having to work with this man in a professional capacity when he didn't know the meaning of the word.

Yes, he got the job done. But the way he went about it—slouching and shrugging on one hand, issuing bossy orders on the other—was going to drive her mad. Madder than the struggle to keep her hands off and her clothes on was making her.

Striving for nonchalance, she turned and waited for his gaze to lift and meet hers. "Why are you here? To deliver an advance warning that you're back to boss me around?"

"And horn in on your power trip?" He carelessly hitched one shoulder. "Hardly. I'm just doing some preliminary fieldwork."

"That's odd." She leaned back against the bookcase, her hands flat behind her on a hip-high shelf. "You told me you never worked hard at much of anything."

"So I did." Jacob left the video on her desk and made his way to stand beside her, leaning one shoulder against the bookcase and tucking his hands into khaki pockets. "Didn't realize I'd made such an impression."

And she would make sure he continued in that uninformed state for the next however many weeks he was in and out of the office. "Don't flatter yourself, Faulkner. I rarely forget much of anything people tell me."

For a long, drawn-out moment he studied her intently. His expression, brilliantly cutting and sharp, possessed a life of its own, as if he was considering whether or not a response was required. Finally, he reached out, and she thought for a moment he was reaching for her. A ridiculous notion, because he obviously wasn't, and because that one thought spawned others. And she found herself wondering what she would do if he did.

If he touched her.

If he moved closer, into her space, breathed her air and brushed the curve of her jaw with his lips.

But he didn't. He picked up the frosted glass figurine behind her instead. He turned it over and around, balanced it on his palm, used his thumb to test the smooth curving surface of the woman's glass bottom, her breasts, her face lifted to the sky.

Melanie's fingers itched to take it from him, to return the sculpture to the shelf and move his hands to her body, but she didn't do the first and certainly wasn't about to do the second, no matter how quickly her heart tripped or how hot and itchy her skin felt beneath her summer-weight sweater.

She nodded toward the figure. "Lauren brought that back from Ireland. I keep forgetting to take it home."

"Nice," he said, before returning it to the shelf. "Why take it home? Why not enjoy it from here?"

"I do," she admitted, surprising herself and moving her gaze from Jacob's face to the figurine. "It's just that I have a collection of this artist's pieces at home. Keeping the lot of them together seems logical."

"Do you like his work? Or do you like the work that he does?"

She frowned, shook her head as she looked back at him. "I'm not sure I understand the difference. Or is the redundancy meant to trip me up?"

Jacob took a step closer. "Do you like his eye, his style, maybe the way he interprets emotion in the figures? Or do you just have a thing for naked bodies?"

The way he asked the question, the timbre of his voice, the flash of teasing fire in his eyes made it easy to imagine that his query was more leading and more personal than he'd intended it to be. Then again, he was a guy. What was she thinking? Leading and personal was the name of the game.

Common sense told her to blow him off, but too much time together loomed in their future, and she was loath to give him any inkling of advantage. "Yes, actually, to both. I like his style, the way he portrays the human form. And, as far as having a thing for naked bodies, I can't think of anything as compelling as a beautiful nude.''

He didn't even blink. Didn't even smirk. Did nothing but ask, ''Are you talking art here?''

''Doesn't the best art imitate life?''

He took a minute to consider the scope of her reply, a minute during which he picked up and fondled the figurine. Yes, fondled, because there was no other word to describe the silky glide of his fingers over the lush glass curves.

Melanie told herself to look away; the words fell on her own deaf ears. And she admitted to the almost painful need to know if he would touch her with half as much awe.

''Is your collection gender specific?''

Melanie's gaze snapped from his beautifully made hands to his face, which was equally compelling in a purely masculine way. ''You mean do I only collect females?'' When he gave a single nod, she lifted her chin and answered with a simple, ''No.''

''Interesting,'' he said, and once again shelved the sculpture.

Now that was curious. ''Why is my equal opportunity collection interesting?''

It took Jacob a moment to drag his attention to her. Once he did, however, his focus was complete, and the look in his eyes unnerving. Unsettling. And stirring beyond belief.

''I can't see many women I know collecting male nudes. Most don't think a man's body is much to write home about,'' he finally said, and while she couldn't help but wonder what woman had given him that impression, she wondered more what he'd look like out of his clothes.

"What do you think?" she asked.

"About men's bodies?" He looked thunder-struck…and that tickled her.

"About bodies in general. You have to appreciate what your camera lens captures, or what you see on a video display." She ran her fingers through the hair at her nape and nervously fluffed. "I can't believe that you don't pay attention to bone structure…muscle tone…angles and contours and curves."

He shoved his hands back into his pockets, an expression of what seemed to be genuine confusion on his face, as if he had never before evaluated what went into his art. "I don't pull a shot apart like that. For me it's more about what the overall concept captures."

"Hmm." That surprised her. "I would think you'd take all of those individual things into consideration to get the result you want."

"Nah." He grimaced playfully. "Too much work."

How quickly she forgot. "That's right. And you don't work hard at much of anything."

His nod was a perfect and teasing touché. "And you, Miss Steel-Trap Mind, work much too hard at everything. Am I right?"

First her partners, and now this man who didn't know a thing about her? "Depends on your point of view. I like to think I have ambition. Commitment. Self-discipline."

He laughed, a deep rumbling sound as attractive as it was annoying. "Self-discipline," he repeated, as if savoring a secret joke.

"You find that funny?"

"Yeah. Hilarious."

Right. Hilarious. She was so glad she hadn't dipped

a toe into the sexual waters and said anything she'd look back on and regret.

"Loosen up, Melanie. If you analyze every detail, take everything so seriously, you'll end up with an ulcer."

"Or get where I want to go," she said. His gaze sharpened. She forced an indifferent shrug. "You said yourself we focus on different things, Faulkner. Different strokes for different folks, and all that. I prefer to steer rather than drift through life. What's it to you?"

His brow furrowed. "Hell, if you're so busy fighting the current—" he took a step closer "—how do you expect to enjoy the ride?"

Melanie swallowed hard, resisting the tug of a current, all right. The man's magnetism was potent, his attention heady, his impression provocative. When he reached to cup a hand around the sculpture where it sat behind her on the bookshelf, her heart lurched.

His gaze cut back and forth between the nude and her face. "So, I'm guessing to you this piece isn't about the total concept. It's more about analyzing the details. The woman's posture. The way she has her hands spread and her fingers flexed to hold herself back."

*Back from what?* When he turned to look at her, his eyes seemed to answer the unspoken question, and Melanie's heart kicked hard in her chest. It shouldn't have. He was only telling her what he thought she might see. Nothing more. Nothing leading.

Nothing sexual.

"And to you?" she managed to ask.

"To me this is all about interpretation. What the woman wants. What she's looking for. Waiting for."

Melanie had to be imagining his suggestion that it was her and not the figurine who was the one looking, waiting. She hadn't revealed any of those truths in the little bit of time they'd spent together.

And she wouldn't. Because they weren't truths at all. "Okay, so, you take in the overall picture. I work my way up through the elements. In the end we both see the same thing, don't you think?"

"I'm not so sure." He blinked, his lashes making a slow lazy sweep up and down. "We didn't see the same thing looking at the view screen the day of the wedding."

Well, he had her there, didn't he? Except she'd never told him what exactly it was she'd been seeing. And he certainly hadn't bothered to share any details about what he'd been looking at when her image had appeared on his screen. Neither had he mentioned anything about where his focus had been while facing that bank of monitors in the van.

She'd wondered about that. The wedding was two months past, and she still wondered if the position of the cameras had anything to do with what they'd been looking at that day. Or if that afternoon had been all about the tension, the same one thrumming between them now like a deep techno beat.

She wanted more than anything to ask him to dance, to hold her close, to slip his hands underneath her sweater and strip her bare. She wanted his hands and his mouth on her body. She wanted to touch him, to smell him, to taste him in intimate ways. And she could barely breathe.

She smoothed the hem of her sweater and took a step closer to him. A step that was so much longer than the distance she actually covered. Screw it. She wanted this. Why was she holding herself back? "Listen, Jacob—"

"Yo, Mel," Chloe called from the hallway outside the office. "You're still coming to the barbecue on Saturday, right? I really need your help. And Sydney wants to know—" Chloe stopped short just inside the doorway. "Oh, sorry. I didn't know you were busy."

*Thank you, thank you, thank you.* Divine intervention when needed most. See? They weren't even yet working together, and she'd already gone mad.

Melanie shook her head. "I'm not busy at all. Jacob, this is Chloe Zuniga. She heads up the gUIDANCE gIRL mentoring program. Chloe, this is the Avatare Productions cameraman who'll be working on the documentary. Jacob—"

"Faulkner," Chloe finished. "You're Rennie's brother."

Jacob turned his smile on Chloe. "You know Renata?"

A blond brow lifted. "I know Rennie. Her friends knew better than to call her Renata."

"Is that right?" Jacob said, and laughed.

That damn laugh again. The echo lingered in the deepest part of Melanie's belly. She pushed off the wall, away from Jacob, and moved to the front of her desk, hoping that, with distance, the echo would fade. But then he laughed a second time, and she was sunk, wanting him out of her office more than she'd ever wanted him to stay.

*Mad as a hatter and Hannibal Lecter to boot.*

And then, almost as if Melanie had totally left the room, Jacob turned and gave Chloe his full attention. "Trust me. Renata's friends still know better. And she doesn't hesitate to correct them. Even in public. I keep waiting for her to snap and bite off an ear.''

''Is she still in town?'' Chloe asked.

He nodded, gestured over his shoulder with a tilt of his head. ''Out on the west side, actually. She's a counselor at one of the Memorial area high schools.''

''I had no idea. All she talked about in school was moving to Arizona or New Mexico to teach.'' Chloe frowned, pursing pouty pink lips. ''I don't think I talked to her but once or twice after I was in Austin. I knew she'd planned to take off a year before going to school.''

Jacob nodded. ''She did, then went to Baylor and made up for it. Went year-round for five years and earned her Master's before moving back here.''

''So she never left the state?''

''Nope. Decided she could kick ass and take names here as well as anywhere.''

*Lame, lame, lame,* Melanie thought, and rolled her eyes.

The other two continued their conversation, leaving her to wonder if she should just abandon her office and give them time to catch up; she obviously wasn't needed. And just as obviously, she'd been imagining all the tension simmering between her and Jacob. Except she knew that she hadn't been.

She'd seen his pulse beating there in the hollow of his throat.

She arched a brow. ''I hate to interrupt you two, but I'm wondering if what Sydney wants might be something I need to take care of.''

Chloe blinked. ''Shit. I mean, shoot. I totally forgot. She wants us in the conference room. You, too, I imagine,'' she said to Jacob. ''The producer and the show's host want to meet the rest of us and go over the taping schedule.''

Jacob headed toward the office door. ''Give me five. I need to grab my notebook from the van.''

''Hey,'' Melanie said, and he turned back, frowning. ''I think you're forgetting something.'' She held up and waved the video cassette he'd left on her desk.

It took him a long moment to decide whether to go or to stay or to answer. A moment during which his expression shifted, his eyes, having darkened, flashed. And his smile nearly brought her to her knees.

He nodded toward the tape she held. ''Actually, I brought that for you.''

Melanie watched him go, shrugged, slid the cassette across her desk before curiosity had her shoving it into her office VCR. She turned her attention to Chloe, whose attention was way too rapt.

''I can't believe you know him,'' Melanie said.

At the exact same time, Chloe asked, ''Did I interrupt anything? It looked like something steamy was going on between you two.''

''Steamy? Hardly. He's too annoyingly self-important to inspire steam,'' she lied.

''C'mon, Mel.'' Chloe narrowed her eyes. ''I know you better than that.''

''Okay. He's cute enough, but nothing was going on. Nothing *is* going on.''

''He's more than cute, and you know it. He's all that stuff dreams are made of.'' Chloe backed toward the office door and peered down the hallway in Jacob's direction.

Melanie found herself itching to do the same. ''I think you've confused Jacob Faulkner with Eric Haydon.''

"Nope." Chloe shook her head and motioned Melanie toward the door. "Eric's a total jock. Jacob's much more…I don't know. Provocative. Evocative. I can't explain it. You tell me."

"Tell you what? That he drives me totally insane?"

"You say that like it's a bad thing." Chloe spoke with the authority of a woman having been there. "Remember Macy's scavenger hunt? When Eric and I first hooked up? It's amazing the man lived to learn a single thing about me."

"Speaking of the scavenger hunt, I really ought to give Jess Morgan a call," Melanie said, changing the subject like the avoidance pro she'd never realized she was. "I can't remember the last time I saw him."

"Right." Chloe's huffy inflection screamed, *Wrong*. "Listen, Jess is a doll. But you've never been hosed up with nothing to say when he's been in the room the way you were just now with Jacob."

"What're you talking about? You're the one who interrupted our conversation."

"Uh-huh. You couldn't find your tongue, and I think Jacob's the cat who had it."

Melanie shoved Chloe out into the hallway. "You're as cornball as he is."

"I knew it!" Chloe laughed. "He gave you that look, didn't he? That one where his eyes get all dark and your panties melt."

Melanie shifted from one foot to the other. "I don't know what you're talking about."

"You are such a liar. And you've obviously forgotten that I knew him way back when. In high school? Half the fun of hanging out with Rennie was getting to see her sexy big brother. Jacob Faulkner is still as sexy as it gets." Chloe's grin reached new prurient depths. "Maybe you'll get lucky and find out if he's as big as rumor had it."

"Oh, honestly." Ignoring Chloe's snicker, Melanie dropped the subject and headed for the conference room at a brisk walk.

She might as well look no-nonsense and eager to get to the meeting because, after that rumor remark? Her mind was destined to stay in the gutter.

## 3

HE WAS *SO* GOING TO PAY for this! Oh, but he was going to pay! Did he really think two couldn't play his stupid video game?

And why had she thought she needed to rush home and watch his little film production, anyway? She hadn't even taken time to work out or shower or eat or unwind with a beer and *The Simpsons*.

Nope, she'd walked through her front door, tossed her keys and tote onto the table in the entryway and headed straight for the entertainment center and the VCR. Big mistake. That had been an hour ago and still she was fuming.

And so what if she was? She damn well deserved to fume considering she'd wasted twenty good minutes of her very short evening viewing Jacob's collection of outtakes from the day of Lauren and Anton's wedding.

The sneaky bastard.

He'd taken every incident where she'd lost her cool, lost her head, lost all semblance of professionalism, and made himself the perfect little movie short of a shrew needing to be tamed.

Like she really needed the up-close, live-action and full-color keepsake of her behavior that day.

Uh, no. She didn't, and would've been quite happy to live her life without the reminder, thank you very much. No wonder he'd laughed in her face this morning when she'd claimed to be self-disciplined.

And now, with this latest stunt, Jacob had guaranteed their relationship would never again be strictly business. Because not only had his video compilation reminded her of their disastrous work-related interaction, he'd caught her off guard with the way he'd managed to digitally capture the lust she'd felt in places other than her heart.

Even while her taped image had complained about the way Jacob had decided to set up his cameras, her eyes had been flashing and brightly focused, her body language signaling her awareness of the attraction simmering between them. An attraction as real as anything in her experience.

An attraction she wished she could toss into the Dumpster with the rest of her trash because, now that he'd be working with her both in and out of the office, the chemistry between them was going to be in the way, getting on her nerves, aggravating her until she did something really dumb.

Like sleep with the man.

The itch was there. A nice itch that she wouldn't mind him scratching. Except she could hardly sleep with him *and* work with him. That was a no-no and a no-win. Seeing him on a daily basis meant living with the increased frustration.

And since no one had ever said all was fair in love and sex in the city, she wanted him as hot and bothered as thinking of him made her.

If anyone was going to hold the upper hand here, it was not going to be Jacob Faulkner.

Working up a sweat while adjusting the lights and camera equipment she kept set up in her condo's spare bedroom, she pressed her lips together, stepping back to eye the layout. At least now, after an hour of pacing and therapeutic scrubbing of toilets and tubs, she'd finally managed to settle on a payback certain to burn off her adrenaline-laced energy.

Yep. Two could definitely play this warped show-and-tell game. She headed for the kitchen, returning with the bar stool she needed as a prop for her sound stage. She might not work as a videographer, but she could just as easily put together a production to suit her needs.

Right now her needs were all about assuaging her pride and about setting her course through the next few sure-to-be-turbulent weeks. She'd have him eating out of her hand, even if she had to play dirty.

And making use of the stripper's pole she'd had installed in the room for exercise was about as dirty as it got.

She stepped back, checked out her setup. The lights were hot, but working up a sweat wasn't going to be a problem. It was, in fact, inevitable and a very good thing. Crossing the room's hardwood floor in bare feet, she moved to the computer station and launched the system's media player.

She chose a file of dance-appropriate MP3s, adjusting the equalizer until the floor fairly thrummed beneath her feet. And then she smiled. He thought he knew the real Melanie Craine? He thought he'd capture the undisciplined truth? He didn't know half of who she was. No one did. Even her partners. At times, she hardly knew herself.

She knelt on the floor in front of the light she'd positioned to cast her shadow onto the wall. Her silhouette faced that of the glass sculpture in a mirrored pose, the sculpture she'd brought home from work and placed on the bar stool. The shadow of the pole ran down the wall in a line between the other two shadows.

Jacob's fascination with the female nude had inspired her, had made her want to show him that she was much more than the single fraction of her personality he'd seen. His harping-shrew video of her was totally skewed. As skewed as the sexed-up version she was about to make.

Satisfied with the placement of the shadows, she closed her eyes, splayed her fingers low on her belly and got into the music. Feeling it first with her head and her shoulders, she nodded and swayed to the bass in the beat. She kept her eyes closed as her torso began to move and the first tingling waves of excitement tickled the base of her spine.

Whenever she danced, she forgot everything but her body. Her brain lost all ability to handicap sensation and she melted into what felt like pure liquid motion. She felt that way now, sliding her hands from her thighs to her knees, dipping forward before raising her arms overhead with sinuous grace, stretching high, grasping for something that remained out of reach.

Something like Jacob Faulkner.

Instead she took hold of the pole.

The thought of Jacob brought another tingle, this one centered lower in her body, deep between her legs. Slowly, she got to her feet, shoulders rolling side to side as she pushed up from the floor, her hands sliding high on the pole again. She turned, faced the room and arched her back, tilting up her pelvis and lifting one knee waist high.

Oh, yeah. She loved the feel of her body when she

danced. The stretch of muscles, the pull of tendons, the strength in her abs and her arms. So sensual, so…sexy. An arousing awareness of all the things that made her a woman. The very things she wanted Jacob to know.

Swaying to the music's rhythm, she spun to face the pole and hooked her knee behind it. She secured her hold with one hand and leaned back, the fingers of her free hand brushing the floor before she slowly rolled back up. Her lower body undulating, she twined both legs around the pole, moved her hands to the hem of her cropped T-shirt and pulled it over her head.

She still wore her bra, the lacy push-up cups giving her the figure she wished she had naturally. The figure her mind's eye pictured Jacob seeing. And wanting. Desperately wanting and aching to touch.

She smoothed her hands up her stomach to her breasts, cupping their light weight and tossing her head back with the pleasure invoked by imagining his hands covering hers. His hands moving to her shoulders and pulling down the straps of her bra.

She left them dangling there and turned to face the wall, taking in the shadowed ridge of material against her arms as her body continued to sway. Oh, but she wished she could see his face when he watched her undress just for him.

While her own nerve endings prickled and teased, she wondered how dark his eyes would grow, how hot they would flash, how long it would take him to get hard. How hard he would get. She wanted to stand behind him, run her hands from his shoulders to his wrists, wrap her arms around his waist and slide her palms down the bulge behind his fly.

Instead, she slipped her fingers between her own

legs, pressing and pulling slowly up the front seam of her leggings until she reached the elastic waistband.

Then she began to sweat.

She felt the first buzz along her hairline, the second between her breasts. She imagined the feel of Jacob's mouth nuzzling her there, breathing in the scent of her skin perfumed with nothing but arousal. Her breathing quickened.

She wanted to cup his head close, to guide his mouth to her taut nipples still covered by padded lace, to thread her fingers into his hair, which she knew had to be the texture of exquisite silk…

…as would be the soft skin between his legs that covered his testicles, and the skin drawn tight along the shaft and over the head of his penis. She moaned deeply in the back of her throat, where she imagined holding him, sucking him.

She wanted to take him as far into her mouth as he wanted to go. Her groan became a desperate whimper and, as she shimmied off her leggings and kicked them into a corner of the room, she imagined her tongue swirling up and down and around his cock.

She was unbelievably wet. The scent of her arousal was musky and mingled with that of the sheen of clean sweat now covering her skin. She stood in nothing but her bra and bikini panties. Even the soles of her feet were damp against the hardwood floor. The music swept her along, the notes reminiscent of the feel of hot sex, erotically potent, electrically charged.

She reached back and released the catch of her bra, all too aware that the video continued to capture her every move. Moves she'd never anticipated, spurred on by feelings she'd never expected to experience when she'd set her plan into motion.

She'd gone too far to stop, but she was not about to share the rest of this intimate dance. As the soft ivory satin and lace slipped from her arms to the floor, she took hold of the pole, swinging around and switching off the videotape.

She watched the garment fall in shadow, realizing that would be the last movement Jacob would see. But she continued to watch. To watch and to imagine that Jacob was doing the same. That he was watching, was touching, was the one bringing his hands to her breasts, tugging at her nipples. Oh, how she wished for his mouth.

With her bottom lip caught between her teeth, she massaged and kneaded until her touch became unbearable and her arousal equally in need of relief. She spread her legs, her hips working the music's rhythm, rocking left, right, pumping forward, back. Bending at the waist, she drew her hands from her ankles to the crease where her hips met her thighs. And then, hooking her fingers into the elastic leg openings, she tugged her panties down and stood there, totally uninhibited and completely nude.

She splayed her hands over her abdomen, sweeping her palms down over the soft line of dark hair until she captured her swollen clit between the tips of her index fingers. She couldn't help it; she cried out, the pressure sending her close to the edge. But she wasn't ready to come. Not until she'd imagined Jacob's deeper exploration.

She reached between her legs, her flesh swollen and bare, soft and sensitive beneath her practiced stroke. *This is how I like it,* she wanted him to know. *Right here, softly, touch me, tease me, circle here, then slip inside*. And she did, crying out at the penetration of one finger, then two.

She moved to the music and to Jacob's imagined caress. Her body responded, and she took herself over, shuddering, shivering, wishing, oh, how she wished Jacob were here to physically finish what his image had started. Instead, she finished herself, released a final trembling sigh and pulled her hand from her body with a last lingering touch.

Several deep breaths later, she doused the hot lights, stopped the music and ejected the tape from the camera. Then she slipped back into her clothes. Jacob wouldn't be in the office again until Monday, she realized, tugging up her leggings. That gave her time to concoct a clever comeback should he ask her what she was trying to prove.

She wanted to watch the tape, to see what he was going to see, but knew she'd never have the guts to send it off if she witnessed herself baring all. No, she thought, tucking the tape into the padded mailer she'd addressed earlier.

As much as she'd rather have Jacob discover the rest of her personality's facets one-on-one, he'd made the first move in this sex, lies and videotape business.

Her striptease was simply move number two.

IF NOT FOR THE CHANCE to spend time with Renata, Jacob wouldn't have come. It was August in Houston, and it was too friggin' hot for a cookout. Damn fool thing to do, he grumbled, forgetting where he'd put his *cajones*. That particular forgetfulness made it hard not to be whipped and dragged around by Chloe's sugary-sweet pleas.

He grumbled again and exited the Southwest Freeway into the historical neighborhood where she and Eric lived. The woman had better make good on her promise of free-flowing beer. That was all he had to say. And Renata damn well better show. Those were the only reasons he was here.

Well, those and the fact that, thanks to Melanie Craine, he'd been walking around for two days now with a World Series bat between his balls. More than once on the way over, he'd had to shift and adjust the goods just to be able to drive comfortably.

The way this group of women stuck together like racked billiard balls, he figured Melanie would be here today. And he had a payback to deliver. In the end, that had been the deciding reason he'd blown off a Saturday afternoon baseball game at Minute Maid Park.

Yeah, that's why he was here. To even the score.

Not because he couldn't wait to get a look at what she was wearing and spend the rest of the afternoon trying to get her out of her clothes.

He pushed away the thoughts long enough to navigate the narrow streets without running his truck up onto a curb. He wouldn't think about Melanie's amazing body again until he'd parked. He'd think, instead, about a lesser reason he'd come: Chloe's claim that the party was a bribe to get Renata to join gUIDANCE gIRL as a consultant.

His sister said she never saw him often enough, so Chloe had begged him to come. Not that he minded being used by a gorgeous woman—witness him offering himself for more of Melanie's games—but Jacob didn't think his sister needed much in the way of persuasion.

She was an expert at dispensing advice, having done

so since grade school when she'd been eight, he'd been eleven and she'd told him to always have extra change for the ice-cream man in case Kelly Sims was broke. Renata, champion of the weak and wounded, crusader for a woman's right to have her ice cream and eat it, too, would fit right in with the rest of the gIRL-gEAR women.

Even recognizing that female bonding potential, he wasn't having an easy time figuring out the dynamics of the group. He was hoping today he'd pick up a few clues. Most of his video work didn't require personal involvement with clients. But this assignment was different.

Documentary or not, if he made this show work, he could write his own career ticket. Any number of NYC-based production companies would wet their proverbial pants after seeing a show of this caliber on his résumé. The inheritance he'd received from his paternal grandmother had allowed him to outfit his own studio and perfect his craft on top-of-the-line equipment. And getting to know the women away from the office would go a long way to making sure the shoot turned out to be his best ever.

He pulled his Explorer Sport Trac in behind a line of two-seaters and sporty status cars parked at the curb. Adding that half dozen to the double row of vehicles running the length of the driveway, he figured this shindig wasn't the quiet and cozy get-together Chloe had claimed.

Not that he was particularly surprised. He wouldn't classify anything he'd learned about the seven female friends' working relationship as cozy. Or as quiet. He had a feeling hair was pulled and mud-wrestling done on a regular basis. Or not. But hey, a guy could dream.

He hadn't seen enough of their off-site playtime to know that game's score. The only true playtime he'd witnessed, in fact, had been Melanie's incendiary striptease. And even then he didn't know if she'd been the one playing, or if she'd been playing him.

He groaned in defeat. How could a two-dimensional, gray shadow be sexier than a living color peekaboo peepshow? He'd lived in a state of unbearable arousal since watching the tape. What the hell had she been thinking? And why the hell had she turned off the recording like that, right in the middle of his left-handed fun?

Talk about *strokus interruptus.*

No matter all the reasons he gave himself for showing up at Chloe's today, the bottom line was that he was here to see how far he could get Melanie to go. He'd spent the morning watching the tape again. And watching it one more time. Not because he'd needed a refresher; Melanie's shadowed image had imprinted itself on his brain the first time he'd popped the tape into the VCR and hit Play.

He'd watched because he knew he'd be seeing her today. And because he couldn't reconcile her shadowy seduction with the woman who worked in a black-and-white office and wore work clothes that were dull and ugly and drove him nuts for wanting to strip them away. Especially after that yellow thing she'd been wearing at the wedding.

That outfit had been all he'd seen when she walked through the sanctuary doors and into his camera's LCD view screen. He'd followed her progress down the aisle and watched the way her body moved, bouncing beneath the nearly sheer top that was as loose and flowing as her short skirt was tight.

The contrast was definitely the sort of which his professional eye took notice. But it was her body underneath that grabbed his more primal attention. That, and the way the heels she'd been wearing did what heels were supposed to do to a woman's ass and long legs.

For weeks he hadn't been able to get that image out of his mind, and now that he'd seen her take her clothes off…forget it. The shadowed striptease had turned him on even more than watching her walk down the aisle.

He hadn't realized how much until he'd been putting together the outtakes in an effort to point out how far over the professional line she'd stepped that day. She'd encroached on his artistic territory, tried to run his show.

He'd wanted her to see that she'd been just plain wrong, that her issues with control weren't doing her any favors. And he'd always been a hell of a lot better at showing than he'd ever been at telling.

Well, apparently, not this time.

He supposed he deserved the bump-and-grind gauntlet she'd thrown in his face. Melanie had been pissed off enough at his effort to come right back and turn the tables. And she'd done a damn fine job.

The three faces of Melanie Craine just didn't click. She'd been a witch wearing yellow, a tease in severe office black, a vamp wearing nothing at all. And he was about to get hard again, dammit. So he pushed away thoughts of Melanie and pushed open the gate of the eight-foot cedar fence into Chloe and Eric's backyard.

The crowd was huge, the pool inviting, the air humid and hot. He wanted a cold beer in a very bad way and he wanted to see his sister, but he didn't want anything half as bad as he wanted to get his hands on Melanie Craine.

PUSHING BACK LONG STRANDS of curling chestnut hair from her face, Renata Faulkner handed Eric Haydon a plate of burgers ready for the grill.

He was a nice guy, but definitely not a guy she would've expected to find living with Chloe Zuniga. Though it seemed time had indeed healed all wounds, the Chloe whom Renata had known had always been too hard-core, bitterly sullen and punk. And here was Eric, amazingly all-American.

Then again, maybe there was more truth than Renata had ever wanted to believe to the theory of opposites attracting. It seemed to be working brilliantly for these two. Her reunion with Chloe might be but days old, yet Renata had seen enough to know her friend had found herself the real deal.

"Hey, thanks," Eric said, trading her for a platter of burgers just short of well-done. "I see Chloe hijacked you into kitchen detail."

Renata grinned. "She always was the bossy type. And definitely never one who took no for an answer when she wanted a big fat yes."

"You're not telling me a damn thing I haven't spent a good year figuring out." Eric dodged another blast of flame and smoke. "She's a piece of work and then some."

"C'mon now, sugar. Don't be talking trash about your woman to her old friends." Walking up and into the conversation, Chloe smacked Eric soundly on his denim-covered backside. "I'd rather Rennie remember me in my more precious incarnation."

Renata laughed out loud. "Precious as a sliver of broken glass beneath the ball of a bare foot."

Her arm snug around Eric's waist, Chloe arched a brow sharply. "I can see leaving you two alone together is not going to be a good idea. A girl needs to know her secrets are safe rather than being shared for a laugh."

Eric lowered the grill's heavy lid, hooking an elbow around Chloe's neck and gesturing with the barbecue tongs he held in the same hand. "C'mon now, princess. We're not laughing at you. Only with you."

"Right." Chloe ducked out from beneath Eric's arm and linked her fingers through Renata's. "We'll be leaving you now to your manly meat business."

Eric sulked. "But I thought you liked my manly meat business."

Chloe rolled her eyes as Renata laughed and let her old friend drag her away. "He's such a doll. Wherever did you find him?"

"It was one of those six degrees of separation things. I knew Lauren, Lauren knew Anton, Anton knew Eric. Hmm. I guess that's only three degrees," Chloe amended, then shrugged and grimaced. "Five minutes. I need five minutes off my feet. I've been running like crazy for hours."

Skirting the newly installed swimming pool, the women settled on opposite sides of the patio's glass table beneath an umbrella of cream-and-green stripes. Propping her feet on the seat of a third chair, Chloe sighed in relief. "Anyway, Eric and I ended up paired for one of Macy's gIRL gAMES. The rest, I suppose you can say, is history."

Renata saw no need to hide her approval. "A period of history I wouldn't mind studying in the least."

"Oh, yeah?"

"Oh, yeah." Renata looked toward Eric and smiled. She took a deep breath and shook her head appreciatively. "One of these days I am going to have to get myself one of those."

"Shopping?" Chloe asked with a laugh.

"Definitely in the market. Though not in any sort of desperate, beat-the-sales-crowd rush." Settling back into her chair, Renata turned her attention back to Chloe. "I've made it this long on my own, and don't see any need to be stupid."

"Hey, no one said you had to be stupid, though you've got to agree that we're all entitled to a bit of questionable behavior between here and there. I've definitely been guilty of my fair share." Chloe glanced in Eric's direction again and Renata couldn't help but wonder what thoughts were going through her girlfriend's mind.

She followed the direction of Chloe's gaze, skipping over Eric and frowning when she caught sight of a guest she couldn't place from Chloe's earlier introductions. A guest Renata had a hard time believing belonged.

He leaned against the trunk of the backyard's massive oak tree, a Shiner longneck dangling from his fingers. His complexion brought to mind the Mediterranean, as did his dark hair, long and loose, hanging in twisted strands to skim his shoulders.

His attitude, however, made the biggest impression, his insolent expression that of the defiant boys Renata saw so often at school. Yet it was more. A sort of wary regard, as if he was protecting his back while keeping a distrustful eye on the enemy camp. She found it hard to look away—a strange response, because she'd never been taken in by the renegade type.

"Who is that?" she asked, nodding in his direction when Chloe looked back to see who she meant.

"Oh. Patrick Coffey, Ray's brother. You met Ray, right? Sydney's Ray?" And that was all she said.

Renata wanted to know more. "Hmm. He looks like he'd rather be swimming in the comfort of shark-infested waters."

"He'd definitely be more at home if he were." Chloe frowned. "I'd say he's harmless but I'm not sure that he is. And it's really a long story."

"Shortcut it for me." Now Renata really wanted to know more.

Chloe pulled her feet close to her body and wrapped her arms around her bare knees. "I see you've still got that dog-with-a-bone thing going on."

"A skill that comes in handy for divining deep dark secrets."

"I'm keeping track here, you know. A month of gUIDANCE gIRL mentoring for every sordid detail."

"We'll talk contract issues later. Just tell me about Patrick."

Chloe rolled her eyes and gave up. "Patrick's been home about a year now, I guess, after being held by—get this—real-life Caribbean pirates. I kid you not. It was really a rough few years for Ray."

"And for Patrick, too, I'd think." Pirates? How out of this world was that?

Chloe shrugged. "I'm guessing so. But since he hasn't said a word about it, no one really knows."

"He hasn't talked to anyone?" This couldn't be a good thing. "It's something he ought to consider doing, to an impartial professional if he doesn't want to talk to his brother.''

"Well,'' Chloe began, slowly tightening her persuasive noose, ''since he shows up at the office with Ray from time to time, you could make him your first gUIDANCE gIRL subject.''

Renata laughed. ''In case you haven't noticed, Chloe, there's nothing girlish about Patrick.''

Chloe waved her off. ''Yeah, yeah. That's beside the point.''

"You're not going to take no for an answer, are you?''

"Not a chance. Not after being subjected to your all-night, Rennie-knows-best sessions in high school.'' Chloe's teasing expression grew serious, her wide violet eyes misty and warm. ''You were there when I needed you, and I've never forgotten.''

Renata reached across the table and squeezed her hand. ''I'm so glad you ran into Jacob. I can't believe I haven't been around for so much of what's happened in your life. I've really missed you.''

Chloe squeezed back. ''Me, too. And I didn't even realize that you were probably a lot of what I felt was missing in my life before I found Eric. But now that I have the both of you...talk about the best of both worlds.''

Renata laughed. ''Well, I hope you continue to think that way after you've worked with me. The kids I deal with? I know better than to involve myself too much in their problems. I have to be able to sleep at night. And that means I end up taking out my frustration on close friends.''

She said it with a quirk of her mouth, thinking back to friends who were now enemies, as well as those who were no longer lovers for that very reason. Then she wondered if she'd learned her lesson, or if she was now putting Chloe into a direct line of not-so-friendly fire by agreeing to work with her.

Chloe only smiled, her lips frosted her trademark pink. "Isn't that what friends are for? I know I've unloaded on Mel more than a few times. She usually smacks me around until my head's on straight and then we move forward."

"I guess I'm just giving you fair warning. If I claw your eyes out after a particularly rough day, don't take it personally."

"Oh, but clawing is on Chloe's list of fetish favorites," said a deep male voice from above her head.

# 4

THE MAN RUFFLED A HAND over Chloe's hair, lowering his body into the chair where she'd rested her feet only minutes before. Renata could do nothing but calmly look on and try to remember to breathe.

He stood a good head taller than the other men here, but it was neither his height nor his impressive build that rendered her speechless. Her tongue had been tied by no more than his presence, by that indefinable quality allowing powerful men to command attention with no effort at all.

She did seem to be the only one starstruck, however. Chloe wasn't the least bit hesitant or shy; she barely let the man get seated before shoving him hard in the chest. He didn't budge or flinch or even wobble in his seat.

So she shoved him a second time for good measure. "You scare me like that again and you won't be able to walk for a week, buster."

All the man did was grin. "You and your cotton candy threats."

Chloe's glare finally withered. She rolled her eyes, her mouth twisting into one of her genuinely rare smiles. "Cotton candy, my ass." Shaking her head, she made introductions. "Rennie, this is my brother, Aiden Zuniga. Aiden, Rennie Faulkner."

Again, Aiden ruffled Chloe's hair. This time he

earned himself a punch to the shoulder before he turned his gaze and grin on Renata. He rubbed at the spot where Chloe's fist had made contact. "Renata, right? You went to school with Chloe."

"Did I know you then?" she asked, knowing full well she'd have remembered this one if he'd been around. That grin. Those eyes. Oh, my. Oh…my. The other Zuniga boys—Colin and Richard and Jay—had been in and out and around the house during those years, but Aiden? No, she'd have remembered him.

Aiden shook his head in answer. "I don't think so. But then, I wasn't home very often."

"You weren't home ever," Chloe accused, propping her feet on her brother's lap. He grabbed her ankle and teasingly threatened to toss her away. "I totally blame Aiden's abandonment for all my psychological issues."

One of Aiden's brows went up. "And, knowing the way your little mind works, no doubt for the national debt, homelessness and Tom and Nicole's divorce."

Chloe huffed. "That last one you could've gotten to a little sooner, you know. Before I hooked up with Eric would've been nice."

Renata couldn't help but grin as she returned her gaze to Aiden, compelled to study him more closely while his sister held his attention.

His hair, she decided, had once been blond but had darkened with time to a rich golden-brown. Like buttered wheat toast, or a jug of tea steeping in the sun. His eyes were the dark blue Chloe's would be if not for her penchant for violet-colored contact lenses. The blue of big sky country, Renata mused, her thoughts spurred by his Wild-West look.

He wore jeans that had been cut from a bolt of

denim, but had faded and softened to what she imagined would be the texture of an aged patchwork quilt. His round-toed boots were black, the heels flat, the leather superb. Turquoise snaps closed a short-sleeved white shirt across his broad chest. A silver belt buckle lay flat against his abs.

She had to stop with the cowboy fantasy because she was finding it difficult to breathe evenly. And because Aiden leaned forward, breaking the spell.

"Chloe's exaggerating about the abandonment, you know." He gave his sister a grin of pure sibling affection, one Renata recognized because she shared the same with Jacob.

One that gave an oomph to the already sizzling attraction humming beneath the surface of her skin. Oh, yeah. This one she was definitely going to like—a lot.

Aiden went on. "She enjoyed being spoiled and learned too damn early what a sucker I was for her little-girl pout."

"I am not spoiled, and I do not pout." Chloe sat back, stretched out her legs beneath the table, crossed her arms and pouted.

Aiden looked to Renata for support and she laughed.

"Uh-uh. I know better than to take sides. Besides," she added, turning her gaze Chloe's way, "there's a lot to be said for the consistency of human nature. If you'll remember, I spent more than a few years watching you at work. I know that pout well."

"Oh, fine." With a huff that was not quite believable, even less so because of her impish grin, Chloe got to her feet. "You'd think a girl could get a little respect at her own party. But no. It's turned into dump-on-Chloe day."

"That girl is some piece of work," Aiden said as his sister stomped off, leaving him with a teasing wink.

Renata settled more comfortably into her chair, owing the other woman in a major way for offering up the one-on-one time with Aiden. "I'm sure she'll be back once she gets that out of her system."

"You know Chloe. All bark, very little bite."

"You have to say that. You're her brother," she said, and brought her gaze back to Aiden's face. She really did like the twinkle in his eyes.

"True," he agreed, nodding. "And I figured I'd better be nice since she took the hint and left like a good sister."

"Hint?" Renata asked as her heartbeat did a tumbling blip.

"Yeah. I gave her a nice swift kick beneath the table." He said it without apology or the slightest hint that he was pulling Renata's leg.

She didn't know what to think other than admitting a burning curiosity to know if she'd truly captured Aiden's interest or was only witnessing Chloe's brother on the make. "Hmm. I don't seem to remember her coming to school with bruised shins. This must be a communication method you've worked on over the years."

He pressed his lips together in a wry smile. "That *was* pretty lame, wasn't it?" he admitted.

She nodded. "It's nice to see a man willing to own up to a failed attempt to impress."

"Damn. And here I was hoping I'd succeeded."

She wasn't about to tell him exactly how well he had. She quite liked the idea of a man being smitten to the point of playing the fool. "I'm game if you want to give it another try."

Aiden sat forward in his chair and leaned toward her. He studied her face for a minute and then boldly took hold of her fingers where her hand rested on the tabletop. He rubbed his thumb from her knuckles to her nails. "Why don't I get us a drink while we wait for Eric to figure out what he's doing with that grill?"

Renata smiled, curling her hand into a fist in her lap when he released her. "Thanks. A beer would be great."

"A beer I can handle. Not exactly impressive, but doable."

The sight of him walking away was worth having had to let go of his hand. She'd never understood the appeal of a cowboy the way she did now. What was it about the fit of denim over lean hips and long legs, the strength in that long, rangy stride? Not to mention the perfect taper to his waist from his broad, muscled back.

From out of nowhere came the urge to skate her palms from his shoulders all the way to the tops of his thighs, where she'd linger. And play. And explore…taking pleasure in the secrets behind the copper buttons of his fly.

He was back in seconds with two ice-cold bottles. She sipped, enjoying the earthy chill, but not anywhere close to the way she'd enjoyed the movement of his body or her rather prurient fantasy. Or even the way she now enjoyed Aiden watching her tongue flick at the moisture on her lips.

Finally, he drank, his throat working hard as he swallowed. Her heartbeat thudded and awareness shimmered in the heavy afternoon heat.

"Tell me what I've forgotten about you," he said, and she couldn't help but grin.

"Tell me what you remember, since I have absolutely no idea what you know."

He laughed. "I do know the boys said Chloe actually studied when you were around."

"I guess that's a good thing, though it makes me sound like I had nothing but school on my mind." Renata tilted her head, tilted the longneck, thought back to the past. "I wasn't any more of a bookworm than Chloe, to be honest. It was just a case of convincing her that without the grades, neither one of us would be going anywhere."

He drank again, his eyes focused intently on hers as he raised, then slowly lowered his bottle. "Chloe told me you're a school psychologist now. On the west side?" When she nodded, he went on. "Why a school district instead of private practice?"

"I like the kids. I like being there where they can find me, where they need me. *When* they need me." She ran her fingertip around the beer bottle's mouth. "It's hard to believe it's been less than a dozen years since I was there myself."

Aiden was quiet for a minute, his thoughts hidden even while his eyes showed his mind hard at work. Renata didn't try to hazard a guess as to what he was thinking. For a reason that had no basis but the churning of nerves in her stomach, she didn't want to know.

But none of that mattered when she sensed he was looking into her past, seeing all the times she'd wished for someone to talk to. The times when she and Jacob had been left at home, had tried to be all the family the other needed but, more often than not, had failed.

A carefree grin lifted both corners of Aiden's oh-so-yummy mouth. "Your kids must be glad to have you on their side."

Renata laughed. "I'm not always on their side. Trust me. The choices some of them make?" She shook her head. "I'm amazed they manage to get to campus, period, much less on time. And forget having finished their homework."

Aiden laughed. "Sounds like you were looking over my shoulder while I dragged myself through high school."

She gave a wry smile. "Actually, I was thinking about Jacob."

"Jacob?"

"My brother. He's the reason I hooked up with Chloe again. He's a videographer, working on the gIRL-gEAR documentary. They ran into one another at the office." She glanced around the large backyard, searching the noisy and milling crowd. "He's supposed to be here, but I can't say I'll be surprised if he doesn't show."

Aiden leaned back in his chair, squaring an ankle over the opposite knee. He continued his concentrated study of her face. "You know your brother's habits well, do you?"

"I should, considering all the years I spent exploiting his weaknesses so I could get my way." Renata offered a hint of a grin in response to the intensity of his stare. The silence between them thickened as she waited for him to respond to her admission.

Finally, he did, wiping condensation from his bottle with his thumb before his gaze snagged hers and held. "Is this where I say I like a woman who goes after what she wants?" he asked.

She touched her tongue to the bow of her upper lip,

wondering if he'd just invited her to act on her recent fantasies. Wondering, too, if her eyes had given her away. "Jacob will be the first to tell you that I don't always get it."

"You two sound pretty close," Aiden said with a curious interest.

She gave a slight shrug while rotating her bottle on the table. "We fought like crazy, but, yeah, we're close. Growing up, we were all the other had a lot of the time."

Aiden frowned. "Where were your parents?"

"Working. Traveling. In their case, one and the same." Funny how he had her admitting things she'd worked half her life to put out of her mind. "It got old, trying to be a kid at the same time I was having to be an adult."

"And now you help other kids deal with the same pressures."

"Except that the kids I work with are a hell of a lot more grown-up than either Jacob or I had to be at that age."

"You're lucky to have him."

"Yeah," she admitted. "I am."

"Listen, Renata." Aiden leaned forward, his elbows braced on his knees. He gestured with one hand while his longneck dangled between his legs from the fingers of the other. "I don't want to break up Chloe's party, but I want to see you. Away from here. Where we can talk without sweating our asses off. Let me take you to dinner."

"Tonight?" Her voice didn't even squeak. Amazing. "Have you seen the amount of food we're expected to eat this afternoon?"

"Coffee, then." He smiled that full-dimple, seductively unnerving smile. "I've yet to meet a woman able to turn down Starbucks."

She laughed without spilling but a drop or two of giddiness. "We can do that. Or we can wait until tomorrow. I might actually have room for coffee by then."

This time he grimaced. "I won't be here tomorrow. I have a buyer coming to look at a quarter horse at noon. I'm heading home first thing."

Heading home. *Heading home.* Renata wondered if the color she felt draining from her face was visible. "You don't live in town?"

He shook his head. "I'm between San Antonio and Austin. Not a lot of room in Houston to raise horses."

So the cowboy look wasn't affected. No wonder he pulled it off so well. "I had no idea."

"Good. That means my sister hasn't given away all of my secrets."

"No. She hasn't." But it sure would've been nice if Chloe had at least pointed out how far away Aiden lived. "Actually, she didn't even mention that you'd be here today."

"I wasn't sure I'd be able to get away." He reached again for Renata's hand, cupping her fingers into his palm and stroking their length with his thumb. "But I'm damn glad I made the effort."

"So am I." And she was, even if his revelation had shifted the dynamics of where they'd been headed. Moments ago she'd been intrigued by the possibilities. Now she knew they'd never share more than this physical attraction.

And that was fine. Better to know where she stood than to fall head over heels for a man who wouldn't be lying next to her in bed at the end of a long hard day. After so many years alone with only Jacob on her side, she'd vowed never to suffer a long-distance relationship.

But she wouldn't say no to having a little cowboy fun from time to time. "And, yes. Thank you. Coffee tonight would be perfect."

"LISTEN, MEL," Chloe began, dragging Melanie away from the table of food to the far side of the backyard and shoving a beer bottle into her hand. "You and Jess are nothing but friends, right? So lose the long face already. He had to work. It can't be helped."

"Right. You aren't the only one here without a date." Melanie felt like a fifth or sixth or even seventeenth wheel, standing here, whining about Jess—who *was* only a friend—leaving her in the lurch. *Puhleez!* So far, today's only bright spot was that she hadn't paid an ungodly sum of money to a therapist to point out the obvious.

Knowing Chloe had invited him to the cookout, Melanie had retreated to the safety of Jess, who she'd known for ages, at the first sign of danger from Jacob.

That damn tape had seemed like *such* a good idea at the time. But now? All she wanted to know was what in the hell she'd been thinking. And why she hadn't yet thought of a plausible story explaining the loss of her mind.

"Don't give me that without-a-date crap." Chloe waved away a fly buzzing over her bowl of potato salad. "You've never hated being alone. Besides, Aiden's here alone. Kinsey's here alone."

"Kinsey's with Doug," Melanie countered, watching the couple dunk one another in the pool, splashing anyone who hadn't left the deck earlier when they'd dived in.

Chloe shrugged. "Now, maybe. But they didn't arrive together. Patrick's here alone."

"Patrick's always alone."

"His choice. I know about fifty women ready, willing but doubtfully able to soothe his weary soul." Chloe glanced this way and that, canvassing the crowded backyard. "Poe's alone. Renata's alone. Well, sort of alone. Aiden's sticking pretty close. Anyway, just quit your bitching."

"I'm not bitching. I'm just…bitchy." A mood unlikely to dissipate until she'd settled on an action plan. One thing was certain. She'd have to play it cool.

Giving Jacob a hint, an inkling even, of her second thoughts regarding the tape would not bode well for their professional future. She had to make as though she'd been in total control. The decision totally disciplined.

Right. Like she'd been able to convince him of that so far.

"Hmm."

Melanie grimaced at Chloe's suspicious-sounding tone. "Hmm what?"

Her pointed gaze shifted suddenly back to Melanie. "This isn't about Jess at all, is it? You're nervous. Something's happened."

"Nothing's happened," Melanie answered, yet again being probed and in not a good way.

"You can't even look me straight in the eye. And you keep watching the gate like you're waiting for someone."

*Uh-oh.*

"Hmm. There's only one no-show unaccounted for…" Chloe mused.

Melanie took a studiously casual sip of beer.

"Are you waiting for Jacob?"

"Don't be ridiculous."

Her friend sucked in a delighted breath. "You're blushing."

"It's the heat."

"Didn't I tell you the man was hot? What happened between you two? Tell me everything!" Chloe licked a chunk of potato from the back of her clear plastic spoon and leaned forward avidly.

Melanie winced. "There's nothing to tell."

"Don't give me that," Chloe began, wagging her spoon, obviously on a roll. "I'm not buying it. When I walked into your office the other day, I had to wave my hand to clear the steam. Good thing I wear contacts."

Melanie felt her shields go up. "Don't tell me you're matchmaking here."

"Me? Match-make? Not a chance." The other woman shook her head vehemently. Almost *too* vehemently. "I've learned way too much about chemistry, friends and lovers from Eric to think my opinion on how you should run your love life amounts to anything."

Love life, ha! "I have no love life."

"Exactly. Or at least, you didn't used to." Chloe scooped out one last bite of salad from her bowl and waited hopefully.

"And I still don't." Unless having sex with a pole counted.

"You're blushing again, sugar. Don't be embarrassed. I can see why you'd want to jump Jacob's bones. There's something about him that you're not going to get with Jess. Could be just his obvious fling potential and nothing you can work with long term, but a fling might just do you good.''

"You think I need a fling. With a man I don't even know.''

"Stop being a prude and listen already. I know you, Mel.''

*Yeah, I'm a real prude, all right.*

"You've been way too uptight lately. I don't know what about, though I'm guessing it's somehow related to the wedding. And,'' Chloe continued when Melanie opened her mouth to interrupt, "Macy hooking up with Leo, Sydney finding Ray and this thing with me and Eric.''

How sweet of Chloe to point out that Melanie was one of only two of the original gIRL-gEAR partners unattached. And more than likely the last one, what with Kinsey mooning over Doug all the time.

Melanie glared at Chloe. "Your point?''

"My point is that you work ungodly hours and make no attempt to meet men outside the office, and suddenly this sexy man literally walks into your professional life. It doesn't make sense to blow off the guy without knowing him better. Now, blowing him is another matter entirely.''

Grinning at Melanie's dropped jaw, Chloe acknowledged Eric's beckoning wave with one raised hand. "Give it some thought, Mel. What's the worst that could happen?''

*I'm going to have to face him and pretend like I haven't done a thing. Like he hasn't seen a thing. Or at least have a viable lie ready to tell about why I made that damn tape.* Melanie relaxed her white-knuckled grip on the bottle. "He's a business associate, Chloe. That's all."

Chloe's exasperated gaze gradually softened. "Okay, sugar. If that's your story, I'll stick to it if anyone asks. But when you're ready to talk, I hope you know I'm a discreet listener."

"Patient confidentiality?"

Chloe shook her head. "Girlfriend trust. It's more sacred."

They shared a warm smile and Melanie forced a swallow of beer past the lump in her throat.

"Um, speaking of business associates..." Chloe let the sentence trail off and nodded toward the backyard gate—

—through which Jacob Faulkner had just walked. Melanie felt heat flush from her collarbone to her hairline. Running her cold longneck over her forehead, she ignored her girlfriend's chuckle and sympathetic pat.

"Steam," Chloe said, before going to join Eric at the grill. Melanie tried to look away from Jacob. Tried and failed.

The man needed to be shot on general principle. And because he'd come out of nowhere to complicate her well-ordered life by refusing to fit any of her preconceived notions of how she was supposed to respond to a man. She was supposed to be attracted to his work ethic, his intelligence, not want to drag him to bed.

Melanie upended and emptied her bottle of beer onto the grass, then turned her focus toward Jacob. He'd moved toward the back patio and stood talking to Sydney and Poe. Both women laughed, watching whatever it was he was showing them on a portable

DVD player. Probably the group interview he'd filmed in the conference room on Wednesday.

The same day Melanie had taken his tape home and performed her infamous striptease.

The thought sent her stomach rolling.

The two women stood on either side of him and Jacob towered over them, not just in height but in the totally masculine scope of his body. She tried to study him with a sense of detachment, but all she could think about was the way she'd imagined his hands on her body when she'd brought herself off.

Her knees trembled. Her temperature soared. The sun beat down on her head and she blamed the heat for the dizzying buzz along the surface of her skin. Had he watched the tape? Had he shared it with his buddies and had a good laugh? Had he tossed it into the trash unopened?

No, that couldn't be the case. That couldn't be the case at all.

Not with the way he was suddenly watching her, his gaze having come up to meet hers.

With Sydney and Poe staring at the DVD player's screen, Jacob turned his full attention Melanie's way. She stood there, alone, feeling strangely more naked than she'd actually been when she'd stripped. And it was all about the way he was looking at her.

Gone was the lazy lounging lizard appearance of not giving a damn. His eyes were bright, his expression determined and intense, as if he had something he needed to say. Something he needed to tell her. A challenge to issue. A dare.

That look answered her question. He'd watched the tape.

And her payback was nothing compared to the one she'd be receiving from him.

# 5

"YOU WANT COMPANY? Or is this seat saved?"

*Da-da-dum* went Melanie's heart into the base of her throat. Ten minutes ago, after being melted by Jacob's gaze, she'd moved out of the backyard sun and into the patio's shade. Now, taking one quick breath, she looked up over the frames of her glasses, better prepared for what she would see.

Only it wasn't what she'd expected. This time his look was totally laid-back, totally tame, nothing at all like his earlier sizzling expression.

*Batty-crazy-nuts.* He was driving her insane. And the trip from here to there was growing markedly short.

"You're welcome to join me." She tempered her voice to a cool indifference—two could play this casual game—and inclined her head toward the chaise longue in the porch's far corner, beneath the awning and out of range of the water splashing from the pool.

"Thanks," he said, grabbing the chair and moving it closer to hers.

He took his time adjusting the cushions and the footrest, took even more time setting his beer on the deck between their chairs. Once he sat, he didn't seem the least bit concerned about making conversation. He only wedged the DVD player's case between his spread legs and leaned back.

And that was it. No more sharp piercing looks. No questions. No movement at all.

Not a single solitary word.

If she didn't know better, she'd think she was sitting next to a different man than the one whose expression ten minutes ago had nearly singed off her clothes. The bastard was back to basking in the sun, a desert reptile conserving his strength, a chameleon fitting in until the time came to put his clever little tongue to use.

*Great.* Just great.

Now she was going to be thinking about his tongue when chameleons were probably not even desert reptiles, and thinking about his tongue was not exactly practicing the self-discipline she'd so recently preached.

But she was at a loss about what to say, what to do, whether or not to be the one to bring up the subject of the tape. And so she said simply, "I met your sister earlier. She seems very nice."

Eyes closed, he nodded. "She is, except when she's being a bossy pain in the ass."

It made absolutely no sense at all, but even closed, his eyes were beautiful. His lashes, his brows, the laugh lines fanning out from the corners that crinkled when he smiled. She wondered how old he actually was. Strange that, here and now, that's what she wanted to know. It was a safe thought, at least.

Unlike thinking of a chameleon's long curling tongue.

She swallowed hard. "If Rennie decides to work with Chloe's gUIDANCE gIRL program, the two of them ought to make some kind of pair. Like minds, albeit bossy ones."

"Hmm. I only knew Chloe as a kid. She wasn't all

that bossy, but she definitely seemed to be mad. All the time. About everything,'' Jacob said. ''I would've thought she'd end up in line to receive guidance, not dole it out.''

Melanie nodded, as if in agreement, when what she really wanted to do was scream with frustration. Why were they sitting here talking about work and other women? Why had she dumped her beer on the lawn?

And why the hell did Jacob have to look like an incredibly rich dessert, best avoided but impossible to resist?

Today he wore denim shorts, leather sandals and a plain gray athletic shirt. Ankles crossed, he'd hooked one arm over the chair's headrest and draped the other across his middle on his very flat, very fit abs.

Melanie wasn't going to allow her gaze to drift lower. Seeing his forearm and his hand resting at the waistband of his shorts, and seeing his fingers tucked beneath the edge, was already giving her fits.

Between her tight throat, the afternoon humidity and his position's tempting invitation to climb on top, breathing had become extremely difficult. His body was absolutely remarkable, nearly perfect except for the way his knees slightly bowed.

She was glad for that, glad to see that he was human, after all, because she'd had at least two beers too many and found herself dizzily elevating him to the status of a god.

A long-tongued chameleon sex god.

And that just wouldn't do.

She cleared her throat and continued to act as if nothing simmered between them but the humid afternoon air. ''Chloe seems to have grown out of that. Now if she gets mad, you know it's for a very good reason. Or at least a reason she deems good enough. Which, now that I think about it, is why she can seem to be mad about everything all of the time.''

*Okay, Melanie. Close your mouth before you get totally stupid.* She was babbling, waiting nervously for the bomb to drop. For all she could tell, the ticking hadn't even begun. At least Jacob's ticking. Hers hadn't let up since he'd walked through the gate.

Jacob, on the other hand, was stretched out on the lounger looking half-asleep, as if he hadn't a care in the world. As if he hadn't heard a word she'd just said. As if he hadn't received her package, after all. Or watched her strip down to her skin before she'd shut off the camera to finish her fun.

Melanie stifled the groan working its way up her throat. She knew he was pulling her leg. The fact that he was so very good at pretending gave him away. No one could have looked at her the way he had not fifteen minutes ago and then fallen fast asleep.

She glanced toward the DVD player he'd tucked between his legs. Right where she couldn't help but see it and have her curiosity raised. ''Was that part of the documentary you were showing to Sydney and Poe earlier?''

''Yeah. Just a few extra minutes of footage around the office.''

''Could I take a look?'' She was dying to see how much of her antagonism—both real and faux—toward Mr. Cameraman here had actually come across on tape.

He seemed to hesitate for a second or two, then said, ''Sure,'' and sat straighter in the chair, pulling the mini DVD player from the carrier and into his lap. He

loaded one of several stored disks, handing her a pair
of headphones he dug from a pocket in the case.

She took them, but lifted a brow in question. He
shrugged. "Speakers on the player aren't worth crap.
They're tinny as hell, and forget picking up the
stereo."

"Okay," she said, and he plugged them into the
audio jack and hit Play before handing her the device.

Setting the compact player on her lap, she adjusted
the volume, joining the group interview in progress,
thinking as she watched that gIRL-gEAR's seven female partners really did make for a compelling picture
of success.

The host was asking a question of Sydney, and the
rest of the women laughed. Jacob had done a great job
capturing the group's comfort level. They knew one
another well, and it showed.

The screen suddenly went dark, then turned to
snow. Just as Melanie reached up to remove her headphones, the picture came back. But what she was looking at was no longer the office conference room.

No, she was looking at her condo's spare bedroom,
at the white walls and the shadow female figure kneeling on the floor. Through the headphones, she heard
the music as clearly as she had the day it had rocked
her system's speakers. Stunned, she continued to
watch the train wreck unfold.

She watched herself get to her feet and take hold of
the stripper pole, seeing exactly what Jacob had seen.
Seeing what she looked like as she danced. As her
body writhed. A body that seemed to belong to another
woman entirely.

Her shadow looked amazing, tight and fit and curvy.
And the dance came across exactly as she'd intended,

voluptuous and erotically wanton, as if the woman performing was in need of a very good time in a very bad way.

It was so much easier to think of the shadow as being that of someone else. Seeing the evidence of her sexuality expressed on the screen, especially while sitting here with what might as well be throngs of people milling around, and with Jacob beside her having watched the whole thing…

What in the hell had she been thinking? How had she managed to be so stupid as to get herself into this mess? She raised her hand and rubbed the ache from her forehead. Oh, if she only had a brain!

And then she heard it, a low moan that she knew was not part of the music or a sound only in her head. No, it was definitely in her ears. And definitely male. And, oh, it was definitely Jacob.

He was talking to her shadow, his voiceover offering a rumbling sort of purring encouragement, punctuated with ''Oh, baby, yeah'' and a few other guttural, less repeatable comments that left her reeling and weak-kneed and short of the breath she suddenly and desperately needed to breathe.

And then it began, the rustle of clothing, the slide of a zipper, the grunt of primal desire. The throaty growl of a man in need, in pain, in a state of arousal that offered but one option involving a woman or a right or left hand. Jacob, she knew, used his left—a thought that led to all sorts of visual imagining as she continued to listen, continued to watch.

The sound of his breathing grew labored and hard, the sound of his voice took on a hoarse edge, as if he'd passed a point of no return, as if her shadowy striptease turned him on as fiercely as the performance had her. As if coming was no longer an option but a vital part of staying alive.

The sounds, the words, the tone of his voice…his arousal was obvious—as was his solution. As had been hers. So why were they both masturbating to their sexual fantasies when they were two healthy, driven adults who wanted what the other offered in the way of physical bliss?

Never in her life would she have believed she'd want a man the way she wanted Jacob Faulkner, a want driven solely by sexual desire, having nothing to do with attributes beyond his body. Her longing wasn't about his intellect or his ambition. It was all about what he had in his pants.

How absolutely clichéd. How marvelously thrilling.

How totally un-Melanie Craine.

Stopping the DVD while her shadow tweaked at bared nipples with back arched and head tossed back, she unplugged the headphones and returned them to Jacob. Then she ejected the disk and handed him the player. But she slipped the evidence of their joint debauchery into her tote, not yet certain why she wanted it or if she wanted it at all. Just knowing that she didn't want to give it back.

Finally, having pulled together what she could of her shattered control, she pressed her lips together and glanced in his direction. He said nothing, but was no longer lying back and letting life pass him by. He was quite involved in the moment, reliving the experience along with her, sharing the heat of bodies and imaginations and the dance.

A bead of moisture rolled from his temple in a line to his jaw. His forearms glistened with perspiration. Sweat soaked the neckline of his T-shirt at the hollow of his throat. They were sitting in the shade of patio umbrellas, in the breeze circulated by the porch fans. Yet Jacob looked as if he was being burned from the inside out.

And Melanie suffered, oh, she ached, she burned, she sweltered in the same consuming heat. She swallowed and said, "Well, that was…quite…"

"Arousing?" Jacob said, and swung around sideways to face her, his legs tucked between their chairs.

"Interesting, at least," she answered, because he was so close now, and he smelled so good and so clean. She didn't want to talk about the tape. She wanted to live it. Every moment. To hear him purr. To hear his whisper. To hear those unspeakable words spill directly from his long chameleon tongue.

He leaned over into her space. His lips parted. His eyes flashed…and then he got to his feet. She looked straight ahead as he stood. Her gaze caught on the swell behind the zipper of his shorts; her heart beat so hard she feared her eardrums would burst.

She looked up. He looked down. And he smiled. "I feel like taking a swim. You're welcome to join me."

She didn't answer right away, what with nearly having swallowed her tongue when faced with his fly at eye level. And so he grinned—first with his mouth, crooking up the corners till his dimples showed, and then with his eyes. She swore his eyes were going to be the death of her. They flickered with pure wickedness, sparked with a challenge that teased.

"Be careful, Melanie," he added, when her silence continued. "Your control is showing."

He turned and stepped over his lounger, walking away and missing the glare Melanie threw at his back. *Control my ass,* she fumed. If he had half the intuition he claimed, he'd realize he'd spun her so far out of control she was dizzy from reeling.

Or maybe from the beer. Whatever.

She watched him walk away; her stomach pitched and rolled. She didn't want him to go. She wanted to go with him. She didn't want him. She did. And because she seemed not to know anything any longer, she looped the straps of her tote over her shoulder and stood.

She couldn't believe it; she wasn't going to stay put and remain seated and sane. She was going to follow the path into temptation. Her toes tingled, a buzzing sensation that weakened her knees on its upward sweep through her body, rendering the backyard conversations as unintelligible as a droning swarm of bees.

She walked through the patio door, into the stainless steel kitchen, and headed for the corner staircase. With each upward step, her stomach tumbled until she doubted she'd ever be able to eat anything again.

*Deep breath, Mel. You're only going for a swim.* Funny, but she already felt as if she were drowning. Anticipation made it so very hard to breathe.

At the end of the second floor hallway, the guest bedroom's door stood ajar. She'd left her larger beach tote on the bed when she'd first arrived. So now she would simply take her suit into the adjoining bathroom and change. Jacob was more likely than not finished; she'd catch up with him at the pool. End of nervous breakdown.

Except when she pushed the door wide open, she found that Jacob wasn't close to being finished at all. He was standing at the foot of the bed, his duffel open as he dug inside for his trunks. He was wearing nothing but his sandals and his unbuttoned denim shorts. When he realized she was there, he looked up.

She'd known from the fit of his clothes that his body was sculpted and lean, but she'd never expected to have her breath sucked away. She was stronger than that; she wasn't taken in by beefcake and bullshit. She knew better than to think a gorgeous body meant anything. But knowing, it seemed, worked better in theory than in practice.

He was absolutely beautiful, his shoulders broad and rounded with muscle, his biceps and triceps equally defined, his chest and abdomen dusted with dark hair. She stepped fully into the room, pushed the bedroom door closed and leaned back against it. The beat of her heart rapidly became a full-body flutter.

"I thought you'd be finished dressing by now."

"Is that why you shut the door?" He slowly unfolded his bright orange hibiscus-print trunks, draped them over his duffel, moved his hands to his hips while she watched. "So I could finish?"

She inclined her head; her fingers flexed so tightly into the cloth of her shorts she expected to find permanent wrinkles in her permanent press. "If you don't want the privacy, I can open it back up."

He shrugged one shoulder. "Well, you being here sorta limits the privacy I do have."

"I'll go then," she said, though the longer she stood here unmoving, the harder it was going to be to ever put one foot in front of the other again. "Is that what you want me to do?"

"You could do that." He left his trunks where they were and moved toward her, his body seeming so much larger in the flesh than she'd ever imagined when he'd been fully clothed. His dark eyes flashed. "Or you could stay."

Her heart beat painfully hard. "You want me to stay?"

"I'm not sure I can tell you what I want without getting graphic." He stood less than three feet away. So close she could feel waves of heat rolling from his body. So close she could think of nothing but sex.

The hardest thing she'd ever done was not reach for him then. She lifted a brow. "More graphic than the recording I just listened to?"

His mouth quirked. "At least as graphic as your dance."

"I didn't watch the tape before I sent it." She glanced away, breathed, looked back. "I knew things had gotten out of hand, but until I saw it just now…"

"I'd say you took things in hand quite nicely."

She pictured shadow hands pinching at shadow nipples and wanted to disappear into the wood grain of the door. "It sounded as if you did the same."

He took another step closer. "You made for great inspiration."

"So did you," she admitted, and her chin came up.

A chuckle sounded low in his throat. "I can't say I've been anyone's inspiration before. Don't women look for that in their sexy novels?"

"You mean the same way men look for theirs in *Playboy?*"

He grinned like the devil he was. "I prefer *Maxim*. Except when I can have the real deal."

She feigned ignorance and managed to find enough voice to ask, "The real deal?"

He nodded. "Flesh and blood. And warm. And willing. Not a glossy magazine page that never breaks a sweat.''

"A sweat?" It wasn't ignorance that had her mimicking a mynah bird, but anticipation flexing its claws.

"Yeah. A sweat."

One more step and he was close enough that she could grab him by the belt loops and tug him forward and into her body. She forced herself to wait. And she waited, because she could tell by his fiery gaze that she was about to sweat like she'd never sweated before.

"I like a woman who isn't afraid to work up a sweat." He dropped his gaze to her breasts, then to her belly, and finally brought up a hand, as if he was thinking about touching her. Taking his own sweet time. Torturing her on purpose. Teasing her unmercifully until she begged for what they both wanted.

The heady sense of being pursued made it so hard to stand still, to lean back against the door and pretend her weak knees weren't on the verge of collapse. He looked back up then, ran a fingertip along her hairline beneath her bangs, where perspiration always beaded first.

"Are you the real deal, Melanie?"

"I'm not afraid to sweat, if that's what you're asking." And she wasn't. Neither was she afraid of what he made her body feel. Her only fear was that if she gave up control to this man she'd never regain any of the discipline she'd worked for her entire life. She loved the challenge, hated the threat.

"Good." His finger slid behind her ear and down her neck, where he wiped the dampness from her nape. "Oh, yeah. Very nice."

Cocky bastard. Far too pleased with her response.

"Thank you. I do aim to please." How she got out the words she hadn't a clue. She could barely draw a breath.

This time when he moved, he leaned his head forward, his hand cupping her nape as his lips drew within millimeters of hers. "Melanie?"

"Hmm?" she hummed back, feeling the warmth of his breath and his body, smelling his clean hot skin, wanting desperately to taste him.

"Can I have you?" he whispered.

She gave an imperceptible nod because she didn't trust what was left of her voice to get the job done. "As long as I can have you."

He leaned into her body then, touching her the way she'd wanted to be touched since he'd hovered at her back and beside her that day in the church. With his palms flat on the door above her shoulders, he brushed his lips from her ear to her temple and down her cheekbone.

Her eyelids fluttered shut and she raised her chin, giving him access to her neck. He took it, nipping lightly at her skin until she finally slipped her fingers beneath his waistband, urging him closer.

She felt every tremor of the groan that rolled up his throat. "Melanie?"

"Jacob?" She blew her answering question softly over his ear.

A shudder ripped through him. "You sure this is what you want?"

"I'm sure it's what I want right now."

He hesitated, then ground out, "And that's enough?"

"You tell me," she answered, her head turning and her open mouth moving toward his throat.

He stood still and let her explore his skin with her tongue, let her nip her way along the resilient flesh of his shoulder, let her leave a trail of tiny damp kisses beneath his collarbone. His skin was salty and wonderfully warm. And she wanted to taste more. To feast. To feed the hunger he'd driven her to feel.

She tingled and ached but not nearly enough. Not completely. Not in the way she wanted, the way his eyes and the sounds he'd made promised to provide. So when he backed away from her mouth and all the fun she was having, it was all she could do not to scream.

"Why did you make that tape?" He glared at her, his chest heaving.

"Because your tape pissed me off," she answered, breathing equally hard.

"That wasn't what I intended."

She didn't care that he seemed contrite. "Then your intentions fell short, didn't they?"

"You say that like you know what they were."

She didn't care that he appeared defensive. "Does it matter?"

"I thought so at the time."

She didn't care that he looked put out. "And now?"

"Now I don't want to talk about it."

All she cared about was getting him out of his clothes. "Why's that? You can't talk and fuck at the same time?"

He took a moment before he answered, a moment in which Melanie's frustration reached an unbearable height. A moment in which she panicked, wondering if she'd actually pushed him too far. Goading was so much more palatable than begging, but right now, here with this man, she wasn't above getting down on her knees.

He ran a fingertip from her temple to her jaw, her chin and down her neck to her chest, where he drew a line back and forth along the scoop edge of her tank top. "Are you sure talking is what you really want me to do with my mouth?"

Finally! "I'd rather you shut up and show me what you can do with your tongue."

His face but inches from hers, he reached for the front fastenings to her khaki shorts. Melanie reached behind her and locked the door, praying everyone wanting to swim had already changed, because Jacob had opened the fly of her shorts and was now on his knees blowing warm breath on her belly. Her eyes rolled back and she closed them as the air-conditioned chill hit more and more of her skin.

She shivered from the cold, from the hot touch of Jacob's fingers where they drifted down her inner thighs. He was even better at taking off her clothes than she was, slowly slipping her shorts down her legs, his hands and mouth following the downward path, tickling, teasing, tasting her skin.

She blew out several short, panting breaths, her hands splayed flat on the door at her hips to keep her from sliding to the floor. Jacob had returned for her panties, and she thought she was going to die. He snugged a finger into a leg opening, his knuckle grazing her sex as he dragged the back of that one finger from her clit to her core.

His mouth opened over the fabric, the moist heat of his breath melting her panties. Or so it seemed since, as damp as they were, they no longer offered any sort of barrier. And then the lack didn't matter because she wasn't wearing them. Jacob had used that one finger hooked over the crotch to pull the scrap of silk to her feet.

She wanted to open her eyes, to read his face, to divine what he was thinking. Instead, she opened her legs and dropped her head back against the door. She wasn't sure what to do with her hands, and wanted to help, wanted to use her own fingers to spread open her sex, giving Jacob full access. But then there was no need.

He'd taken his thumbs, dipped them briefly into her entrance, then used the moisture to spread open her folds, revealing the hard knot where sensation stabbed in sharp, prickly bursts. The bursts intensified with no more than a brush from his thumbs, from the hot breath he blew, from the pressure he applied on either side of her clit.

He rubbed both thumbs in circles, pushing into the bundles of nerves just beneath her skin until she had to catch a cry, letting it go as no more than a whimper. And then she felt the flick of his tongue and she moved her hands to his head, sliding her fingers into his hair.

Absolutely amazing, what he was doing with his mouth, the way his lips sucked at her there between her thighs, pulling at her flesh until the ache in the core of her body was the only thing she knew. She felt herself slipping—her back down the door, her fingers out of Jacob's hair, her control toward an orgasm for which she wasn't ready.

First she wanted more of what he was making her feel; she'd felt nothing this intoxicating in years, if ever. She'd lost her spine, her strength, lost all feeling but for the sex. Lost all awareness but for knowing it was Jacob giving her this bliss. Jacob, whom she wasn't even sure she liked, doing things with his tongue about which she'd only dreamed.

Licking and lapping and—oh, yes, yes—pushing into her, pulling out—oh, again, please again—eating her so thoroughly she wondered if she would ever get enough, knowing she might never have this again because this was all about a fling. All about the moment. All a part of the tension that had been keeping the air charged between them.

But the reminder fell on ears that no longer worked because she was a total morass of physical sensation, a sexual creature taking pleasure and forgoing thought. Engaging fully in the sort of behavior she'd prided herself on rising above. Right now she wanted to sink as low as she could go.

Jacob made it easy and beautiful, made her crazy with the way he used his fingers to stroke her, following with his tongue, opening her up to his attentions and humming his encouragement into her sex. He pushed two fingers inside of her, drew on her clit with a suction that was torturously slow and intense. Again and again. Fingering her. Sucking on her.

It was too much all at once, and she came. Shuddering, quivering. The spasms seemed never to stop, what with Jacob knowing exactly how to ease her beyond the first initial flash into the long lingering tremors that she thought would never end. Inevitably, they did, and when the end came she wanted to collapse onto the floor. She had absolutely no idea what had just happened.

She only knew she wanted more. More of what Jacob had given her. And more of Jacob. She started to reach for her shorts, but he lifted her foot and pulled both her shorts and panties off her ankle. Then he got to his feet, his body heavy where he leaned into hers, chest to chest, belly to belly.

She closed her eyes, wanting to lie beneath him, to bear his weight, to take him into her body. Her hands again found their way to his waistband; she dipped her fingers beneath to his belly, where his fly remained open. Her heart thudded in wild anticipation. She'd come like she'd never come before, yet still arousal ran through her veins.

Moving her fingertips slowly from his hipbones toward the erection that filled out the front of his white Calvin Kleins, she opened her eyes, looking straight up into his, which flashed with a heat that raised her temperature by immeasurable degrees. She nudged her hands closer together, closer to his penis, and then she was there, the sides of her index fingers in contact with skin so amazingly soft for covering an erection so amazingly hard.

She took her time, stroking her fingers up and down the side of his cock's head. He let out a long hissing breath, a sharp staccato curse, a deep rumbling growl that sent a shiver to settle at the base of her spine.

And then he took both of her hands in his and pulled them from his shorts before he grinned like the cocky bastard he was and said, "My turn."

# 6

JACOB SWORE HE'D HUNT down anyone who dared knock on the door and interrupt.

He didn't have the patience to deal with bullshit. He barely had the patience to get Melanie across the room. Getting inside her sweet body was already taking way too long.

Forget bothering with kisses and foreplay and pretty pillow talk. Later. They'd get to all of that later. Right now his mind was in sync with his body and they shared but one goal.

He kicked out of his shorts and boxers, turned and dropped into the overstuffed easy chair in the corner of the room. Melanie climbed onto his lap, her knees hugging his hips. She raised up as if to settle down and take him inside.

It was all he could do to stop her. "Wait."

"What?" she whispered hoarsely, sitting back on his knees.

"Grab my shorts. I need a condom."

She did, coloring slightly as if embarrassed that she'd been so carried away.

But when he started to tear open the packet, she boldly took it from his hands, freeing him up to strip off her top, take hold of her rib cage and scrape his thumbs back and forth over her nipples.

He leaned forward, took one pebbled peak between

his lips and sucked until she whimpered and pushed him away.

"You're distracting me."

"No. You're distracting me." He moved to the other breast, flicked his tongue over the other nipple. She shuddered there in his lap and made him a very happy man. "I love your tits. They're so soft. So sensitive."

She snorted. "I thought bigger was better."

He grinned against her skin, loving the softness against his, which was much rougher due to his fast-growing beard. "Size only matters when it comes to a man and his cock."

"So say men, anyway."

"Now, sweetheart. That's just jock talk." He leaned back in the chair, invited her to cover him up. Watching her slender fingers work their way over and around the head of his cock was torture, visually, tactilely.

Waiting until she was ready again was going to be damn hard. He'd be lucky not to come there in her hand, which held him so right. "We know it's all about using what we've got."

She kept her lips pressed together while rolling the condom to the base of his shaft.

"What? You don't believe me?" he asked, and her lips moved in what he thought was a smile, though one that seemed directed inward rather than in response to his teasing comment.

And then she raised up on both knees, scooted closer to his hips and took him fully into her hand. "Oh, I believe you. I'm just afraid that if you use this even half as well as you use your mouth then we're going to be seeing more of each other than either of us planned."

"If you can live with that, I'm good to go." And then, because waiting any longer wasn't an option, he surged upward, driving himself into her body in one smooth thrust before he collapsed on his back.

She gasped. He stopped. She sat back with her hands on her thighs, blew out several short, panting breaths before she shuddered and groaned. He didn't know if he'd hurt her; hell, he wasn't that much bigger than average.

But something here was definitely not right. This was way beyond anything he knew about the way a woman enjoyed sex. "Melanie? Are you okay?"

She closed her eyes, shook her head, gave a derisive-sounding snort that started to piss him off until she said, "You have no idea how good you feel."

Oh, well, that he could handle. Not to mention relate to. He chuckled, and then groaned because she moved, leaning forward and bracing her hands on his shoulders. Sitting as he was, the move put her breasts right at his mouth level where they belonged.

"You're laughing?" she asked.

"No, sweetheart. I'm enjoying. I don't think you know exactly how tight you are. How hot." She lifted her hips and he hissed. He retaliated by nipping at the firm flesh of one breast, pulling on one nipple until she whimpered. "Crap, Melanie. You keep that up, I'm not going to be much good down here."

"Keep what up? This?" She lifted her hips until only the head of his cock remained inside her, then sank back down slowly, burying him to the hilt, rotating her hips in an amazing figure eight as she repeated the entire process.

"Yeah. That. Mel, stop. Stop." She did and he ground his teeth until he thought his jaw would break.

Sweat pooled at the small of his back. "The way you sound. Those noises you make. That thing you do with your hips. I think I'm about to die."

"Die in a good way, I hope." Leaning back into the palms she'd braced behind her on his knees, she tilted her pelvis upward, the motion putting everything right where he could get an eyeful when he looked down.

Her pussy spread open by his cock, her clit exposed there beneath the line of dark hair above her beautifully naked lips. Bare lips, so delicately soft. Her sex glistening with her juices, which he knew tasted like warm saltwater and sweet peaches.

Seeing himself there where he entered her, his cock thick and red, her sex a pale pink, the condom slick with the fluid of her arousal…he groaned and pushed upward, as far as their position would allow. He wanted more, wanted it harder. But she wasn't finished making him wait.

Using nothing but her knees at his hips and the muscles of her abdomen to hold her body still, she brought her hands to her stomach and slid her palms down over her belly. She didn't stop, even when her fingertips reached her mound, but went lower, pulling back on the hood of her clit, circling her entrance as he filled her.

He died a little more when her touch grazed the sides of his cock. Died even further when she leaned forward, sucking him into her vagina, and pressed her hands to his abdomen, digging the heels of her palms into the muscles there at the base of his shaft.

He couldn't take it anymore. He grabbed her wrists and held her arms to her hips, driving upward, again and again. He held just as tightly to her gaze, refusing to close his eyes or look away as his orgasm rocked through him. He had to know, to see. *Yes!*

She followed him into completion, her mouth open, her chest heaving as she labored to breathe. Shudders swept through her body, swept through his; he felt the contractions of her climax and pumped harder, rubbing her clit with every thrust of his cock.

Finally spent, she had a series of quick tremors. He slowed, making sure she slowed with him. Her silent nod gave him permission to pull away. He exhaled, unbelievably sated. And sleepy.

He sat there for a long moment, sprawled naked while she backed off his lap and out of the chair. He continued to sit and watch while she found her clothes scattered across the carpet from the doorway.

She dressed without looking at him, and his lethargy faded. He didn't want her to feel bad about anything they'd just done. He wanted her to feel good. And he wanted her to feel more. He wasn't halfway finished with having her.

He pushed himself to his feet, disposed of the condom in the room's attached bathroom, walked back into the bedroom buck naked just in time to see Melanie slip her feet into her shoes. He didn't even stop to pick up his clothes. He headed straight for her, hooked an elbow around her neck and forced her head up. Her eyes were doe-wide and doe-bright, and she gasped.

"You scare me," she said, but that was all she got out before he brought his mouth down on hers. He slanted one way, brushing his lips lightly at first, then with the pressure he'd been holding back. Her responsive nature made it hard to go slow.

But this time her response was to pull away, to step

back from his embrace, grab up her purse and the bag with her bathing suit. "I really need to go."

"Go? Where?" *What the hell?* He frowned, bending down to grab his shorts and drawers and pull them both on. "You're leaving? Just like that?"

She kept her gaze averted and headed for the bedroom door, digging in her bag for her car keys. "I've just…got to get home. I've got to go."

He fastened his shorts, tossed his trunks back into his duffel and pulled on his T-shirt. This wasn't happening. He didn't believe this was happening. That she was running out after what they'd done here in this room, after having the sort of sex they'd just had.

Sex she'd been into just as much as he had, goddammit.

He was not going to start feeling guilty over… He didn't even know where the idea of guilt was coming from. It wasn't as if he was at fault here for whatever she was accusing him of. If she was accusing him of anything.

He didn't know what was going through her head. He only knew he wasn't going to let her get away without making things right.

Or not.

She was halfway through the door and obviously in no mood to talk. She hadn't even looked back once. She'd just gotten up and dressed and the hell out of Dodge. Fine, he mused with more than a touch of irritation. He zipped up his duffel, stuffed his feet into his sandals and followed.

He'd just take Dodge to her.

JACOB PULLED HIS TRUCK away from the curb and in behind Melanie's sparkling black Infiniti Coupe. He was not about to let her pretend nothing had happened between them—even if what had happened between them was nothing but sex.

If she thought what they'd done was something she could turn her back on, well, that wasn't going to happen. He had his pride, but he also had a strangely vested interest in Melanie now. As long as he didn't lose her on the drive to her place, he planned to let her know the extent of that involvement.

He needed to do it before she could get on the phone with one of her girlfriends and "bond" over the size of his dick or the way he played too rough or whatever it was about sex and guys women gabbed about. *He* sure wasn't going to call her up and gab about whatever was going on with her.

Yet knowing all that, he still wasn't clear on why he was chasing her down, why he had this urgent need to set her straight. Pure selfishness on the part of his dick was undoubtedly the biggest reason. He wouldn't work this woman out of his sexual system anytime soon.

And, sure. His pride was involved. He didn't like thinking he'd disappointed her. Or left her dissatisfied. Ego or no, however, he *knew* that hadn't happened. She'd come twice during the, what? Ten minutes they'd been in the bedroom? Fifteen tops?

Women didn't come like that if they weren't having fun. What he couldn't figure was, if she'd been having all that fun, why the hell had she taken off the way she had? He hadn't exactly kicked her dog or burned off her cat's whiskers.

What he should do was back away, let her tuck her tail and go. It wasn't like he was looking for a relationship. Sure. He could get off nicely on spending a lot more time with her naked. But soon enough he'd be outta here, off to New York, maybe to L.A., once he hooked up with the right project and made the right connections. He never had fooled himself into thinking a guy could afford a woman along with his career.

Career obsession aside, he'd spent enough time with Melanie in the office to know he wasn't imagining the more personal tension sizzling between them. Acting on it had pretty much been inevitable. The when and the where there in the middle of the cookout might not have been his best-ever exercise in spontaneity, but the bait itself?

"Give me a friggin' break," he muttered, rolling over a freshly patched pothole and bouncing in and out of another. After seeing her shadow work that pole, he'd never flinched once about adding the voiceover to her video production. She knew her body; she knew what she liked. She knew what he liked. And his edited version of her video had shown her exactly how right she'd been.

He'd told her he was visually inclined and she'd given him a hell of show to watch, offered him more to look at than skin and lingerie. She was creative. Innovative. Spectacular. Not the type of woman to panic over a wrong step, a mistake. What they'd done was not a mistake.

No, he thought, easing his way down the narrow streets into Midtown, cursing foully as Melanie shot through a yellow traffic light, making him run the red. She had to be all bent out of shape about how she'd lost that control she prized so highly. He shook his head.

What better time to let it go than during sex? Any man would appreciate the way she'd come undone. As smart as she was, as sharp, how could she not know that? She had to know that, and she had to be in denial. The woman was some piece of work.

And, for now, she was his.

He pulled through the security gate and into the parking lot of her small complex, stopping his truck in the space beside her car. She cast him a brief glance that he was hard-pressed to interpret before heading down the shadowed walkway between the converted condominiums. All he could do was follow and hope she didn't bust his chops for stalking or trespassing or just plain pissing her the hell off.

It was when she reached her front door, shaded by a brick archway covered with ivy, that he realized how shaken she was. He walked up behind her and hovered at her back, watching her hand tremble as she tried to work the key into the lock.

The tremor turned the simple act of opening the door into what appeared to be a major feat of motor skills. And that made him feel like shit.

Without looking up, she took a shuddering breath, reached back and offered him the key. He took it, deftly shoved it into the lock and turned. With her push, the door swung open. Taking two steps inside, she held out her hand. But he'd already reached around her and dropped the key onto the table in her entryway.

Her bags slid from her shoulder to the floor. She let them fall, using one foot to shove both toward the table. But before she had a chance to move even a step away, Jacob took her hand and pulled her into the living room. He'd learned his lesson; he wasn't giving her another chance to escape. This time—if the fact that she'd let him inside meant there was going to be a this time—they were going to do this right.

She gestured toward the rear of the condo. "The bedroom's in the back."

"I'll keep that in mind." He wrapped his arms around her waist and pulled her body to his. She was such a perfect fit. "For later. For now, this'll do."

He lowered his head, determined to finish the kiss they'd started earlier. But Melanie wasn't having any of it. With the tip of her tongue caught between her teeth, she watched his mouth descend, then turned her head so his lips brushed her cheek.

*Okay*, he thought, and left them there, nuzzling the soft skin along her jaw and beneath, sliding his hands down to the swell of her ass and drawing her close.

Well, hell. She wasn't having any of that, either. She wedged her fists between their bodies and pushed him back, causing him to bite down on the several nasty things he wanted to say.

Instead of asking what the hell her problem was, he settled for, "What's up, Melanie? I can kiss you below the waist but not above?"

"I don't need to be seduced." She reached for the hem of her white cotton tank top and, once it was off, unhooked the back clasp of her bra. "I mean, it's nice, but it's not necessary."

With the bra's cups and straps dangling, she pulled his T-shirt over his head and off. Only the silk-and-lace lingerie hanging loose between them kept their skin from making contact. "I assumed you'd rather get straight down to business."

The woman had a chip the size of King Kong's hairy butt on her shoulder. One corner of Jacob's mouth twitched. He wanted to laugh even more than he wanted to tell her the fuck off. His reaction wasn't about anger, but about wondering whether or not she was worth the effort.

Or if he was totally wasting his time here, doing what he could to show her how to have fun.

Then he wondered if having fun was against whatever personal rules she lived by. Just his luck she'd be all work and no play in bed as well as out. Except he didn't believe that for a minute, not after living through the last few hours and having her straddle his lap.

No. This was all about kid gloves, mint juleps and magnolias, and he figured the investment would be time well spent. "Believe it or not, Ms. Craine, foreplay is not proprietary to women."

"I don't recall saying that it was," she said, her mouth getting all uppity and bowed.

He rocked his hips against hers. "Yeah, but actions speak louder than words, sweetheart."

She huffed, rolled her eyes.

And he grinned, slipping his fingertips beneath the waistband of her shorts and teasing the skin there above the curve of her ass. When she shuddered, he held her closer, his hands drifting lower to cup her sweetly rounded bottom. At that more intimate contact, her full-body shivers set in.

"Cold?" he asked.

"Hardly."

"Hot?"

"Sizzling."

"Hmm." Now they were getting somewhere. "I'd say sizzling's only about half as hot as you need to be."

"Promises, promises."

"You think I can't take you there?"

"Actually, no," she said in that snotty tone that he'd be quite happy never to hear again. "I'm sure you can. I just didn't know if you wanted to expend that much effort."

"Trust me. It's no effort."

A brow went up. "That sure of yourself, are you?"

Easy answer. He shook his head. "No. I'm that sure of *you.* Unlike when making your little skin flick, you weren't exactly alone in that bedroom earlier, you know."

She wanted to look away, but his gaze held hers. "That was just…the heat of the moment."

"The moment, huh? That was it? You're saying *you* can't do that again?"

"Good grief, no," she said, and frowned. "I'm not saying anything of the sort."

"You think *I* can't do that again?"

She gave a small shrug and looked away. "I'm wondering why you would want to."

"Why would I want to have sex?" he asked after picking up his jaw.

Melanie closed her eyes. "No. I know why you would want to have sex. It's just that we already did. You came, you conquered, made your conquest and all that."

"Wait a minute." Where in the hell was she coming from? He raised a hand and forced up her chin. He wanted to see her eyes, to know what she was thinking. "You think because I had you once I don't want you again?"

"It's been known to happen. More than a few times, I'm sorry to say," she said flatly. Then honesty widened her eyes and she softly added, "But, no. I'm hoping that's not the case with you."

It really was unbelievable the way some guys screwed over women and made the rest of the male population pay for their sins. Still, as much as he wanted her to understand exactly how hot she was, he didn't want to get in too deep. He wasn't here to save her from her personal demons.

He picked his next words carefully. "Here's the deal, Melanie. I want you in ways I doubt you've ever imagined. But one furtive quickie a day is my limit. This time, let's take our time and make this more of an adventure."

The look in her eyes almost made him think twice. The hope, the need, the uncertainty—all elements that could easily mean death to a single man. He might have been worried if not for the fact that both of them were fully aware they were offering one another nothing but fulfillment in bed. That he could handle.

So, as much as he hated what he was about to do, he found the clasp of her bra and hooked it back into place. Then he scooped up her tank top from the floor, slipped it over her frowning forehead and down over that soft skin that was making him righteously insane.

His own shirt he didn't care about. But getting Melanie out of her clothes, stripping her naked in his own time and way…that was something he wanted more than he'd thought possible. And handling that realization was going to require more work than the other.

"Now." He stepped back and held both of her hands. "I want to see your pole."

She blinked. Then her eyes widened as she understood exactly what it was he was asking. And, at that, her faced flushed a beautiful shade of peach.

"Why?" she asked, pushing a hand up through the hair at her nape. "It's just part of my workout routine. It's not like I have a stripper fantasy or anything."

"Yeah," he said, taking her hand and more than a bit of pleasure in getting in the last word. "But I do."

He led her down the hallway, past a dark bathroom and a bedroom as starkly black-and-white as her office. At least she was consistent—and obviously Little Miss Sunshine at home, as well as at gIRL-gEAR. He'd have to buy her a gallon of bright orange paint for her birthday, he thought, and frowned.

O-kay. That was strange, thinking of her birthday and buying her gifts. He shook his head and pushed away the unsettling thought as he reached the last room in the back of her place.

The room with the pole in the center.

The pole that he'd thought about every time he'd dreamed about her and come awake with one of his own.

She followed him to the doorway, and when he glanced at her from over his shoulder, she gestured for him to feel free to take the tour. But he shook his head. He was not here to look around.

He was here to be entertained. To see the live show that her tape had captured. To watch the very uptight Melanie Craine let it all hang out. He took a seat in her desk chair, swiveled it forward and booted up her PC.

"What are you doing?"

He glanced back to see her still standing in the doorway with her arms crossed over her chest. So uppity. As if the world would end if she let herself go. "Looking for your music files."

"Why?"

He found the bulk of her MP3s and a collection she'd saved as "dance.m3u" in her My Music folder. He launched her media player and opened the file, adjusting the volume of her speakers. Then he turned back around, looked her up and down, and grinned. "Because. I want to watch you dance."

He thought for a second that she was going to get huffy and stomp away. She did that thing with her nose, lifting it enough so she had to look at him through the bottom half of her lenses.

He wondered why she didn't wear contacts—not that he was complaining. He sort of liked the way she looked hiding behind her black retro frames.

*Hiding.* Hmm. He wondered what she was hiding from. And why, now that he'd figured it out, it didn't bother him more than it did. More than it probably would if he stopped to think about it—which he wasn't going to do.

Finally, Melanie made her decision. She walked into the center of the room and took hold of the pole, wrapping one knee around it. She shook her head slowly, her gaze direct and challenging as she told him no.

"I've danced for you once already. I won't do it again. But," she added, her hips now swaying to the music's bass beat, "I'll dance *with* you if you want to dance."

He thought about that for a minute. About dancing with her. About being too close to watch her body move the way he wanted to. Too close to watch, but right there up against her and able to feel. All of her. Every move.

The bumps and the grinds and the cha-cha-cha. Her legs winding in and out of his, her hips pressing to him. Her arms raised, her breasts lifted and rounded, the perfect handful he so wanted to get palms and fingers and mouth back around. Her chin up, her head back and all that soft skin of her neck his to nuzzle and kiss.

He could taste her already.

Yeah. He liked the concept. Liked it a lot. He pushed himself out of the chair, caught off guard by the surge of lust that drove through him as he stood and faced her. She wasn't doing anything but standing there, leaning into the pole, her eyes lit brightly with his favorite sort of mischief.

But he felt himself seconds away from pulling a caveman stunt and dragging her off to his lair to mate.

Her mercurial moods intrigued him, enchanted him and made him wary as hell. But right this moment nothing mattered except here and now and making sure she understood that he intended to fully enjoy every inch of her body, every moment they spent together naked in bed. Or wrapped tightly together while standing.

When he reached her, he kept the pole between them, lifting his arms and grabbing it with both hands high overhead. He remained still, watching as Melanie moved, her hips swaying side to side, her pelvis tilted toward his, first on one side, then the other, never making contact but coming close to his thighs with each pass.

The music switched gears and so did Melanie. She placed her hands on his bare chest, slid her fingertips toward his sides and stroked with her nails from his armpits up to his wrists. When she reversed direction for the trip back down, he had to brace himself so he wouldn't grab her and haul her straight to the floor.

By the time she reached his waistband, she'd worked him into a sweat—and seemed pleased about it. Her fingertips slid from his sides to his belly, just there above the line of his shorts.

He ground his teeth, unsure which would break first—his jawbone from the pressure or his cock from the anticipation.

With beautifully nimble fingers she released the button of his fly and dragged down his zipper, never touching his erection the way he wished she would...more than anything. Even more than he wanted to let go of the pole and grab hold of her, he wished she would grab hold of him.

What she did, though, was a worse sort of torture. Because now that she'd eased his shorts and his boxers down his hips to the floor, now that he was the one standing bare-assed naked while she remained clothed, she was back in control.

And he couldn't remember ever in his life feeling so close to the edge of his own.

All his best intentions to take his time and do this right were quickly flying in the face of his desire. Especially since Melanie had slipped around to stand between him and the pole, and was shimmying out of her shorts. Her hair tickled his chin, and the scent of her perfume rose in intoxicating waves. She was right here, right now, inches away, and still he waited while arousal grew.

The file of songs that she'd saved and he'd chosen rang in his ears with the rhythm of sex. Yet that provocatively carnal striptease on tape was nothing compared to the live action version of having Melanie take off her clothes.

It was when she bent over that he couldn't take it

anymore. She held on to the pole for balance, leaning forward and lifting her sweet cheeks right into his groin, rubbing back and forth over his cock with an invitation designed to cause a saint to fall.

He reached down and dug a condom from his shorts, kicking out of his sandals and the garments binding his ankles. And then he caressed the backs of her knees, drawing his hands up her thighs until he reached the crevice of her bottom.

He slipped his erection between her legs, slipped his hands beneath her top and her bra, massaging her bare breasts until she whimpered. He couldn't wait any longer.

Not with Melanie shoving back against him, writhing against him, lifting and opening and pushing against him. He moved his hands to her backside and spread her cheeks, thrusting forward into her sweet little sex. She squeezed, and he thought he was going to go off. Grabbing her hips, he stilled and shuddered and hissed at her when she tried to move.

But she was having too much of a good time, and the sounds she was making fueled his lust until he knew nothing but the way she felt, all wet and warm and soft, and the way the rhythm of his stroke was taking him to oblivion.

He continued to pump and to thrust, but reached down between her legs and found her clit, circling the tiny hard button and selfishly enjoying the way she squirmed. And then he held his breath and gritted his teeth and turned off what sensation he could to concentrate on her pleasure—a noble determination that lasted about five seconds.

He couldn't take it anymore. She was just too much, holding the pole, her feet spread wide, her sex vividly exposed where he could once again see everything going on—his cock sliding in and out, her pink flesh so swollen and wet and stretched wide to accommodate his girth.

Her lower body ground wildly against his. How was any guy supposed to hold out?

And then she came, crying out and grabbing hold of his hand there between her legs, using his fingers the way she wanted, pressing them on either side of her clitoris before sliding them down with her own to wrap around the base of his shaft.

Unbelievable. She was fuckin' unbelievable. And he was in deeper than he'd ever thought possible. A depth that had nothing to do with how far into Melanie he'd buried his cock, but was all about the sensations flooding through him.

And then his balls drew up and he was done. He unloaded hard and fast, unable to focus on anything but the burst of pleasure taking him apart. She took him in and took it all until he had nothing left to give.

And when he was empty and spent, he held her to him, sinking down to the floor, keeping their bodies joined. He wasn't ready to let her go. Not yet. Not yet. He held her there in his lap, wrapped his arms around her waist even as she continued to face away from him, her forehead braced against the hands she'd stacked on the pole.

When she lifted her hips slowly and eased him from her body, he moved back far enough to pull off the condom. But then he reached for her again and drew her close, settling her into the "V" of his spread legs.

Neither spoke, as if what had happened between

them was far beyond explanation, too important or enigmatic to be put into words. Words. Jacob's worst enemy.

He wasn't even going to try.

# 7

MELANIE SHOVED ANOTHER forkful of lemongrass chicken into her mouth, giving no more than a passing thought to what her fellow diners might think of her manners.

She was starving, and the only person in Mai's Restaurant she would ever see again already knew the truth about her unlady-like appetites.

Besides, Jacob was sitting across the table shoveling down his own food just as fast and as furiously. Or he had been last time she'd stopped eating long enough to look away from her plate.

She did so again and saw that he was simply staring at her while she fed her ravenous gut.

Oh, yeah. Definitely unlady-like.

"What are you looking at?" she finally asked, once she realized he wasn't going to go away or stop staring.

Forearms propped on the table, he gestured toward her with the tines of his fork. "You. I'm sorta getting off here watching you eat."

*Lame,* she thought, though the response was admittedly more automatic than heartfelt. "I don't see what you find so fascinating. It's fork to mouth, wash, rinse and repeat, just like it is for everyone here."

"Well, not exactly." Jacob cast several bold glances around the Asian restaurant, where the placement of the tables left little room for privacy and even less for the servers to squeeze between. "You're the only one eating with such...gusto."

She finished chewing the bite of food in her mouth, then laid her fork along the edge of her plate and laced her fingers over the napkin in her lap. Arching her eyebrows, she pressed her lips together for a moment, trying to work out whether he was teasing her for a reaction or just because he was who he was.

And, in reality, weren't they one and the same thing?

Finally, she queried, "Gusto?"

He nodded and wiggled both brows. "Yep. Gusto."

"I see." Lifting her napkin, she dabbed at one corner of her mouth, hoping to hide what felt like a smile. "Well, any gusto I may exhibit is solely because of you."

His responding grin was devilishly rapacious. "I'll gladly take full credit."

"As well you should. You caused me to miss out on the burgers at Chloe's cookout," she said, enjoying herself even more than the flush of perceived insult showing in his face.

He snorted, then leaned forward and growled, "Burgers my ass. Sure. I'll take responsibility for you running out on the food. But you ran because you couldn't wait to get home and show me your pole."

If she'd been drinking, she would've choked. As it was, she covered her laugh with the napkin and pretended to cough. "The culprit here is your pole. Not mine." She paused, wondered how ready either of them was for honesty, and forged gamely ahead.

"Still, I doubt I'll ever be able to exercise in that room again without..."

"Without thinking about me?"

That much of a confession she wasn't ready to make—not to herself, and certainly not to him. "Without thinking about sex, at least," she admitted, toying with the last bite of chicken on her plate.

"Good. That means I'm doing my job here well."

Her fork stilled. "And your job would be?"

Jacob chewed a mouthful of lettuce-wrapped spring roll, washed it down with a swallow of green tea. "To inject a bit of fun into your life. You need to think about sex more often. And now you will."

"Inject, huh?" Keeping a straight face around this man was growing increasingly difficult, even as she felt an odd relief that he wasn't going anywhere just yet. "And since when are you an expert on how often I think about sex?"

"Not an expert." He peered into his teapot and gestured to the server for a refill. "More like a trained observer. A good cameraman sees things not everyone sees, remember?"

Ah, yes. They'd had a similar conversation that day in the church. About how his profession had changed the way he looked at life. The peek at his hidden depths still intrigued her to this day. "Well, then. What exactly do you see that leads you to believe I don't think about sex often enough?"

He waited for the server to leave before answering. "Sweetheart, look at yourself. You're too seriously black-and-white. Your clothing, your office, your condo, your car. The frames of your glasses. Even the dance you did for the tape."

"The dance?" She smoothed down the knee of her black linen slacks, curious how the striptease factored into his color-coded analysis.

Jacob dunked his tea bag, frowning as he obviously tried to put his thoughts together. And then he returned the lid to the ceramic pot and looked up with that fascinating darkness flickering in his eyes.

"As sexy as the dance was—and it was, trust me on that—it was still a shadow. It was flat and it was gray. Like you didn't want me to see how firecracker-red you really are."

God, if he kept looking at her like that she was going to have to throw out her entire wardrobe. "Next time I'll be sure to colorize the tape."

"Don't do that. Just…loosen up. Wear red." He leaned forward as if sharing a confidence. "It's like a trigger, like wearing sexy lingerie next to your skin. No one else needs to understand the reason you've jazzed up your closet. But you'll know."

"And I'll think about sex."

"Sure." He shrugged one shoulder. "Do it often enough and it'll be a Pavlovian response."

"So…you've decided that because I have a preference for simplicity and uncomplicated design instead of wearing fussy accessories and come-fuck-me red pumps, I'm not sexy?"

"Yes. I mean, no. Shit. That's not what I was trying to say." He scrubbed a hand through his hair. "It's not about whether or not you're sexy, because you're spicy as hell. This is more about the way you see yourself, whatever the reason is that you pretend you're not a chili pepper."

Spicy or not, she tossed her napkin to the center of her plate and crossed her arms over her chest. "I'm sure you know you're digging yourself one hell of a deep grave here."

"Uh, yeah. I figured that." He blew out an exasperated breath. "Okay. Here. The day of the wedding. The first day I saw you. You were wearing yellow. It was soft and sheer and all marshmallow-bunny pastel."

An eyebrow went up. "Marshmallow-bunny pastel?"

"Wait for it." He picked up his knife and fork as if his motor skills drove his thought processes. His voice dropped to just above a whisper. "You were hot. Sizzling beyond belief. You have no idea how hard it was not to drag you out to the van, strip you out of all that yellow and screw your brains out."

"I see," she said, marginally alarmed by the hint of a tremor in her voice, soundly aroused by the idea that he had wanted her that much, absolutely fascinated by how appealing she found the idea of being ravished. "So, what you're saying is that marshmallow-bunny-pastel yellow turns you on."

"No, Melanie. You turn me on. I don't care if you're wearing yellow or black or khaki or white." He returned his flatware to the table and sat back, staring at her with an intensity that had her reaching up to push her glasses solidly up the bridge of her nose.

The nervous gesture gave her away. She saw realization dawn in the gentle shake of his head. "Making that outtake video backfired on me, big time."

"I don't understand." The rapid-fire beat of her heart demanded he be clear.

He dragged both hands down his face before looking at her through a veil of frustration. "I meant to show you how out of line you were in trying to tell me how to do my job. But all I did was remind myself how sexy you are."

Enchanted, she forced herself to snort. "Next you'll

give me a big cliché about how beautiful I look when I'm angry.''

"Not beautiful. That's too tame a word for what I saw. You were…mesmerizing.'' He noted her gape and shrugged. "I forgot that you won't ever see what I see when I look through a camera's view finder.''

Finally! Another glimpse into Jacob's mind, a glimpse of what he thought of her. Mesmerising. The revelation thrilled her in unimaginable ways. "But isn't that basic psychology? Men are more visually inclined? Women communicate on a different level?''

He looked incredibly tired. "I guess I should've added a voiceover to the outtakes.''

Not quite an apology, but a decent enough explanation. "I wouldn't have gotten so angry if you had.''

"True,'' he said with a laugh. "But then I would've missed out on your retaliatory striptease.''

"And we wouldn't be sitting here now.''

He cocked his head to one side. "I'm not so sure.''

Her ears perked up, along with the beat of her heart. "Why not?''

This time his mouth quirked in that way he had that made her want to kiss him. That cute sort of lift to the left corner, and that plump little pout beneath. She wanted so badly to kiss him.

Sleeping with him was all about pleasure, but kissing him? No. Kissing was personal in a way that involved more emotion than required by straight unattached sex. The very same emotion that had brought her to the edge of tears and reason when he'd held her in his lap not an hour ago.

Never in her life had she felt more cherished than when she'd been sitting naked on the hardwood floor in the circle of his arms. How twisted was that, that

Jacob Faulkner would be the one to show her the tenderness she'd longed for desperately in the relationships she'd had?

"Uh, Melanie?"

"I'm sorry." She shook off the dangerously distracting thoughts. "What did you say?"

He rolled his eyes. "I said that I've watched every frame of footage I've shot for the documentary. And I know I'm not imagining that you like what you see when you look at me."

Conceited bastard. "What if I do? I'm sure you walk past the occasional mirror. You're not exactly Yoda."

He arched a wicked brow. "More like Han Solo?"

"Uh, no."

"Damn."

He was so irresistible that, well, she couldn't resist. "Okay, yes, Han Solo. Rakish and conceited and incredibly beddable."

"Hmm. Beddable."

She nodded. "I concede the point. We would've ended up here together, striptease or not."

"Here, literally, as in eating Vietnamese?"

"As opposed to…?" she asked.

He shrugged. "The figurative 'here' of coming together and dancing naked with your pole."

She blinked and stared, wondering if he was as unsure about what was happening between them as she was.

"Don't get me wrong," he said when she didn't reply. "I'm not complaining. It's just that as exceptionally cool as I find the idea of your pole, I would love to get you into bed. A real bed. A padded mattress with soft sheets and pillows."

"I see."

"No. I don't think you do." He glanced around at the closest tables, as if making sure he'd pitched his voice low enough for this particular conversation. "I'm a pig. Selfish and greedy and totally unrepentant. And you're passionate and uninhibited and confident and daring and creative—"

"And you want to get into my pants."

"Repeatedly."

"You're talking about an affair."

"We've gotten a pretty nice start on one, wouldn't you say?"

"I suppose…."

"Uh-uh. No supposing. Yes or no. Is what we've done together nice?"

She glanced down, picked at a knotted thread on her coffee-colored, sleeveless linen top. "I'm not sure I'd call it nice."

"Then call it not-so-nice. But not-so-nice in a way that knocks you on your ass because it's so hot, so tight, so—" he clenched one hand into a solid fist "—so genuinely real that even if you do go back to the way things were before, nothing will seem the same. We go ahead with this fling, and we make this documentary shoot memorable in ways neither of us ever counted on."

Her heart a captured wild thing trying to beat its way out of her chest, Melanie sat breathless. Looking into his eyes, listening to his voice, loving every second of what he was making her feel. Never in her life had she felt this sort of connection, which went far beyond anything she'd ever thought of as sexual.

This…this untamed sense of being ruled by her

body instead of the mind, the intellect she'd cultivated all of her life. What was wrong with her?

Who was this masked man, and why was she suddenly so susceptible to his cocky, bad boy charm? At least he was right about one thing. She would never be able to go back to living in her black-and-white world.

He wanted to continue what they'd started. He wanted to call it an affair.

She said the only thing she could, a very simple, "Yes."

RENATA PICKED the Starbucks in the Galleria Barnes & Noble for the evening's coffee date with Aiden.

She'd decided the books would give them something to talk about should they run out of things to say, or should things between them get too intense as they had so unexpectedly, so…effortlessly earlier this afternoon.

Besides, the distraction of sharing reading tastes and learning Aiden's preferences would tell her a lot about the man he was—assuming she figured out by then whether or not she wanted to know.

She was having a lot of trouble resolving how best to handle the attraction. But she did know her level of comfort would be much higher in a crowd than in an intimate one-on-one situation.

As much as he intrigued her, he also thrilled her in ways that were wildly enticing. And that frightened her on a very personal level.

She'd always thought herself immune to the sort of intimate temptation he offered; she knew too well the danger in taking that particular emotional risk, in letting herself become involved, grow attached, develop an affection for a man who could fulfill her physically but could not be the partner she needed at this time in her life.

There were women who could compartmentalize relationships that way, and a very big part of her wished she belonged to that group. She would love to have a strictly sexual, no-strings-attached affair; she missed lying in bed with a man, feeling his skin so warm against her own. Testing the resilience of his muscles beneath exploring fingers. Shuddering at that first breach when taking him into her body.

But her emotions refused to quit the equation.

Latte in hand, she wandered through the upstairs fiction section, moving from the horror shelves into those housing romance. She had an insatiable love for a happy ending. And the relationships portrayed in the novels showed love the way it was meant to be. Healthy and whole. Two individuals bringing out the best in each other.

Renata sighed and sipped her latte. She swore she'd have that kind of love for herself one of these days, when she found a man who shared her passions, one who understood the importance of time spent together doing nothing more than enjoying the morning's first cup of coffee, or the late-night news while spooned together in bed.

At the sound of a softly cleared throat behind her, she started and pressed her free hand to her chest. And then she hid her grin with another sip of her coffee before glancing back to find the very man she'd been casting in her fantasy leaning one shoulder on the corner of a seven-foot shelf that was eight inches taller than he was.

Except he looked nothing like she'd expected. He

was vibrant and brilliant; he was strong and complete. All those things she knew as well as she knew herself. Yet she shouldn't know him at all. She'd done nothing but engage him in one long conversation in the middle of a hot afternoon.

Hands tucked in the front pockets of his jeans, he nodded toward her paper cup. How could she have forgotten in such a few short hours the way he took her breath away?

"I see you started without me."

She turned toward him, but stayed where she was, keeping distance between them. "I've been here a while. Browsing. I think if they rented out tables and chairs I could easily make this my office."

His mouth lifted in that gorgeously carefree grin he had. "Sounds like the dream of a first-class bibliophile."

She smiled at his observation. "I suppose I am. I have a hard time walking out of any bookstore—but this one especially—without buying one book at least. Buying two or three makes me so much happier."

He moved his hands from his pockets and crossed them over his chest, his shoulder still propped against the shelf. "And four or five?"

"Absolutely ecstatic."

She laughed and ran a hand along the colorful spines on the closest shelf, feeling as giddy as a schoolgirl bewitched by an adolescent crush. "My budget, on the other hand, complains mightily. As do the shelves built into the wall beside my fireplace. They've taken to groaning every time I walk in the door with another green-and-cream bag."

"You'll have to start shopping with one of those reusable canvas things." Aiden took a step into the aisle, coming closer and heightening her anticipation. "Lull them into a false sense of security, then spring the surprise."

She adored him. Absolutely adored him for playing along. How many men had she known who would've done the same—and looked so damn good while doing so?

He still wore jeans and his plain black boots, but tonight his shirt was a simple blue oxford. He looked more urban cowboy than horse rancher. Like one more corporate type dressed down for the weekend.

She wished that's all that he was.

Wished that he lived in an uptown high-rise, worked in a converted warehouse like so many young entrepreneurs. That he partied in downtown's jazz and Latin clubs and knew nothing about horses but what he learned every February during the city's wildly popular livestock show and rodeo.

But he wasn't. He was who he was. She needed to get over her fantasies and decide how she wanted to deal with that reality. Though, she mused, seeing his naked backside exposed between a pair of leather chaps was one cowboy fantasy she might want to hold on to.

"Hmm. A canvas tote might work. Except those tote bags tend to be rather bottomless, and that defeats the entire purpose. No," she said, refusing to indulge her book-buying addiction, as well as all unproductive trains of thought. "Discipline is the name of the game." She held up two fingers. "Two books. No more."

"You want help picking out titles?" he asked, having moved fully into the aisle, where he now stood so close that she caught the scent of clean, fresh air on his clothes.

She pulled in the deepest breath she could manage and cast him a sideways glance. "This *is* the romance section."

He shrugged, his lips twisting to stave off a grin. "I think I can handle it."

"Well. I'm not sure I know what to say. But—" she pulled a new Barbara Delinsky paperback from the shelf "—if you're game to delve into the secrets that make women tick, let's see what we've got here."

She handed him the book. He glanced at the back cover copy, taking his time absorbing the words. The interval gave her a chance to study him more closely, to notice again how thick were the lashes fringing his eyes, which were that blue of big sky country.

What would it be like to look into those eyes when waking every morning? Or when dozing off by candlelight late into the night? To run her fingers through his hair, so thick and so beautifully layered in a sharp *GQ* cut? To feel those lips open beneath hers as they kissed?

She gripped her paper cup until foam bubbled through the hole in the lid, when what she needed to get a grip on were the runaway hormones making a mess of all her good intentions to enjoy this time in his company and do nothing more daring than pick out a good book.

Finally, he said, "Hmm. Maple syrup and the redemptive power of love. Sounds…sweet."

"Give me that." She grabbed the book and used it to smack him on the arm. Silly man. "It is sweet. And it's touching."

She thought of how many romances she'd read and

how much more than entertainment they'd offered. "That's the reason I love sharing these books with a lot of the girls I counsel. They don't see much sweetness in their lives and don't always make the best relationship choices because their experience is too limited."

He hovered at her back while she flipped through the book's pages. "I never would've thought about applying popular fiction to psychology."

"You'd be surprised how many authors really get it right, at least as far as relationships go." Renata was surprised herself—that she hadn't melted from the heat coiling down her spine. She wanted more than anything to back up into his body.

He moved to stand in front of her, leaned back on the divider between two sections of shelf. "I'd be more surprised if it was only your students who enjoyed reading love stories. It would make a lot of sense for you to share what worked for you."

"Professionally?"

"That. And personally."

She shrugged because his comment was taking their conversation where she didn't want to go. Where she couldn't go and still keep this a nice friendly coffee date. "What can I say? I'm a romantic at heart. Not to mention a sucker for happy endings."

And that wouldn't happen between the two of them, no matter how exciting the idea of exploring that very possibility was. Not when he lived where he did, she lived where she did, and she'd seen the toll taken on her own family with her parents' constant travel. She started to return the book to the shelf, thinking that if he planned to help her pick titles, she might do better in the horror section, after all.

Scaring herself back into a state of common sense certainly couldn't hurt.

But since he'd opened the door, and she was having such a hard time convincing herself to close it, she invited him into her life.

"And, yes," she continued, tucking the book into the crook of her arm instead and walking down the row, scanning titles as she went, picking out an older Deborah Smith. "I think there's a lot to be said for hopes and dreams."

Aiden, obviously, was not needing the distance she suddenly found herself wanting because he followed her. Oh, but she was confused. Wanting him. Wanting to walk away. Knowing the latter was what she had to do, no matter how warm he felt there as he moved to her side, how comfortable she felt in his shadow.

"What are yours?" he asked.

"Hopes and dreams? Oh, the same as those of most women." She blithely tossed off the comment, trying to find the balance she'd lost the minute she'd turned around to see him standing behind her. "Spa vacations, cucumber facials, an unending supply of calorie-free chocolate. Oh, and did I mention the Starbucks?"

She stopped browsing because Aiden had moved to block her forward motion and stood head and shoulders above her. She was caught between the choice to look up at him or to back across the aisle and away.

Choosing to stand her ground, she lifted her gaze and looked into his eyes, unbelievably stirred by his harshly striking beauty, by the expression he wore that was so very hard to define or to turn away from.

And so she didn't turn. She stood there and took it all in. The tenderness and the heat. The desire that was barely banked. The fire of a wild mustang restrained by his Thoroughbred breeding.

"What about you?" she asked, when he made no move to back off or to come closer. When he remained still, as if caught between a push and a pull that even he couldn't define. When he didn't say a word in response, and only watched her as she continued to watch him.

It was at that moment that she realized she'd bitten off a big chunk of trouble by agreeing to see him tonight after this afternoon's encounter. Because when he finally responded, he did so not with words but by raising his hand and tucking an unruly lock of hair behind her ear.

He lingered there, his touch tender, his intent innocent. Or so she wanted desperately to believe. Yet innocence had never before come with such a burst of raw emotion. Emotion threatening to undo all her good intentions to stay sober, when the look in his eyes was so intoxicating.

For this one moment in her life, unlike any other ever before, she wished she was not the nurturing sort. She longed to reach out and take him into her body rather than into her heart, and he'd done nothing but tame her flyaway hair.

"Dreams I have would be more about gentling horses," he said, stroking fingers through the thick chestnut waves of her shoulder-length strands. "Getting them to trust me, to know me. My touch and my scent. The sound of my voice. To equate all of that with their needs being met."

Renata had no idea how to respond. What was she supposed to say when he held her spellbound? She clutched both books and her latte to her breast. "What happens when you're not there any longer? When they're sold to a new owner? Sure, the words and the commands might be the same—'' she turned her head until her cheek barely brushed the inside of his wrist ''—but it won't be your voice they hear when they prick up their ears. Or your scent they catch when they lift their noses to search the air.''

"No," Aiden said, moving into her personal space so that he touched her hands where she held tight to the books and the stiff paper cup. His fingers slid from her ear to thread into the full mane of her hair. "But they'll be more prepared to have their needs met by someone who shares my philosophy.''

"And if they wind up with someone who doesn't?" she asked, thinking that if she didn't make her way toward the checkout now it might be years before she did.

"I suppose it could happen." He gave a small shrug, as if the possibility that he'd make such a mistake didn't truly exist. "But I screen my buyers carefully to lessen the chance that it will.''

"Then I guess your horses are lucky to have you for as long as they can.''

"I suppose, though I doubt they derive half the amount of pleasure I get from simply taking care of them.''

Renata laughed, though the sound had nothing to do with amusement and everything to do with fear. "Oh, I have a feeling the pleasure is mutual.''

Aiden lowered his head. His mouth stopped mere inches from hers as he said, "I'd like to think so.''

And then he kissed her. Right there in the middle of Barnes & Noble, in the center of the romance novel aisle, Aiden Zuniga kissed Renata Faulkner, and she thought she was going to die.

It was the most tender, sweetest kiss she'd ever shared. His lips played lightly over hers, slanting perfectly so that when she parted hers she tasted the tip of his tongue. She felt the urge to press against him, shoulders to knees, breast to belly, but didn't want to spoil the moment's magic.

Not when she couldn't remember having ever felt anything like this kiss. She would've remembered something so sublime if she'd known it before, if she'd ever experienced anything so exquisite. Her lips tingled and she shivered from the sudden rush of sensation.

And then he was gone, lifting his head and taking away the taste of fresh air, the scent of freedom, the feel of strength restrained and boundaries respected. She followed him upward until she realized she'd raised up on her toes. Then she lowered her heels to the ground.

"Well," she began, on the one hand embarrassed, on the other hand not. "I'm not sure I know what to say."

"You don't have to say anything." Aiden took both books from her hands, gestured for her to continue browsing. "All you have to do is shop."

"Shop?" After that kiss, he wanted her to shop?

He nodded. "Unless you've settled on these two books."

"I'm fine with those," she replied, because she couldn't imagine browsing further with his body behind her and his taste on her lips. "Did you want to get coffee?"

He shook his head. "What time does this place close?"

She frowned. "Eleven, I think."

He glanced at his watch, then took hold of her elbow and guided her to an open area, where he pulled two plush armchairs into a private corner.

When he gestured, Renata sat, tucking her legs beneath her long skirt and leaning toward him. And when he smiled, she felt her heart burst.

"We have three hours. I want to know everything about you by the time we leave." Legs stretched out, he laced his fingers together and propped them on his belly, so flat behind his silver belt buckle.

"I'm twenty-seven years old. That would mean cramming nine years into each hour." She set her books on the table between them, cradled her coffee cup in her hands. "That won't give me time to hear anything about you."

"You can bend Chloe's ear for whatever you want to know. And when I'm back in town next weekend, I'll straighten out all the lies she tells you about me." He pressed his lips together, then smacked them once. "But I could use a sip of your coffee first, if you don't mind."

"Sure," she said, offering him the cup, tickled that her taste had lingered on his mouth.

Aiden pushed forward in his seat and leaned toward her, taking her coffee and setting it on the table next to her books. Bracing both hands on the arms of her chair, he bent to kiss her again. Pulse fluttering, she looked up and watched his mouth descend.

But this time her hands were free and she couldn't keep herself from placing her palms on his chest. His heart thudded there where she touched him, and then all she knew was his mouth. This time he wasn't the least bit gentle or restrained, but was hungry and wanting her to know it.

He devoured her lips, slanting his hard enough over hers that she felt the abrasion of his late-evening beard. She flexed her fingers into the fabric of his shirt and pulled him closer still. And then she slipped her tongue under his and followed it into his mouth.

He groaned and ground harder, kissing her as if she offered him sustenance. His chest beneath her palms was firm and solid, and she wished they were anywhere but here so she could feel his skin sliding against her own.

Another groan and he pulled away, staring down at her as his breathing settled, as the fire in his eyes abated. She returned her hands to her lap, bunching them into the fabric of her skirt and waiting for the roar in her ears to subside.

Except it didn't. Because it wasn't in her ears. It was applause from the small audience who'd witnessed the show. Heat flushed her face as she stared into Aiden's. But he only sat back in his chair, cocked one ankle over the opposite knee and grinned like a cat with a mouthful of canary.

Finally, Renata gave a small nodding bow to their spectators, who were drifting away. And then she returned her attention to Aiden. "Are you sure you don't want a cup of your own? A full shot of caffeine might keep you awake."

"I'd love it. But I'll wait."

"For?" she asked, knowing they weren't talking about coffee now any more than they'd been talking about horses earlier, and loving every minute of the conversation, anyway.

"For the right time."

"And when will that be?"

"When a sip is no longer enough." He laced his hands behind his head and leaned back. "Now. Years one through nine. Tell me everything."

# 8

---

MONDAY MORNING FOUND Melanie back in her office at her desk and unable to walk any better than the day before. She couldn't imagine how much trouble swimming would've been on Saturday if she'd ever made it into the pool.

But she hadn't even made it into her suit. She'd only made it out of one leg of her shorts and panties and onto Jacob's lap. At least that's as far as she'd managed to strip there in Chloe and Eric's second floor bedroom.

Later, in her own bedroom, she'd let Jacob strip her down to her skin, but only after she'd undressed him first. Except none of the bedroom action had happened until after the pole dance incident and the dinner out at the restaurant.

She didn't remember having ever screwed away an entire Saturday, from midafternoon to midnight.

Stopping for dinner that evening hadn't been a date as much as a matter of survival. She'd been starving. If she'd simply ordered in Chinese or whipped up something in the kitchen, she doubted she would've ever gotten Jacob back into his clothes. Or wanted to get back into hers.

The man had absolutely no self-consciousness about parading around in the nude. As much as she enjoyed the show, co-ed naked cooking offered as many drawbacks as advantages. The idea of burned body parts had been unappealing enough to force her to dress and encourage him to follow suit.

And the breather had done them both good. They'd actually talked, even though most of what they'd talked about was the sex. It was almost as if that was all they had in common, though she knew they had to have more.

Besides, listening to Jacob's explanation about finding her sexy had made her feel marginally better. Or would have, if not for the confusion that followed.

She prided herself on remaining calm, competent and professional in every situation. That's who she was, and that's the Melanie she wanted men to like and admire.

The fact that apparently Jacob was more attracted to an aberration than to her true personality...well, it just plain sucked. Especially since her bedroom behavior had only solidified his first impression.

What would he do when he learned his fantasy stripper was all smoke, shadows and mirrors?

*Run like hell, of course.* They all did, eventually.

Relaxing her grip on the last unbroken pencil in her office, Melanie shook off the disturbing thought of Jacob and, as distasteful as work seemed today—and as angry as that distaste made her—glanced at the open page of the gift catalog she'd abandoned last week.

She had managed to include six more items in her list of possibilities, but doubted she'd end up adding a single one to her product line once she went back through and classified them by price and fun factor.

The fact that she had no head for business today wasn't increasing her chance of success. Or doing much to boost her confidence that she'd be able to carry on an affair with Jacob and remain productive at work.

And wasn't that the whole reason she'd known better than to get involved? What in the world had she been thinking, agreeing to his indecent proposal?

A sharp rap on her door brought her head up in time to see Chloe invite herself into the office, plop down into a visitor's chair and glare.

Melanie didn't give her girlfriend the chance to launch into the bitchy tirade she saw coming. "Don't start. I know what you're going to say. And I'm sorry for not telling you I was leaving on Saturday."

Chloe remained unsmiling. Her hands gripped the chair's black leather arms. Her crossed leg swung. Her eyes, made up in shades of pink, glowered.

Melanie tossed her pencil onto the legal pad, leaned back and sighed. "Fine. Make me suffer. I know this is about me ducking out before the end of the party, so have at it. Just do me a favor. Tell me exactly what you're thinking, because I'm fed up with hearing people talk in circles. What's so hard about making a point? Or saying what's on one's mind?"

Chloe's leg stopped swinging and an expression of curious regard crossed her face. "Well, now, sugar. From the way things are sounding, I'm thinking you're the one who needs to unload first. You seem to be a lot closer to the edge of the proverbial cliff than I am."

"I *am* on edge." Melanie pushed up her glasses to rub the bridge of her nose. "And it's making me crazy. I've been a basket case now for thirty-six hours."

And that wasn't even counting back to the day she'd sent Jacob the tape. Only to the moment she'd decided to follow him upstairs. The moment the full-blown crazies had taken over her life. "I'm supposed to be calm and rational and totally in control."

"Says who?" Chloe asked with a frown.

Melanie sputtered out a big fat raspberry. "Me! But it's like I've been in a permanent premenstrual cycle for almost a week now. Piss and moan and bitch and snap. The only thing not on my list is tears. And it's not even that time of the month."

"So cry already," Chloe offered sagely.

"Ha," Melanie barked, shaking her head briskly and fluffing up her hair with both hands. "That's the one thing I refuse to do. It's the last straw between me and insanity. And you know what?" On a roll now, she was! "If I'd stayed at your place and eaten a damn hamburger and taken care of the leftovers like I told you I'd do, I wouldn't be sitting here fighting off a nervous tic."

*Or sitting here wondering if I'll ever be able to walk straight again.*

One of Chloe's eyebrows went up as she studied Melanie's face. "Actually, sugar, you cutting out of the party early is not why I'm here to smack you around."

Hmm. So it could be a couple of other things, one involving the state of Chloe's guest bedroom, but Melanie preferred not to go there. At least not with Chloe. "So, you're mad over something other than the fact that I didn't help with the cleanup?"

"Well, yes, because you promised, but that's a small blip on the big screen of my anger." Chloe pouted. "You could've at least told me you were leaving."

"Uh-huh, right." Melanie looked the other woman

up and down over her rectangular frames. ''And your pissiness isn't about me not saying goodbye.''

''Exactly.'' Chloe leveled an accusing finger. ''If you'd said goodbye, I would've seen firsthand that you hadn't left alone. But, no. I had to hear from Rennie that you'd left with Jacob.''

Time to prevaricate. ''I didn't exactly leave with Jacob. Only at the same time.''

''And?'' Chloe's brows went up.

''And what?''

''And, how was he?''

''What kind of question is that?'' Melanie countered, feeling the heat of a rising flush while working to keep a straight face. A calm, cool and collected face.

''The kind of question a best friend shouldn't have to ask.''

Maybe not, but it wasn't one Melanie was sure she wanted to answer. ''So, I could ask you the same about Eric, then?''

''Sugar, I've told you everything there is to tell about Eric.''

''You haven't told me much of anything in well over a year.''

''Well, okay,'' Chloe hedged. ''But that's only because we got serious. I spilled all the details when he was still a boy toy.''

''So?''

''So, spill all the details already.'' She tilted her head to the side, blinked, pouted and considered. ''I know I'm not psychic, but my boy toy radar never fails.''

Melanie sighed again, hating to admit that Chloe might be right. Talking to a much-trusted friend couldn't hurt, and might actually relieve the pressure causing a headache of monstrous proportions.

"Fine. If you must know, he's amazing in bed. And on the sofa, against the wall. Sitting in a chair. But that really doesn't mean anything, does it?"

"What do you mean, it doesn't mean anything? It means everything!" Chloe gestured expansively with both hands. "Are you kidding? Finding a guy who knows what he's doing in bed and all those other places? How can you think that doesn't mean anything?"

"Well, sexually, yes. It means everything."

"But?"

"C'mon, Chloe. You know there's more to life than sex."

"And?"

"And Jacob may make for a perfectly good boy toy, but that's it. He's got an attitude that's half know-it-all, half don't-give-a-shit."

Chloe signaled a time-out. "If this is only about his boy toy potential, what does it matter if he's a bum?"

"I suppose it doesn't. Except that I know he isn't. A bum, that is." She shook her head. "But then this isn't about who he is. This is about me."

"You having problems with your id?"

Melanie rolled her eyes. "You've been hanging out with Rennie too much, and no. What I'm having a problem with is facing that I'm lusting over a man because of his body. Period. End of story."

"Just his body. Hmm."

"And the way he looks at me." She didn't even have to close her eyes to relive the feel of the heat. "That panty-melting thing. It's like his eyes flash and I want to take off my clothes."

"Well, of course you do."

Melanie took off her glasses and closed her eyes. God, but her eyes were tired. As tired as she was, she couldn't remember why she wasn't supposed to want to spend her life in Jacob Faulkner's bed.

*Groan.* Now she was including him in her future. This was not what she'd expected from a purely sexual affair. She looked back at Chloe. "What happened to being attracted to his intellect? Admiring his ambition?" And him admiring hers, dammit.

Chloe shrugged. "If that's what floats your boat."

"Lust does not last."

"Says who?"

"Okay. It can. You and Eric are proof." Even though Chloe's quiet grin indicated her agreement, Melanie couldn't help but be curious how much of the couple's emotional involvement fueled that physical attraction. And then she frowned.

Ugh. No. She did not want to fall into the trap that paralyzed so many relationships. She refused to fall in love with the man she was sleeping with just because she was sleeping with him. And, yes. Unfortunately, she spoke from personal experience.

But she was years older now and years wiser and way too levelheaded to let her emotions ruin the best thing that had happened to her in ages. The best thing physically, she rushed to amend. Half a week of working with him, a weekend of sleeping with him and she was already looking forward to more.

As she'd said, how totally un-Melanie Craine.

Still, no matter how much fun she was having with Jacob—even out-of-bed fun—she refused to start attaching anything emotional to their pseudo relationship. He might have breached her underwear, but he was not going to breach the walls of her heart.

AS MUCH AS MELANIE HATED taking long late lunches, Thursday's two hours spent at Frankie B's had been worth the time away from the office—not to mention worth every bite of the fried green tomatoes and Cobb salad.

In addition to wiping out lunch and dinner in one meal, she'd finally managed to pick up several ideas for expanding her gIZMO gIRL line. And the best part…

She hadn't been stuck doing her individual in-office documentary interview. She'd been late enough getting back to the office that the production crew had called it a day.

It wasn't the interview she dreaded. After five years in business, she was used to publicity profiles and probing questions. A one-on-one with the show's host didn't faze her in the least. Except it wouldn't be a simple one-on-one.

It would be a ménage à trois with a voyeuristic cameraman rounding out the party.

And she didn't know how much of her true self— the self that existed fully clothed and out of bed, the self that the documentary host would be digging deep to reveal—she was ready for Jacob to know.

As much pleasure as he provided—and he did, oh, how he did—she should be listening to the advice of her practical nature rather than relinquishing control to her selfish and greedy physical side. Here she was, waffling again, reversing the conclusion she'd come to earlier in the week.

Because no matter how much *fun* he'd *injected* into

her life, gIRL-gEAR business and Jacob Faulkner did indeed make for a very bad mix.

She was having the absolute worst time keeping her mind on the job. And that just wouldn't do. Not when she was the one taking up the slack left hanging by the lovebirds surrounding her everywhere she turned.

She supposed it wasn't just Jacob, that the same would hold true for any man. But, she supposed again, never before had a man gotten under her skin the way Jacob had managed to do.

Putting a stop to the sex had crossed her mind more times than she could count since she'd climbed off his lap in Chloe's guest bedroom Saturday afternoon. Almost as many times as she'd wondered why she was considering giving up such a guilt-free and no-strings pleasure. It wasn't as if Jacob was a permanent fixture in her life.

The documentary shoot was scheduled to wrap in another month. Surely she could forget about drive and ambition and do thirty days worth of living for the moment, since the moment would be but a speck in the timeline of her life. She could easily regain her sanity once Jacob was gone.

And, really. She'd always performed best under deadlines, anyway—a thought that brought a wry grin. Wouldn't that drive Jacob to drink, benefiting from the very obsessive nature he complained about?

Then again, he was a guy, and as long as he was getting laid often and laid well, why should he care about the attitude she had toward her work? Why was it so important to him to show her the fun he claimed she was missing? The selfishly sexual part of his reasoning she totally understood.

But that was all she understood. She didn't get his

"mission" to spice up her life. What was in it for him, besides the obvious? Unless he got off on the power trip as much as he did on the sex. If that was the case, he'd done himself proud. Look at her, sitting here mooning over him like some sort of lovesick cow!

As much as she hated to admit it and as much as that admission riled her, she needed to get her head out of Jacob's pants and back into the entrepreneurial game. She pulled up her in-box, scrolled down the queue looking for priority messages, finding only one from Sydney and…wait a minute.

An e-mail from jf@avatareproductions? It wasn't marked priority but still it caught her eye.

Why would Jacob be e-mailing her when they took care of business at the office during the day and took care of pleasure at night? In her bed. Beneath her new comforter of Moroccan red and gold, and Egyptian cotton sheets.

Still, the fact that it *was* from Jacob brought a moment of indecision, not to mention nails tapping on her desktop as she stared at the screen.

The part of her that was a savvy professional and wise to the ways of distraction told her to ignore him until she'd finished the more pressing matters of work. Dessert was always best savored as a reward for a job well done.

Except when it was eaten first because it was irresistible, and the thrill of indulging in being bad beckoned. She couldn't wait to see what he wanted, and that was the very reason she wished she could hate him.

He'd totally destroyed her ability to focus on anything. She'd worked so hard for so long to get to this point, and she certainly knew better than to let herself fall prey to a cocky bad boy—no matter how good he was in bed.

And that was the thought that fueled her decision. In addition to being a lovesick cow, she was now officially an unrepentant and insatiable horndog. Work could wait because Pavlov had whistled.

She double-clicked on Jacob's e-mail, only to bring it up and see that he'd simply sent her two hyperlinks. She tapped her finger on her mouse and debated on whether or not she had any interest in what he wanted her to see.

But it wasn't much of a debate because she had never been much of a debater.

She clicked the first link, which took her to a Web page into which opened a Webcam feed. She rolled her eyes, started to close the window, but realized the feed she was seeing was familiar…. She frowned. What the hell?

It wasn't just familiar. It was her office! She was looking at herself sitting behind her own desk.

Again she started to close the window, but remembered the second link in Jacob's e-mail. A quick click on that one and she found herself looking into another office, one she didn't recognize but had no trouble guessing to whom it belonged. Or at least who crashed there when he wasn't busy harassing female entrepreneurs with his camera, *grrr*.

The man should be shot on general principle—not to mention for being a spy, *and* for worming his way into her bed and her life so completely that she was less angry than amused by his invasion into her privacy. So what, exactly, did he expect to see? And where, exactly, was the camera?

After a brief study of the Webcam's angle, she

glanced up into the corner of her bookcase, ran her
gaze along the top shelf to the center partition. There
it was, the sneaky bastard. Wired in unobtrusively beside her television and the cables for the office satellite
feed.

Spy boy had been busy, hadn't he? Obviously tapping into the Internet via the office's dedicated service
line. Taking full advantage of the run of the office
Sydney had given the documentary team. At the very
least, the bastard was way too sure of himself. At the
very most...

That *most* was what intrigued Melanie, what had her
sitting here in her chair instead of climbing up to tear
the camera out of the wall. She supposed it was his
turn to throw down a gauntlet in this strange battle of
wills they called an affair. But she wondered. How far
would he actually go?

Before she decided what sort of show she would
offer up for his viewing pleasure, she needed to know
more specifics on the setup—primarily, how secure
was his connection. He obviously had the camera's
feed streaming to his capture software. Still, until she
knew for sure, she had no intention of doing the wild
girl party thing for an audience like some sort of coed
on a locker room cam.

Using the eraser end of her pencil to push her
glasses back up her nose, she looked back at her monitor and hit Refresh. Then hit Refresh again. The software wasn't broadcasting the live feed, but seemed to
be taking a snapshot every five seconds or so.

And that was when her plan began to come together.
He seemed to have forgotten whom he was dealing
with here. Or maybe he just didn't know. Melanie

Craine was not an easy conquest, no matter that *easy* was exactly what she'd been with Jacob thus far.

She needed to remind herself of that fact, as well as show Jacob Faulkner a thing or two about the imaginative use of technology. She hadn't spent all these years keeping her nose to the motherboard, keeping company with geeks instead of bad boys, for nothing.

FRIDAY MORNING, Jacob tossed his satchel at the base of the coatrack in his office before collapsing into his chair, and rubbed both hands across his face. He was dog-tired. Just plain beat. This invincibility thing was obviously all in his mind because his body was dragging ass in a very big way.

Sleep. He needed sleep. Tonight he would go home to his own bed and catch up. Then again, sleeping in his own bed would mean missing out on *not* sleeping in Melanie's. He wasn't sure that he wouldn't regret giving up a night of sex more than another night of sleep.

What was a few hours, anyway? They were nearing the end of August and the shoot was scheduled to wrap next month. Once he finished with the documentary, he doubted they'd be seeing one another as often since he'd pretty much booked up October with interviews and photography showings in NYC.

He'd worry about making up the deficit in his shut-eye quota then—the same way he was spending this morning making up for the time he'd missed in the Avatare office while working at gIRL-gEAR. He had paperwork to process and more than a few calls to return, not to mention dodging a couple of his work buds who were going to kick his butt the minute they saw him.

Since hooking up with Melanie this past week, he'd cut out on a couple of the Astros baseball games he and his friends had made plans to attend. Neither Asa nor Harry would let him off the hook easily.

Again he scrubbed both hands down his weary face. Yeah, well, the suckers could just bring it on. He was young and hale and hearty and could stand up to a little bit of ass-whupping.

Or he could have if he wasn't so friggin' beat!

Legs spread wide, he swiveled his chair around, hooked up his PowerBook to the Avatare office network and booted it up, watching through bleary eyes as it came to life. First things first meant cleaning out his in-box, since this was the only day he'd been to the office all week.

He'd been scheduled to shoot Melanie's interview yesterday afternoon, but she'd had to cancel due to a luncheon meeting that ran long. The documentary host had flown back to L.A. last night for the weekend, freeing up Jacob until Monday morning rolled around again.

He'd slept in this morning until he'd heard Mel's keys jangling as she was leaving for the office, then he'd decided what the hell. Tomorrow was Saturday. He'd get up and get going before she got that look in her eye that called him lazy.

He wasn't, really. He had money for everything he wanted and needed, and he'd gotten there without giving himself an ulcer in the process. He wondered whether or not Melanie had one—or if her body had grown used to the years of uptight living and figured, why go to the effort?

This last week, though, he had to admit that she had loosened up a bit. Full credit in his court, of course.

He still hadn't quite figured out where her uppity attitude came from, and doubted he would in their limited time together. Her interests weren't like those of most females he'd known; she even thought about things more like a guy than a girl.

The fact that sex was a big part of that equation made him a very happy and satisfied man. So much so that he found himself wondering once or twice what it would be like to stick with her for the long haul. A totally stupid thing to think, because it wasn't going to happen.

Homer Simpson's announcement of, "The mail is here! The mail is here!" brought Jacob back to the present. He glanced up and blinked to clear the clouds from his vision as his in-box filters magically screened out the junk and the spam. All that was left were the notes needing his attention.

Oh, yeah. He'd sent himself the same links to the Webcam feeds he'd sent to Melanie. He wondered if she'd ripped the camera off her bookshelf yet or if she was going to be a sport and go along with the fun they could have watching each other. He clicked on the link to her feed, returning to his in-box while waiting for the page to load.

Yes, cool! A response from one of the New York companies he'd queried. But just as he opened the e-mail and before he saw more of the content than the word *interest,* a knock on his door brought an immediate invasion of his office.

Asa Brennan and Harry Schott. Jacob closed the e-mail and leaned back in his chair as the two thugs barged in. "You know, most people wait for an invitation after they knock before waltzing in."

Asa glanced at Harry. Harry glanced back. Both

men dropped into Jacob's visitors' chairs, ignoring him completely. "I dunno, Harry," Asa began, crossing an ankle over a knee and lacing his hands behind his head as he leaned back. "Looks like Faulkner." Nose up, he sniffed the air. "Smells like Faulkner." Mouth in a grim line, Asa shook his head. "But sounds like some prissy-assed puss who's been hanging around a bunch of women."

"Very funny," Jacob said with a snort, though he was having a hell of a time keeping a straight face.

Asa wasn't through, giving a girlie singsong lilt to his voice as he repeated mockingly, "'Most people wait for an invitation after they knock before waltzing in.' Waltzing. Shit."

Harry nodded in agreement. "Yeah, Faulkner. If that's who you really are. Who'd you sleep with to get that gIRL-gEAR gig, anyway?" His dark slash of a brow went up on the left side. "Or who've you been sleeping with since getting it?"

Jacob only shook his head. "You guys can't stand it, can you? You know management only gives the sweet assignments to the best of the best."

"More like to whoever happens to be in the right place at the right time," Harry said, slumping back onto his tailbone. "You lucked out and you know it."

"What can I say?" Jacob shrugged. "Some guys have it all. And some?" He offered up both empty palms. "Some of you schmucks got nothing."

"You wish you had my nothing," Asa said, a grin of cosmically cocky proportions widening the mouth that his last girlfriend had called her own private rock 'n roll show. "My nothing just got me invited to Milwaukee to accept an award for that short I shot last year."

"Hey, man. That's excellent." Jacob leaned forward, extending his hand across the expanse of his desk to shake Asa's. "The one about the dart tournament, right?"

Asa nodded as Jacob sat back, and that was when the trouble began. He caught site of the browser window he'd left open on his screen—the URL where he'd set up his system to show the feed from Melanie's office Webcam.

Holy crap! He sure as hell hoped she'd locked her office door. She'd obviously moved the camera because the shot wasn't angled down as far as it had been originally. It was more...straight on.

And straight ahead in the center of the frame, Melanie stood wearing a classic black business suit with a hip-length jacket and a skirt that fell beneath her knees. She'd leaned back against her desk, her palms on the surface at her hips, one ankle crossed over the other there where he could not look away from her feet.

No doubt about it. He was gonna need paddles to jump start his heart. Because in addition to the suit, she wore a Mardi Gras-type mask, with long ribbons of pink, red and white and plumed feathers to match. She also wore the sexiest pair of shoes he'd ever seen. Yep. Even better than the ones she'd been wearing that day in the church, because these heels were stiletto and bright cherry-red.

But that was only the first stretch in the torturous route up her body, because her legs—at least what he could see of them between her ankle and the middle of her calves—her legs were wrapped in matching fishnet stockings.

Jacob groaned, deciding he was going to die.

"You okay, man?" Asa asked, reminding Jacob that he wasn't alone in the room.

And then he groaned because he wasn't alone in the room. "Yeah. I was just thinking that I'm going to have to cover your ass while you're gone. And that is seriously going to cut into my downtime."

Harry laughed. "Dude, your entire life is downtime. What're you talking about?"

"I'm talking about the fact that you had damn well better keep your cell charged because I refuse to take up all this man's slack on my own," Jacob said, jerking a thumb in Asa's direction.

Harry frowned, turned to discuss scheduling with Asa, giving Jacob the distraction he needed. His Powerbook sat open in the center of his desk, meaning he had to look over the screen to make eye contact with either of his buds.

It also meant he could pretty much continue to check out Melanie without rousing either man's suspicions. But one look back at the screen and he knew checking her out would be better done in private.

Ha! As if he could look away now that she'd turned her back to the camera and stood bent over her desk ninety degrees, balancing first on one foot then the other as if doing a slow-motion dance.

She had the most fantastic ass. And those heels and what they did to the whole picture…well, now his cock was talking to him, reminding him exactly how it felt to slide between her sweet cheeks. He was about to be in a hard-on of trouble here.

And as much as he was enjoying the view, he said a silent thank-you when Melanie finally stopped shakin' her booty and stood up straight. Except then she turned back around and went to work on the long row of buttons fastening the front of her black blazer.

He just barely managed to bite down on his next groan, and glanced briefly at the other two photographers to make sure they hadn't overheard the sound of grinding teeth. But Asa and Harry were busy coordinating schedules on the PDAs both had pulled from cases at their waist.

So Jacob looked back at his screen. One by one, Melanie flicked the suckers open, a whole lot slower than Jacob would've liked, except he was liking just fine the sight coming slowly into view.

She was wearing a red bustier, for crissakes. The boning hugged her body and pushed up her breasts into temptingly plump mouthfuls. He wanted to slurp her up and suck her hard.

He swallowed, but his mouth was dry, so he reached for the bottle of water on his desk. He drank and nodded at whatever Harry had just said. Something about splitting time over Asa's assignments. For all Jacob knew, he'd just agreed to cover the other man onehundred percent.

Right now, he didn't give a damn about anything but watching Melanie strip. She shrugged out of the blazer and stood there in the stilettos, the fishnets and the bustier. All of it red and all of it about to make him dig his cock out of his pants.

"Look, guys," Harry said. "I've gotta run. I'm doing a first birthday party in River Oaks at noon." He returned his PDA to his case as he stood.

"Parents doping the kids with sugar before naptime?" Asa asked.

"Something like that." Turning to Jacob, Harry got to his feet just as the cellphone at his waist rang.

"We'll catch up on scheduling early next week, right?"

Jacob nodded, but Harry was on his way out the door, leaving Asa to drill Jacob with a piercing gaze.

"What's up with you, man? For someone working such a choice gig, you look like shit."

Jacob shrugged, his peripheral vision trying to draw his full gaze back to the computer screen. "Women. Can't live with 'em. Can't walk out on the job when the exposure's going to take me where I want to go."

"Hey, man. I'm there. Between you and me, I'm looking for a lead in Milwaukee to pan out."

"You're still thinking of going back home?"

Asa nodded. "I've been wanting to head that way for a while."

And then, in a case of mounting interruptions, Jacob's desk phone rang. He glanced at the caller display. "I'd better get this."

"Yeah, I'm outta here, anyway." Asa slapped palms to thighs and pushed himself to his feet. "Ball game tonight, right?"

"Yep. I'll be there," Jacob rashly promised, reaching for the receiver as the other man waved goodbye on his way out the door.

"Faulkner," he said for his co-worker's benefit, before hitting the mute button and cutting off the tele-marketing recording so he could get back to watching the show that had become the very center of his world.

Melanie still wore her skirt, but now stood with her legs spread as far apart as the slim black garment would allow. Her hands were at her waist and were moving up the corset-tight bustier. She took her time, as if enjoying the feel of her own hands sliding up her ribs to the swell of her breasts.

She tossed back her head, then looked straight into the camera, wetting first one index finger then the other with her mouth. With her bottom lip caught between her teeth, she ran both fingertips down the slope of her breasts and beneath the red satin, lifting both of her nipples free and circling slippery fingers around the tight pink buds until they practically sat up and begged.

Jacob slammed the receiver back into the cradle, got up and closed his office door. He leaned back against it and reached into his pants, compressing the base of his cock with the ring he made of his fingers until the urge to come backed off. Eyes closed, he took several slow, concentrated breaths.

And then he returned to his desk and the live action striptease that was so much better than the shadow one on tape. With her stance still wide, her chin up and shoulders back, her nipples puckered there above the lacy edge of the bustier, she moved her hands to her back and the fastenings of her skirt.

Jacob sank down into his chair just in time for the rest of the show.

Palms flat on her upper thighs, she swiveled her hips side to side while sliding the black skirt down her legs. She bent forward in the process, completely exposing her cherry-tipped breasts.

He was pulsing again, ready to blow, and if Melanie's act went much further, he was going to be finished. Her skirt was now around her ankles, or it was until she stepped out of it and moved closer to the camera.

She slipped her fingers beneath the red garters holding up the stockings, popped both against her thighs before moving her hands into a V around her mound, which was covered in nothing but a thong of red netting.

No woman in his life had ever aroused him this fast or this completely. She stood there covered from the lower swells of her breasts to the barest patch of her tummy visible between her garter belt and her thong.

But the things he most wanted to see were the very things she was showing him. She was a cherry. A head-to-toe sweet piece that he wanted to consume.

She teased him then, her hands returning to pluck at both nipples, her tongue circling her parted lips as she did. And then she hooked one ankle around the leg of a visitor's chair and dragged it into the frame.

She didn't sit immediately, but turned and took hold of the chair's arms, giving him yet another beautiful shot of her bare ass. And then she crawled up into the seat on her knees, her legs open as she simulated the up-and-down ride she'd taken on his lap that first time.

He leaned back in his chair and ran the flat of his hand down the length of his shaft behind his fly. Their offices were only six miles apart, but it would take him a good twenty minutes to get there, and she could very well be dressed and off to a meeting before he even made it halfway.

Then again, in his condition, driving was not necessarily recommended. But then driving wasn't even a factor, because he wasn't moving out of his seat.

Melanie had turned around in the chair, sitting forward on the seat and draping her knees over the arms. He could see everything there between her spread legs, except it was still covered by scraps of red netting and silk and lace.

He would have growled if he could've shoved the sound past his heart, which was beating in every square inch of his chest, but he could barely even breathe.

The fingers that had played with her nipples now dipped beneath the scrap of material covering her mound, and then she pulled the thong away.

When once again she wet her fingers, Jacob grunted and flexed his abs. A crowbar, a jackhammer, the jaws of life. Nothing was going to separate him from his chair or his Powerbook screen. He couldn't even move to activate the camera's zoom.

Besides, he wanted to see all of her—not just the action going on there between her legs. Even if it was the sleekest, steamiest, most realistic and raw self-gratification he'd ever witnessed.

She separated the folds of her sex and slid two fingers inside. Not one, but two, while her other hand played back and forth between her nipples and her clit.

He took it all in—her head thrown back, the pinching and tweaking, the roughed-up nipples, the flushed pink clit. He brought his fist down on his desk; goddamn, but he wanted to be the one there getting her off, fingering her to the slick rhythm she'd set.

In and out her fingers went, and she was peachy and juicy and he wanted to eat her up, to lick her clean, to bend her over and bury his face in her incredible sex.

And then she came. Came all over the place. Her hips arched up off the chair, and he could've sworn she buried three fingers to the hilt.

Her head went back and she stuffed her fist to her mouth to cut off the cry that rang in his ears and rocked him from his throat to the hard rise of flesh between his legs.

His balls ached and he felt pre-come spill from the

tip of his cock. But he stayed where he was, waiting and watching Melanie's finish. Watching her collapse exhausted. Watching her breathe deeply and grin. Watching her take up a pair of insulated wire cutters and…snip.

The screen went blank.

He sat there, unmoving, unblinking, unable to fathom anything but what she'd just done. And she'd done it for him. Solely for him. Never in his life had any woman given him so much of herself. And he wondered when the time came how hard it would be to walk away.

Right now, the hardest thing he knew was in his pants and needed to be taken care of. He grabbed up his satchel and, holding it strategically, headed for the men's room down the hall.

One thing had just been made exceedingly clear. Melanie's power trip attitude was all about knowing what she wanted, and making sure she got her way.

Once he figured out how to get her back for this, he'd make sure he got his.

# 9

MELANIE BARELY MANAGED to get back into her suit, dispose of the fishnets, change her shoes and dump the camera and wiring detritus before she heard chatter and laughter in the hallway outside her office door.

She unlocked and opened it, then settled in behind her desk with the work she'd used as an excuse this morning to beg off from accompanying the others to career day at the high school where Rennie Faulkner counseled.

For the past three hours the executive office wing had been a virtual ghost town, silent and still. But now the girls were back, putting an end to Melanie's privacy. It seemed she'd timed her show perfectly.

She shoved her gym bag farther into the kneehole beneath her desk, hearing the clatter of cosmetics rattling in her mini train case as the contents shifted. Oh, shoot! Her hair and makeup had to be a mess!

Pulling her glasses off, she grabbed the mirror and the hairbrush she kept in her desk drawer and quickly repaired her chunky textured cut. Her compact was next. Nose and T-zone dusted, she smoothed her smoky-taupe eye shadow until only a bare hint remained, blotted the red gloss from her lips and reapplied her usual nude frost.

She had no idea if Jacob had actually been in his office to see her production live, or if he would watch the captured stream later. All she knew was that the feed was encrypted and her show would remain private.

She would never have given him that particular performance if she'd thought for a moment she couldn't trust him with the goods. Still, the safety net of the Mardi Gras-style half mask made her feel a bit better. Now all she had to do was sweat out the wait for his reaction.

As she took a deep breath, it hit her. She was absolutely exhausted. Of course, good sex with a good man did that to a woman. And nobody ever said the man had to be in the same room at the same time.

But being able to breathe again was also a huge relief. How any woman had ever survived the era of confining corsets Melanie had no idea. She wasn't even certain the bustier hadn't left her with at least one broken rib!

She'd just returned her glasses to her face and her hairbrush and mirror to her desk drawer when there was a knock at her door. She looked up to find Rennie Faulkner waiting for an invitation to come in.

"Come in." Her smile welcoming, Melanie motioned the other woman forward. "We are absolutely informal around here. Don't feel you ever have to knock. Chloe certainly doesn't."

Rennie walked in and took a seat in one of the black leather visitors' chairs. A teasing light glinted in eyes that were a light amber shade, a contrast to Jacob's, which were the color of rich coffee. "Well, if we all based our behavior on Chloe's…"

"True," Melanie acquiesced, laughing. "But you haven't spent time with her for a while. You have to admit she has settled down this last year."

Adjusting the folds of her long, flowing skirt, Rennie smiled; the lift of her lips seemed to be driven by a private thought, as much for her own sake as for Melanie's. "The love of a good man, I wonder?"

"Must be." *And here we go.* Melanie prayed the inquisition would be swift and painless. "Nothing else has ever seemed to work."

Sighing, Jacob's sister crossed one leg over the other and jiggled her foot. "It gives a girl hope, you know? To believe there are others out there like Eric."

Melanie's thoughts went immediately to Jacob, as Rennie had no doubt intended with her probing. Yes? No? Did she suspect any of what was going on? Was she here to finish the job of driving Melanie insane?

Or was Rennie simply musing over men, as single women were wont to do?

Surreptitiously, Melanie ran fingertips along her nape, where perspiration had blossomed. "Well, except for one or two perennial holdouts, the ones that have crossed my path this last year have been snagged by my best girlfriends."

"Then that should give both of us even more hope. Now the odds are in our favor." Rennie chuckled, then released a long sigh and shook her head. "Notice how I'm already including myself in the group with you and Kinsey and Poe."

"And why not?" Melanie marginally began to relax. Maybe this wasn't about Jacob at all. "We're all in this man-hunting gIRL-gEAR business together."

"My thoughts exactly. With the lucky partners already attached, when the next man comes along…" Rennie let the thought trail off.

And Melanie picked it up with a laugh. "…the competition pool won't be quite as crowded."

The other woman followed suit. "You know, it's good to be able to laugh about it. Especially since that didn't exactly come out sounding very charitable."

"How so?"

"I only meant that good women obviously attract good men, and you girls are the absolute best. I finally did tell Chloe that I'd decided to work with her, but I swear I didn't base my decision on the hopes of finding a date." A self-amused expression crossed her face. "Though I have to admit I've never met so many amazingly gorgeous guys as I have since being here."

"It's like flies to honey. Our own personal match making reality show," Melanie said, glad to see Rennie was really no different than the rest of the gIRL-gEAR women. "We do have our raging bitch moments, but I think you'll love it here."

"Oh, I'm sure I'll fit right in," Rennie stated. "Jacob reminds me every time he sees me that my attitude could use an adjustment."

"He called you bossy," Melanie said, before she stopped to think to whom she was speaking. "I mean—"

Rennie waved off the remark. "He tells me the same thing all the time. About myself. Not about you."

"Oh, I'm sure next time you two talk, he'll come up with something much worse than 'bossy' to say about me." Again with the runaway mouth. "Anyway—"

"No. Hold on a minute." Rennie tilted her head to one side, giving Melanie one of those omniscient sisterly smiles. "That's right. Jacob told me he'd worked with you at Lauren's wedding."

Melanie suppressed a snort. "I'm not sure he

worked with me, but I was there. I wanted to make sure he knew what he was doing.''

Rennie tossed back her head and laughed. "Oh my. I would've paid to sit in the audience for that. Jacob is the biggest control freak when it comes to his work. I can't imagine him letting anyone keep an eye on him.''

Melanie started to sputter out a contradiction, then realized she would be giving away too much. Besides, Jacob was so good at being the bum he was that she forgot how much of his attitude was for show.

For the first time since she'd known him, it came to her that she didn't know why. She wondered if his sister could offer any insight. Then she wondered how best to ask without spilling the details of their involvement.

"He didn't exactly *let* me. I just didn't give him any choice. It was Lauren's wedding, after all.'' Melanie thought for a moment, then said, "And, yes. He did seem rather dictatorial about having his way.''

Rennie nodded knowingly. "Without listening to any of your input.''

"He listened. He even told me he considered what I had to offer. But in the end—''

"Let me guess. All Jacob, all the time.''

Melanie shrugged, grabbed for her pencil. "It was, but he ended up being right.''

"That's the problem.'' The other woman sighed, reached up to push back her long fall of chestnut-red hair. "For once I would really love to see him have to admit that he doesn't have all the answers.''

Hmm. This was getting interesting. "Why would you say that?''

"Oh…'' Rennie waved an expressive hand. "He

thinks he can do no wrong. And, unfortunately, he rarely does. I'm not sure that's good for him.''

''I don't get it.'' Melanie frowned and adjusted her glasses. ''Having that sort of success and confidence in his work? How can that be a bad thing?''

''Oh, my fault for not explaining. You're right. His skill is going to take him far, and his Superman attitude will see him go all the way.''

''Able to leap tall buildings in a single bound?''

''Exactly. Career-wise he's quite indestructible. But in his personal life? I don't think he's quite the man of steel he thinks he is.'' She glanced down at her hands while rubbing her thumb across each of her fingernails in turn. ''So, yes. I'm a bossy, interfering sister. It's just that with all that attitude, I'm afraid one day he'll crack.''

Biting her tongue on the man of steel comment, because this *was* his sister, after all, Melanie gave a small shrug. ''He really doesn't seem the crackable sort.''

''They never do,'' Rennie said bluntly. ''Don't get me wrong. I don't think Jacob's a danger to himself or to anyone else. And I'm probably just borrowing trouble. But he makes me crazy that way.''

Now, to *that* Melanie could certainly relate. ''I don't know anything about his life outside of work. Not that it matters,'' she hurried to add when she suddenly realized how much it bothered her not to have learned more about Jacob. ''But it is a little strange. People usually do spill details in the course of normal conversation.''

Rennie shook her head. ''Not my brother. Without divulging family secrets that need to remain old and buried, let's just say he's let his work eclipse his personal life. Work he can control, down to the very last frame. Editing in what he likes, editing out what he doesn't.'' She sighed. ''I've quit trying to figure him out.''

Melanie scrambled for something to say, her thoughts racing to incorporate what Rennie had just revealed and what few details about his life Jacob himself had put on the table. ''He's definitely an enigma,'' she murmured.

''He is. And he shouldn't be. Not to me, anyway. Not after the way we grew up parenting one another. Latchkey kids of the first order,'' Rennie said, then gave a little disgusted grunt. ''Or of the worst order, since more often than not our parents tucked us in via a long-distance phone call.'' She sighed and seemed to slump deeper into the chair. ''I'm sorry. Here I am dragging up all those family ghosts I swore not to bore you with.''

''Don't worry about it.'' Captivated was a much more apt description than bored. Melanie thought about being tucked in most every night by both her mother and grandmother, almost up until the time she'd left for the University of Texas. She'd taken for granted the very security Jacob had never had.

Yet here she was, with everything in its place and a place for everything. Never wanting to lose the control over her life the two women who'd reared her insisted she'd need to survive in a male-dominated world. Afraid if she didn't rule her emotions as well as her financial portfolio she'd lose the independence that protected them all.

Instead, she'd tightened up into a protected old prune who felt nothing and tempted no one. At least not until Jacob had come along. Oh, God. No. After all this time and all these years, had she actually let a man's influence challenge her way of thinking?

She thought she'd known it all. Now she thought she was going to be sick. "I suppose it's no better than a platitude to say that at least you had each other."

"Platitude or not, it's the truth." Rennie's eyes and smile grew misty. And then she laughed. "You wouldn't believe how one minute we were tattling on one another and the next watching the other's back."

Melanie tried to picture Jacob as a seven-year-old with scraped knees and bandaged elbows. "I don't have siblings, but that doesn't sound much different than most I did know as a kid."

"Oh, it's not. Except that Jacob swore then—we both swore, actually—that neither of us would ever develop such a case of career tunnel vision that we forgot how much more there is to life."

"The way your parents had," Melanie guessed.

"Exactly."

Well, that explained Jacob's struggle to appear nonchalant about his work. It probably fooled most people but him, poor man. "What did your parents do?"

"They were, they are, historians. Truthfully, I think they're perfectly suited to one another. They read each other's mind, finish sentences the other has started. They can sit for hours pouring over ancient documents in any number of languages and never say a word. They just never should've had children."

"As is the case with more than a few couples I've known."

"Oh, it's definitely not a unique situation. It just feels that way, being the children involved."

Melanie really wasn't sure what to say. She only

knew compassion had joined the tumultuous emotions expanding her heart.

She rolled her pencil the length of her legal pad and back. ''I guess it would be a challenge to analyze your own situation objectively. But you both seem to have learned how to cope. I'm not sure his way is healthy....''

''How so?''

*Way to go, big mouth.* ''He's incredibly talented, gifted even. But he acts like he doesn't give a damn. It's got to tear him up inside when you think about it.''

''Or when *you* think about it?''

So much for secret affairs. Melanie glanced down at the yellow pad on her desk. ''I guess it's more obvious than I thought.''

''Not really. I was just guessing.'' A tentative smile passed over Rennie's face. ''I've seen the way Jacob looks at you, and so I wondered.''

Jacob looked at her? How did Jacob look at her? ''Wondered?''

''If anything was going on between the two of you.''

*Oh, why not?* Melanie sighed. ''Something is, though I'm not sure I can give it a name.''

''Don't. Not for my sake, anyway.'' Rennie's probing gaze grew concerned. ''Hey, I'm glad you got past his attitude and under his skin. Not many women do. He's a great guy, but he doesn't let many people see that.''

''Yeah. I've noticed.''

''So, ask him about it,'' Rennie urged. ''I'm curious to know what he'd use as his defense.''

"You mean if he knows himself as well as you do?"

Rennie shook her head. "He knows. Deep down, where guys don't like to hang out. I just wonder if you're the woman who can get him to spend time there, because I sure can't. He's basically told me to mind my own business."

Melanie chuckled. "And he called *you* bossy."

"Well, there ya go. He *has* told you something personal."

"I suppose so. Though it's not much."

"No, but it's a start. Now, see what else you can get him to give you. Er, get him to reveal." Rennie's face flushed. "I'm sorry. Usually I love a good double entendre. Just not when my brother is playing a starring role."

In that case, Melanie decided, she'd be better off not sharing anything else about her relationship with Jacob. Time to change the subject. "Thanks for the advice. But surely you didn't come by just to talk about your brother."

"Actually, no. I was wanting to talk to you about possibly setting up a database for gUIDANCE gIRL."

Finally, something safe. Something familiar. Something well within Melanie's ability to handle. "Not a problem," she told Rennie, wishing the same were true of the other woman's brother.

JACOB LEANED BACK in his chair and stared at the e-mail on his screen. The one he'd forgotten about earlier when faced with Melanie taking off her clothes. *No. Not now. Don't go back there, buddy.*

He didn't have time to replay or even revisit the show because he was looking at his entire future in black type on a white screen. Equity Beat in New York wanted to see him earlier than originally planned, and for an extra day or two—if he could manage.

What a question! He'd manage as much time as they wanted. He'd have to get together with Asa to cover what couldn't be rescheduled. The way Jacob figured, the other man would be back from Milwaukee by then, and it would be payback time. Such was the beauty of having seniority at Avatare.

Too bad he wouldn't be able to take Melanie along. The two of them could have some kind of party in the Big Apple together. He wondered if the Mets would be in town. He wondered if Melanie even liked baseball….

Damn, what was he thinking? He was making the trip for business, not for a piece of out-of-town nooky. If he couldn't keep it in his pants for a couple of weeks, he was in serious need of therapy. The thing was, he knew that wasn't the case.

He'd kept it in his pants for months at a time, most recently for almost a year. Not that he planned to share that fact with his buds. Well, maybe with Melanie. Eventually. When they got closer to having that sexual history conversation. That sharing of test results they'd need to do before ditching the condoms for sweet skin-on-skin love.

Whoa! Wait just a hell of a minute. He held up both hands, rolled his chair back from his desk. This was getting out of control, this thinking that sounded as if he was headed for commitment. He had no intention of permanently tying himself down.

It was a known fact that a guy couldn't have both a woman and a career. Not the kind of career Jacob wanted. Free to hit the road when the muse and opportunity called. He couldn't do that if he had obligations, a family, a woman, waiting for him at home.

He hadn't been lying the day he'd told Melanie that he didn't do whipped. He was his own man, and he wasn't a slave to anyone or anything. He'd learned a long time ago to rely solely on himself.

Once in a while he leaned on Renata. But never on their parents, neither of whom had managed to be home enough during his early years for him to form an attachment. He was closer to Asa and Harry than good ol' Mom or Dad.

And, yeah, lately he'd gotten pretty overinvolved with his work, but film had always been his passion. And now it was his future. This gIRL-gEAR documentary was shaping up to be the very ticket he'd been hoping for.

The work he'd done so far had kicked major ass. He'd impressed the hell out of himself—a mighty feat indeed. He couldn't say whether it was the subject material, or if he'd just hit some sort of unconscious stride.

Whatever it was, getting paid to keep his eye on seven gorgeous women was definitely sweet. He'd be hard-pressed to ever draw another assignment to match this plum. What he had going on with Melanie was a perk he'd never expected. If he'd started seeing beyond the big picture into the individual frames...so what?

He refused to start thinking she'd had any impact on his work. If he thought that, he might as well hang up his cameras for good. Another week and she wouldn't even be around. And where would that leave him? Where it would leave him would be on his way to New York. Exactly where he wanted to be.

He'd just finished composing a reply to Equity Beat when his phone rang a second time. He saved the draft to read through again and glanced distractedly at his caller ID on the third ring. Shit. Full alert. He'd almost missed her. Jacob quickly grabbed the receiver.

"Faulkner."

"Jacob? It's Melanie."

"I know."

"You do? Oh. Caller ID, duh."

"Well, yeah. But actually, I recognize your voice."

"Oh, sorry. I wasn't thinking."

He felt the beginnings of a grin. "Or maybe you weren't giving me credit?"

"No. That's not it."

"You sure?" he asked, picturing her frown. He loved giving her a hard time. She was so easy to rile, and so cute when she finally caught on that he was pulling her leg. "I mean, being the bum I am and all, you probably figured I hadn't been paying attention."

"That's not funny."

He laughed, because she was. Funny. He liked that about her. Liked it a lot. "You're right. I'm being an ass. What's up?"

She hesitated for a minute before he heard her sigh. "Do you have plans for tonight?"

"Plans with you? Or just plans period?" He thought about all those missed baseball games. Then he thought about all of that amazing sex. Harry and Asa might just have to hit Minute Maid Park without him. Again.

"Either one. I was thinking if you don't have any-thing set up, maybe we could get a drink?"

Jacob blinked, frowned, wondered if he'd mistaken her voice, after all. This was the woman he was sleeping with, and she was asking him out for a drink? "Sure. Should I come to your office? You want to come here? Or were you wanting me to pick up a bottle and meet you at your place?"

"None of the above. I was thinking I'd meet you later. Maybe at a club. Or downtown at one of the bars in the theater district. Would that be inconvenient?"

"What? To meet you downtown?"

"Yeah. Sydney's dad owns a wine bar on Main. Paddington's Ford. It's quiet. And dark. And he sells a mean cigar."

"So, this isn't about going dancing then."

"No. I much prefer to dance at home."

Jacob cleared the sudden horny frog from his throat. "Works for me. And, sure. Paddington's is great. What time you want to meet?"

"Is nine good for you?"

Nine would give him at least a good hour and a half at the ball game. And Minute Maid Park was only ten blocks or so from Main. Save his ass from total annihilation for skipping out on the boys again. "Yep. Perfect."

"Okay then." She hesitated, breathed softly, then added, "I'll see you there."

He opened his mouth to ask her what was going on, but the dial tone was already buzzing in his ear. So much for small talk. He hated small talk anyway, and, besides, Melanie was all business. Except when she was making like a wild woman and tumbling him in bed.

Strange, that phone call. Though he supposed it wasn't, really. They weren't exactly running around hiding their affair, but neither had they talked about taking what they had and moving it out of the bedroom. Dating, he was pretty sure the practice was still called.

He could hardly blame her for wanting more than the games they'd been playing in bed. Sex never was enough for a woman. Except that Melanie had seemed to be okay with the arrangement up until now.

Still, he could be a good guy. He'd have a drink or two, maybe a cigar. And he wouldn't even talk about sex until they got back to her place and into her bed.

# 10

SITTING IN Paddington's Ford, where she'd chosen a booth halfway between the bar and the entrance, Melanie watched the glow from the lantern over her table catch in her glass of chardonnay.

Why in the world she was nervous, she hadn't a clue. She'd seen Jacob butt naked. She'd done things to his body she'd never thought of doing to a man. She'd discovered all the heres and theres that got him off.

And yet she was nervous about meeting him for drinks.

This was all Rennie's fault, for peeling back just enough of her brother's camouflage to tease Melanie's curiosity. Until now she'd been able to convince herself that their sexual relationship was enough to keep her satisfied. Until now. But after talking with Rennie, Melanie knew there was much more to Jacob Faulkner than she could ever learn about in bed.

That was why she'd come here, hoping time spent in his company—in public and fully clothed—would disprove what her intuition was telling her. She needed a hint, a clue, an admission even, that he wasn't the goal-driven man she suspected, the overachiever he tried so hard to hide.

At least that was what she needed if she wanted to continue their affair.

And she wanted to continue their affair. An affair or a fling she could handle as long as the man involved wasn't the type she'd eventually want to get serious about. But right now when work had to be her focus, a relationship with a driven, career-oriented man wasn't possible—not if she wanted to keep her wits about her.

Because once he'd gained her respect and admiration, as well as her lust, she'd find it impossible to concentrate on all the things she had on her plate. He'd become a distraction, and she was afraid she'd come to resent him for that, for destroying her concentration.

She couldn't have Jacob and her job—not if she hoped to do her best by both a relationship and a career.

God, who was she kidding? Jacob Faulkner had her respect and admiration in spades. She'd known deep down from the very beginning that he wasn't a bum. That he wasn't lazy in the least. That he was smart and so much more than a boy toy. She also knew that for some reason he didn't want anyone to see that truth.

Too bad for him. Her future depended on verifying just that. Instinct told her the driven ambition he denied was the reason for the success he pretended meant nothing.

And that same ambition was at the root of their sizzling attraction.

Opposites might attract in theory, but rudderless men had never commanded her respect—much less her lust.

Jacob did both.

And, yes. That admission was much easier to understand than thinking she'd only been after his, uh, assets. But it also complicated the hell out of her life. Which was why, unless she relished living in a cardboard box under the Pierce Elevated, she probably should call off their fling. And since Jacob had made it clear that he didn't want to continue what they had beyond the documentary shoot, putting an end to their involvement here and now made the most sense. She had to cut him out of her life while she still had the strength to do so.

Frowning, she lifted her glass for several long cool sips of wine, wishing she'd chosen a place with a less intimate ambience. A place better suited for the end of an affair. A place with bright lighting and a garish decor and music conducive to something other than seduction.

She needed to be concentrating on her career and gIRL-gEAR's bottom line, essentially one and the same when she got right down to it. If only her own fate was at risk, she might have considered relaxing her guard. But she also supplemented Mama's and Nana's incomes each month.

Melanie lowered her glass to the table, her mouth twisting in disgust. Both her father and grandfather had gone AWOL on their marriages, leaving wives with broken spirits. Despite preaching the rewards of setting high goals or the mantra of independence they'd instilled in her as a child, neither woman had possessed the means to pursue either.

Keeping a roof over three heads and food in their mouths—not to mention paying for Melanie's tuition and fees not covered with grants and small scholarships—meant her mother and grandmother had had to continue in their secretarial positions rather than strike out after their own dreams.

When Melanie had met her future partners at university, she'd sensed kindred spirits and rejoiced. Independent, smart and sassy, mistresses of their bodies, hearts and destinies, the six founding "gIRLS" had always agreed to keep men in the bedroom and out of their company's boardroom.

Or at least they had until this recent rash of partnering-up by her partners. Now sex, or relationships, anyway, seemed to be eclipsing everyone's priorities. Until they got back with the program, like it or not, Melanie was the lone business ranger.

Business was where her head needed to be. Period. End of story.

Snorting, she checked her watch. Jacob was running late. Or worse, he wasn't going to show up at all. Great. Rejected. Dumping her before she could find out the truth and decide whether or not to dump him. Wasn't that just like a man, always wanting the upper hand?

She'd chosen to face away from the door, not wanting to be tempted into watching for him to arrive. She planned to play this as coolly as she possibly could, but the way her palms were already sweating, she was beginning to wonder if cool still remained a part of her repertoire.

Since that day Jacob had walked down the dais steps in the church sanctuary and circled around her as if judging her lines and her markings, she hadn't gone to bed one single night without thinking about him. A fact she resented and had vowed to change tonight.

Now that he might be standing her up, she perversely ached to see his smile and duel wits with the dangerous man. He stimulated her mind, as well as her passionate sexual nature. Quite frankly, she would miss the hell out of having him around once he was gone.

"Miss me?"

She took hold of the stem of her wineglass before the whole thing tumbled over, glancing up just as Jacob slid onto the opposite bench. "Now why would you think that? I had an entire day to myself without my every step dogged and my every word recorded."

"Yeah. Those cameras can be a real pain in the ass." He gestured to the server to refill her drink and bring him the same. "Still, it's a tough loss to have a good one taken out of commission. I'm guessing it ended up in your building's Dumpster?"

Melanie snorted. "Go fish, if you want. But that piece of junk couldn't have cost you more than fifteen dollars. I'm surprised it even worked long enough to, well, to work. Just wait till you get the bill for the stolen bandwidth."

"Not a problem." He sat back, stretched both arms along the back of the booth. "I'll make a fortune when I offer the video for download."

This time it was Jacob who shot forward to catch her wineglass, but not before half her remaining drink sloshed onto the red-and-indigo tablecloth. Once he righted the stemware, he slowly lifted his guilt-ridden gaze. "I was kidding, Melanie. You know that, don't you? Tell me you know that, or I'm going to have to shoot myself over here."

She wasn't sure she was going to be able to stave off the sudden burning rush of tears. Her heart pounded until she was certain a wide hole had to be gaping in her chest. "It was a joke."

"Yes. God, yes," he hurried to confirm. He reached

a hand across the table toward her, but hers remained twisted together in her lap. "A joke, Melanie. And a very bad one at that. One I won't make again. I swear."

Breathing slowly, deeply, Melanie pressed her lips together while her blood pressure calmed. Calm, cool and collected, as Kinsey would say. That was the ticket. And the cocky bastard was not going to get away with scaring her to death, bad joke or no.

Feeling more like herself again, she arched one brow as inspiration hit. "And what's an oath you make worth, Faulkner? Do you take your honor as seriously as you take your work?"

He paused. "Is this a trick question?"

She lifted one shoulder and smoothed the wrinkles her fingers had put into her short linen skirt the color of plump eggplant. She wondered if he would notice. The color, not the wrinkles.

She forced her hands to be still. "No tricks on my part, but I'm beginning to think you have a few up your sleeve."

He fought a frown that appeared to be half wariness and half anger, laced his hands over his abs and leaned back. "Okay. I'll bite. Tell me what you think I'm hiding so I can at least defend myself."

*Fair enough.* "For starters, you pretend that what you do doesn't define who you are. That it doesn't rule your every decision."

"Hey, sweetheart." He slumped back farther. "I'm not the one here ruling my life and any number of others with an iron fist."

She somehow kept from flinching. "If I flex an iron fist, I have my reasons." He didn't have to know she'd believed all her life that being in control gave her power and protection in a man's world. "But we're talking about you, *sweetheart*. Not me. Don't avoid the subject."

He frowned in earnest. "The subject bores me."

"Humor me, then." Lacing her fingers together on the table's edge, she leaned toward him. "Tell me that you don't know exactly where you want your career to be in five years. Tell me you don't know exactly how you plan to get there. Tell me you're a temperamental artist with no head for business. Tell me with a straight face, and I'll believe you."

*Tell me, ease my mind, and then great sex will be enough for me. If you're really the bum I know you're not, I won't be looking for more.*

He glanced toward the center of the room, obviously not certain how to answer, or if he wanted to answer at all. His fingertips now flat on the base of his wineglass, he pushed the glass forward, pulled it back.

Finally, he returned his gaze to hers. It was as if he'd wiped away everything he'd been thinking; his expression was sadly blank. "It sounds to me like you've been spending too much time with my sister the psychologist."

Another diversion, Melanie noted with a sinking heart. No denial. "Why? Because it's not possible that I might possess any insight into human nature?"

She sat back and drained her second glass of wine, uncertain if she wanted to go for three. Then again, the look now darkening Jacob's face might be easier to deal with were she under the influence and passed out flat on the floor.

His voice dropped to a rough whisper and he said,

"Don't do this to me, Mel. Don't do this to what we've got going for us."

Odd that the strength of purpose she found irresistible seemed a source of shame to him. "Don't do what? Try to have a conversation?"

"Don't start analyzing. Don't pick it apart."

"And what exactly do we have going for us, anyway, that I'm ruining by trying to understand you better?"

"Do I really have to spell it out?"

She waited for a moment, looking into his eyes, wishing she saw more there than what appeared to be regret. What was it he regretted?

Ever getting involved with her in the first place? Or the fact that she liked him as much out of bed as in? That she could fall in love with a man who never sacrificed his convictions and goals to her own considerable will?

She grabbed her purse, inexplicably hurt by the fact that he wouldn't want her love—even though she had no intention of offering it. "No. You really don't. Because there's nothing to spell out, is there?"

Jacob got to his feet before she could manage to beat him to hers, and slid into her side of the booth, blocking her route of escape. She did not want to sit here and argue; she did not want to sit here and sulk. But it seemed she was stuck and doing both.

"It's bothering you, isn't it?" he asked, once she'd sat back and he was at her side, his knee cocked up onto the bench, enabling him to face her, one arm along the booth's padded back, his fingers teasing strands of her hair.

"You disturbing my hair? Yes. It's bothering me," she said but she didn't move away.

Neither did he move his hand. "The Webcam performance. You're wishing you could take it all back."

How could he be so smart, yet so clueless? Still, sex was a safer subject than love. "If you're going to be offering it for download, yeah. I'm wishing exactly that."

His hand moved to her nape, where he began to massage, his fingers firmly working away the stiffness and tension. "No downloading. I told you. That performance is mine. Period. Unless...you'd like to watch with me. We could take the wine back to my place."

She shook her head, shivering as his hand slid away from her neck and lower, his wrist resting on her shoulder and the touch of his fingertips teasing the bare skin above her collarbone. Her nipples tightened and she was glad the room's lighting was dim and her top a loose fit.

And then she realized he'd invited her to see where he lived. For sex, of course. Progress, of sorts, when she'd finally given up and decided to cut her losses. "No thanks. I'd just as soon forget the existence of that recording, if you don't mind."

"Why?" He scooted closer to her and she was so tempted to cuddle into his body that staying where she was required willpower the likes of which he had no idea. "You were wondering what we had going for us. Your willingness to go that far, knowing you could trust me. That's a big part of it."

She gave a sharp snort and tried to slump down in the seat, away from his hand. But he followed suit, closing the distance she'd been determined to keep. "That...that performance. That was so not me. I mean, yes. I love the sex. And I'm not looking for a white picket fence. It's just..."

His second hand, which had been inching its way into her lap, stilled. "It's just what?"

*Here we go,* she thought. The commitmentphobe was giving her the out she'd come here looking for and had forgotten along the way. "I can't pretend you're a stranger anymore. I know you too well."

He hesitated a moment, then moved his hands and his hip and his entire body, sliding down the bench away from her. "I doubt it, sweetheart."

Missing his nearness already, she prepared to drive him away for good. "I know you don't want to believe that you might actually be letting your career take over your life. I know you don't want to believe that you've fallen into the same trap that your parents did. Because that would mean you didn't learn anything at all from their example. And that you've let down your sister, as well as yourself."

His narrowed eyes glittered. He picked up his wineglass and drained it dry. And then he shook his head. "You've definitely been talking too much to my sister."

"Am I right?"

He shifted around on the bench to face her. "I have plans, Melanie. I'm not sure what Renata told you, but one thing even she doesn't know is that this documentary is going to take me where I want to go."

"How so?"

He shook his head, as if what he was thinking had nothing to do with her question, but with what he was seeing in his mind. "This is the best work I've ever done. Everything I've captured is real. Nothing is forced or set up. It's spontaneous. Every single detail. That's why I could see the way you were looking at me. And that's why…'' He hesitated, as if uncertain how much more to say.

"Why what?" she prompted.

"Why I can't think of this as a relationship," he said quickly. "I like you a lot, Melanie. I'm pretty sure you know that. But a true relationship would cut into the time I need to spend on my work. The time, and especially the focus, I need right now. I'm at a really crucial point and I don't want to screw it up."

And she would screw it up. Who was driving whom away? She pursed her lips for a moment before saying, "Then my timing is really perfect."

"Timing?"

She nodded. "I've realized lately how much I've neglected work since you and I have been involved. And it wouldn't be so bad if I hadn't been watching that same sort of neglect happen all around me."

"I'm lost here, sweetheart. But feel free to enlighten me."

"Lauren can't go without calling Anton at least five times a day. Macy's lunch hours always run two hours, no doubt taken in Leo's corporate rest room. Chloe repairs her makeup at the end of the day, but on company time, because getting home to Eric is all that matters." God, where was all of this coming from? "Even Sydney spends too much time daydreaming, looking like the cat that ate the canary."

The dreaded relationship distraction. Melanie expelled a long sigh, trying to keep her voice steady. A steadiness that would've been easier to maintain if what she was thinking and what she'd just said didn't make the women she loved and worked with sound like unprofessional dweebs.

But the minute the other women became part of a couple, nothing else seemed to matter in their lives.

The entire gIRL-gEAR paradigm was falling apart. And Melanie couldn't stand it.

Feeling righteously justified in what she was doing, even as her heart twisted, she looked Jacob straight in the eye and said, "I think we should call this whole thing off."

"Call it off," he repeated.

"Yes. We're not involved except physically, so it shouldn't be hard. We can both get back to our priorities. When you think about it, it's the smart thing to do."

"It's the chicken thing to do," he countered bluntly.

She blinked. Twice. "Chicken?"

"Chicken. Taking the easy way out. What are you afraid of? Your loss of control?" He smiled wryly. "Don't look so surprised. Did you think you were still a stranger to me? Not hardly."

She found herself totally speechless.

"Don't you realize what a turn-on your passion is?"

"Yeah, right."

"What's the problem then? You think putting an end to this affair is going to help your concentration? Screw your partners and what they might or might not be doing to ruin the company. This isn't about them. This is about you. We stop what we're doing? You'll be frustrated and just as distracted as they are, obsessing about the sensational sex we've had."

Her heart thumped wildly in her chest. "Much ego there, Faulkner?"

This time he snorted. "Is that it? You think I'm going to dump you, so you're doing the dumping first?

We don't have a serious thing going on here. There's no real dumping involved, is there?''

His arguments were too logical. Her pride too great. And her heart aching. This had to be what her mother had felt, her grandmother, too—this pull between sex and sanity, love and self-protection.

But Melanie was stronger than them, she told herself. She would not be weaker when he left. "Fine," she said firmly. "So we don't call it off. Where do we go from here?''

"Back to your place.''

"It's so nice to be wanted for my body.'' She said it teasingly, sarcastically, though in reality she was putting more emotion than challenge on the line.

"Hell, Melanie.''

He slid out of the booth and waited for her to follow. And only then, when she was standing beside him, her shoulder rubbing against his chest and absorbing his warmth…only then did he add in a whisper, "A body I can get anywhere. It's your brain that makes this an adventure.''

SATURDAY MORNING FOUND Melanie having just finished working out when her cell phone buzzed. Bent forward at the waist, she continued her cool-down stretch, counting to ten.

A girl couldn't even enjoy a quiet sweat, she mused, taking hold of the pole for support with one hand, the other braced on one knee. She breathed slowly, in through her nose, out through her mouth, until a bead of perspiration fell from the hollow of her throat to puddle on the room's hardwood floor.

She'd used her remote control a few minutes ago to shut off the music. She preferred cooling down in silence, enjoying the sound of her own labored breathing and the imagined drumbeat of her heart.

But when her phone buzzed again, she picked up her towel and headed for her bedroom, where the device sat in its charging cradle on her dresser. ''Message Received'' read her display screen.

She frowned; not many of her girlfriends shared her cell service and none ever utilized text messaging. The incoming number wasn't familiar, though that wasn't saying much. She didn't make a habit of memorizing numbers.

That was the entire purpose of having a cell phone and a PDA. She pushed the combination of buttons necessary to read what had been sent. And then she rolled her eyes.

*Let's go, Adventure gIRL. Be in your car in fifteen minutes.*

Jacob thought he was so clever. Adventure gIRL her butt. He was determined to ignore everything they'd talked about last night. And the things they'd done after tumbling into bed, having killed two bottles of wine between them.

The alcohol had lowered inhibitions. And she didn't doubt for a minute that this morning found Jacob regretting the things he'd said.

If he even remembered them.

Wouldn't that be just her luck, that all his talk of the things she made him feel turned out to be nothing but drunken ramblings. Drunken horny ramblings. He didn't want to lose the easy sex he was getting.

And, honestly. Why was she putting so much stock into what he said in bed? Bed was…bed. Sex. Much more important were the things they talked about when they had their clothes on. Except Jacob never wanted to talk.

Or he wanted to talk about anything except the things she thought mattered. Until last night, anyway. Last night he'd finally given her the glimpse into his head she'd been wanting.

Of course, once he realized how much of himself he'd revealed, he'd immediately backed off and suggested more sex instead. Such a typical man. And a man she was falling for in a very big way.

He made her laugh. She couldn't remember the last time a man had made her laugh, catching her off guard with the outrageous things he said. His attitude. His observations.

The thought of him not being around the office and, even worse, being half a continent away…the idea was almost unbearable. Even though she'd sworn less than twelve hours ago to keep this purely sexual, she couldn't stand to think of him leaving.

Her phone buzzed again. She pulled up the message. *Chicken.*

That did it. She wasn't going to stand around here and be called names. Not by a man who was a bigger chicken than she was.

## 11

FOLLOWING THE DIRECTIONS Jacob sent as text messages to her phone wasn't hard in the least. Granted, she'd taken forty-five minutes to get to her car, not the fifteen he'd ordered. But she figured he'd rather have her arrive for her adventure smelling better than she had when he'd first rang.

By the time she headed out it had been almost noon. She was able to easily map the entire route using his play by play instructions. She'd never realized how close he lived. Well, closer to the warehouse loft Poe had just bought from Lauren and Macy.

In fact, Jacob's address was also a warehouse, his being farther east of downtown. He was almost within walking distance of Minute Maid Park. She wondered if he made it to many ball games.

She parked where he'd directed, using the security code to open the gate leading to his private carport. She pulled her Infiniti in next to his Sport Trac and got out. He'd told her that the bunker-style door ahead would open into a maintenance room where she'd find his elevator.

She was beginning to wonder if she'd ever find *him*, what with all this subterfuge. But then she heard the electronic whir of a camera zooming in, and it was all she could do not to look up into the corner as the elevator ascended to the second floor.

Spy boy was not going to rattle her that easily.

The elevator opened into a cavernous room with a floor tiled in large black-and-white squares. And *he* accused *her* of needing to add color to her life. Oh, there were red squares, too, she noticed, moving farther inside. And purple, she saw on further inspection. But there wasn't much else in the room.

A kitchen space took up one end, complete with track lighting above a stainless-steel island like something off the starship *Enterprise*. Especially when she factored in the row of television screens above cabinets that were white with black trim.

Except for the missing sound track, it was like being in a funky club with random music video images flashing from one screen to the next. A syncopated relay of sorts.

Or so she thought until she reached the last monitor in the row and found herself looking at her own image. A live image. Nothing he'd recorded earlier in the office or on the Webcam. But a security feed much like the one she'd heard being made in the elevator.

Nope. He wasn't going to get to her. Not today after last night's decision to simply enjoy his brain and his body as long as he was around.

She turned away from the kitchen space, hearing another camera whir and ignoring that one, too, as she made her way into what appeared to be the main living area, or would have been livable if furnished.

It wasn't. At least not in a conventional way. He had what she supposed passed for two sofas, but had started life as automobile bench seats before being given a designer touch. The coffee table between was the tailgate from a pickup, with legs made from the supporting bases of jacks.

Halogen floor lamps sat in critical locations beneath the high warehouse windows in the long brick wall. At the far end of the room, a spiral staircase led up to a second floor. Hmm. Must be his lair.

She headed that way, wondering what kind of guy didn't have a monstrous big screen TV and stereo system. What was she thinking? A guy like Jacob, of course, who didn't analyze but went for the overall concept. This overall concept was strangely spare. And strangely strange.

Since she didn't need to understand him more than she already did, she let it go as she reached the stairs. It was then that she realized the windshield frame hanging there on the far wall wasn't framing a picture. It was broadcasting another camera feed.

And he claimed to be able to separate work from the rest of his life. Ha! Taking a walk through his loft pretty much drove home her theory that videography *was* his life. Amazing, really, how well she knew him. And sad, as well, that the man she knew best would never be a long-term fixture in her life.

Blowing out a long, slow breath, she gripped the iron railing and ascended the stairs, feeling her own image following her progress from below. A mightily disconcerting situation, she had to admit. But it was nothing compared to the shock that throttled through her when she reached floor number two.

The high-set windows of the long main wall were blocked by a television screen. But it wasn't a single screen. It was a video cluster that showed one single broadcast. And, of course, that broadcast was her. Talk about disconcerting, seeing oneself literally the size of a building and cut up into a dozen squares.

She took another step into the room. The camera

capturing her image zoomed in so that she saw only
her mouth to the far right of the top of the screen, a
shoulder in the lower left. The center of the picture
was the hollow of her throat. And the nervous beat of
her pulse was visible there.

She wanted to know where Jacob was but she refused to call out. He'd no doubt make his presence
known when he was good and ready. And watching
his mind at work, gauging that readiness by the ad-
justments he made to the camera angle and zoom, intrigued her to no end.

When, after several seconds, the picture on the wall
of screens hadn't changed, anticipation blossomed on
her skin in a fine sheen of sweat. Before Jacob, she
would've been much more ladylike and perspired. But
her response to him had long since been anything but
ladylike.

She continued to watch the monitors, not wanting
to miss a minute of what was coming and, yes, admittedly hesitant to spoil the suspense. This had to be
his bedroom. And she was certain they'd end up in
bed. But she wasn't ready for the end game when they
had so many rounds yet to play.

It was then that she caught movement behind her
video image. She looked beyond her own shoulder and
watched Jacob come into the scene. Every part of her
body tensed with expectation. Breathing became more
chore than unconscious thought.

When he finally came into focus, she caught nothing
but glimpses as he used her body as a shield. But she
did see that his shoulders were bare and, it seemed,
the rest of him, too. She saw the long lean length of
both hip and thigh before she blocked him completely.

And then, at that moment, the music came on. The

same mixture of Dirty Vegas and Moby, Vibrolux and Zero 7 that she'd used in her original striptease. The man did not play fair, because now he was directly behind her and the air fairly screamed with the tension.

She couldn't see him and she wanted to see him, but she saw nothing but his hands as they settled on her shoulders. His hands and, as he shifted position, a sleek headset and mike.

"Zoom in one," he said, after lifting one hand to a sound control at his ear, and the image on the cluster became no more than her body from shoulders to waist.

"What are you doing?" she whispered, watching her throat work as she spoke.

"You wouldn't watch the tape. I want you to see what I see when you take off your clothes."

"I know what you see. I know the equipment."

"You know the parts. You don't see the whole."

They were back to that, but she wasn't going to argue because his hands had slipped down to the row of buttons beneath the deep V-neck of her sleeveless top. Big round buttons, the color of sunflowers, holding together the matching blouse she wore over her shirt.

She wondered if he'd noticed, but he didn't say a word. He only continued to unbutton.

He finished, and one hand went back to his headset. "Zoom in two."

Melanie watched as her chest filled the video screen. Jacob's hands returned to pull her top off her shoulders, exposing her sheer, ivory lace bra and dark areolas. And then he released the back clasp of her bra and took the straps down her arms until the lace edges of the cups caught on her nipples, drawn achingly taut.

She hated watching; she loved watching. She couldn't decide if she was more aroused by what she saw or what she felt or by seeing what she felt.

And she *was* aroused, beyond belief, and clenching the muscles between her thighs made it worse, made her long to take him as deeply into her body as she possibly could, made her want to feel the firmness of his erection when she squeezed.

And now Jacob's fingers were tweaking where the cups of her bra held fast, tugging at her nipples, his palms dipping below to cup the slight weight of her breasts. Eyes wide open, she watched the play of his very masculine hands, broad-palmed and long-fingered and with a dusting of dark hair, over her very feminine coloring and curves.

The music throbbed to the pulse of her body; her body thrummed to the music's rhythm. She couldn't separate the two sensations, the rush of her blood from the beat. The lighting here on the second floor wasn't overly bright, but it was strategic. The video movements played between light and shadow, as if a strobe flashed from one screen to the next.

She was mesmerized, a voyeur in her own seduction. And then Jacob slipped his fingers beneath the sheer cups and covered her breasts completely. Her bra fell away, leaving nothing for her viewing but her naked torso and his hands. She leaned her head back onto his shoulder and closed her eyes. For this moment she only want to feel.

He tugged at her nipples, kneaded the firm flesh, ran the flat pad of a finger around the pebbled surface of her areolas before starting again from the beginning. But then he moved lower, his palms sliding over her abdomen to her skirt.

''Zoom out one,'' he said into the mike, then added, ''Zoom out two.''

Melanie looked on, and once again found herself gazing at her body from shoulders to waist. Only this time she was bare but for the short denim skirt that rode at her hipbones, and the belly chain circling above. Jacob slid his fingers beneath, splaying them over her abs while the chain across his knuckles seemed to hold him in place, hold him imprisoned.

The concept totally turned her on—as if she wasn't turned on already. The lights, the music, the feel of Jacob's hands on her skin and the very visual proof of what she was feeling taking up an entire wall...how could she not be on the verge of going out of her mind?

And then there was the obvious fact of Jacob's arousal, and knowing that behind her he was naked. She'd caught glimpses as he'd moved, but none of what she'd seen satisfied her curiosity. Not when she could feel the hardness of his erection as he pressed himself to her bottom.

''Zoom down one,'' he said into the mike, and the video cluster showed her belly chain and her skirt. Jacob's hands worked the zipper down in back, and then he placed his palms on her hipbones and slid the skirt down her thighs until she stood in nothing but her sheer ivory thong.

The elastic edge ran along her trimmed line of dark hair, and the sheer material beneath hid nothing. Her clit stood out between her plump labia, and she was dying for Jacob's touch. She watched as if disembodied, as if she was an uninvolved voyeur, as his hands framed her mound, his index fingers slipping beneath the thong and between the folds of her sex.

She whimpered and spread her legs, giving him better access to what he was seeking, there, where his fingers were holding open her sex and, oh, yes, he had her. He circled her body's wet opening and dipped a finger inside, withdrawing before she could do no more than sigh in relief at his touch.

Frustration mounted higher when he pulled his hands away. "Take off your thong," he ordered, and she hurried to oblige, feeling the heat of a blush travel over her skin.

Seeing her naked sex so…big and so…bare was as disconcerting as it was an erotic thrill. And then she heard the tearing sound of a condom wrapper at the same time Jacob said, "Touch yourself."

What? Between her legs? It had been one thing doing so for a camera, but watching her own hands play in her own sex with Jacob behind her looking on? She moved her hands to her breasts and cupped the spare curves, moving fingers to pinch at her nipples as the fantasy settled in to stay.

Jacob had dipped his knees and, holding her hips, thrust his penis between her legs, rubbing from back to front through the folds of her sex, teasing her wildly with glimpses of the covered tip of his cock.

She wanted to feel him inside her, wanted to see him inside her, wanted more than the sensation of her bare bottom pillowed by the cushion of soft hair there at the base of his shaft.

His sharp intakes of breath signaled his want of more, too. But he made no move to take her to bed or to push himself into her body. And so she leaned back against him and slid her hands into the folds of her sex.

She pulled herself open so she could see everything

Jacob had seen on her Webcam performance, as well as when he'd buried his face between her thighs. She pressed her fingertips to the sides of her clit and shuddered as sensations rocked her to her toes.

And then Jacob's hands were there with hers and she let him take over. Nothing she'd watched herself do in any way compared to having him please her. But suddenly it wasn't enough. Not nearly enough.

And so she stepped away, turned around and wrapped her arms around his waist, sliding her palms down to his backside, where she squeezed.

"What the hell are you doing?" He ground out the words even while pressing his erection into the softness of her belly.

"Taking my adventure into my own hands," she replied, and settled her lips at the base of his throat.

She kissed him there, nipped at his skin, sucked and soothed the teeth marks. His hands, which had settled on her hipbones, slid up her rib cage; his thumbs rubbed the plump sides of her breasts and she shuddered.

"Jacob?" she murmured into the muscle and skin of his shoulder.

"Melanie?" he answered, his voice hoarse and gruff.

"Is there a bed in here?" she asked. "Or am I going to have to take you down to the floor?"

He chuckled then, and she felt the rumble everywhere he touched her. "Yeah. There's a bed."

"Then unless you consider a cold tiled floor beneath your back a turn-on, maybe we could move there?"

"A bed? Isn't that rather pedestrian?"

"This is my adventure, buster." She slapped him on the ass. "Now, move it. And lose that thing on your head. Making love to a droid is taking this beyond kinky and into obscene.''

He looked at her for a long moment, his eyes doing that dark flashing thing that made it so very hard for her to breathe. She didn't know if he was pondering the kinky comment or the obscene.

So it surprised her when the corner of his mouth finally crooked into a grin and he said, ''Making love, huh?''

But she didn't have time to form a response because he activated the mike, commanded, ''Zoom right one,'' and then jerked off the headset and nearly dragged her to the bed.

What was she supposed to say? She'd stopped fooling herself the minute he'd walked up naked behind her. This wasn't solely about sex any longer. Not for her. Emotionally, she hadn't yet uttered the *L* word. But physically this was no longer about getting off. It was all about giving back. And, yes, about giving up control.

He tumbled her onto sheets of soft cotton, sheets that were as warm on her back as the heat of his body was, covering her front. She didn't even wait for more foreplay, but reached down between his legs and took his cock in her hand.

She guided him to her sex and surged upward, taking him inside with a cry of delight. Her hands on his back felt his shudder as he struggled to hold himself still.

She didn't want still; she didn't want to wait. She wanted to drive him over the edge before he had the chance to calm down. With her fingertips gouging the muscles of his backside, she pulled him close, refusing to release him when he hissed out a plea for her to stop.

"No," she said. "This is my adventure." And what she wanted more than anything right now was to kiss him.

And so she did. She moved her heels to his buttocks, moved her hands to his head. His eyes widened marginally before she pulled him down for her kiss.

He tasted like sorrow and secrets. Like a man who rarely kissed, who wasn't sure he was wanted. His hesitance broke the very heart she'd sworn not to involve. But his hesitance was short-lived and the sadness banished the moment his tongue entered her mouth.

They battled there with lips and tongues, as if each sought in the other a missing part of self. Melanie had never known this sort of hunger because this need was all about Jacob.

He ate at her mouth, his hands cupping her head as he held her still and feasted. And then the kiss was over, ended when he pulled away and stared down at her from the sharp edge of control.

"God, Melanie." He tightened every muscle he had. "No more. No more."

She turned her head to the side and watched him come. She watched on the video cluster as he slammed into her body with an urgency she'd never sensed before. She watched his face, watched him screw his eyes tightly, watched the tendons and veins in his neck pop to sharp relief.

She watched his buttocks flex, his triceps stretch. And she watched his penis slide in and slide out.

That was when she knew she was done. She pushed up onto her elbows, braced her feet flat on the mattress and thrust her pelvis upward rhythmically, repeatedly, meeting his every stroke, which matched the music's hard beat.

She closed her eyes when she came. She tossed her head back and looked at nothing but the picture in her mind, the picture of Jacob the way she'd seen him that first time. Sensation took her apart and she fought the end of her orgasm and the sharp edge of tears.

She was afraid he was more than her lover. She was afraid he was her life.

MONDAY MORNING, Melanie tried not to pace around her office while the production crew arranged the visitors' chairs in front of her bookcase in preparation for her interview. Instead, she stood behind her desk and faced the windows, staring out at the Southwest Freeway's frantic lunch hour traffic.

She'd worked out extra long and hard this morning, preceded by a half hour of meditation and followed by a steaming shower that went on until she'd depleted her hot water supply. The calming techniques had seemed to help at the time.

But then she'd arrived at work and walked into her office to find Jacob had already been there, and had left behind two stand-mounted cameras and the lighting equipment he'd need. The cocky early bird was preparing to get the worm—while the worm wanted nothing more than to squirm out of what was beginning to feel like a pressure cooker.

After watching herself make love with Jacob on camera and giving up so much of her heart in that incredible kiss, how was she supposed to sit here and expose even more while he looked on?

A voyeuristic participant in her undoing.

The very cause of the same.

The man had merely repeated her confession when she'd said the words *making love*. That was it. Nothing else. Nothing to indicate if he disagreed or agreed. No hint at all if he shared her assessment of what they'd done together there in his bed. Just a simple echo of her statement.

A statement that was a slip of the tongue she really shouldn't have made.

She'd agreed to continue their affair for the sake of the fun and the sex. Not because she was hoping for more. She wasn't hoping for more. Even though her attraction to him had finally come to make sense, even though what she was feeling went a lot deeper than she'd previously had the courage to admit, even though everything he was made him her perfect mate, she couldn't mate.

Not when her focus had to be on gIRL-gEAR.

Not when his had to be through a lens.

Making love. What a big fat mouth she had. A roll of duct tape would've really come in handy. After she taped up her mouth, she could've tied him to the bed frame and completely had her way with him. As if she hadn't done just that. She had. In spades. She'd made sweet and poignant love to him. God, but she was screwed.

"Miss Craine?"

She jumped, then turned, smiling at the host's inquiry. "Yes?"

The other woman, Ann Russell, very much a Barbara Walters clone, chose the chair that offered her best personal camera angle, and patted the seat of the second as an invitation for Melanie to join her.

Melanie would have preferred to stay where she

was, *thank you very much,* but then Jacob walked into the room. Whether or not she was ready, the interview was on.

She had no more than a brief moment to look at him, to see that his expression was all-business, that he was intent on the job at hand. If he'd glanced her way, she hadn't noticed. And, dammit, her feelings were hurt.

He looked incredible, once again clothed in his trademark working wardrobe of a high-fashion and fitted black T-shirt, today worn with baggy black linen pants.

She had to curl her fingers into her palms to keep herself from reaching out and grabbing his butt, or from running her fingers through his hair, which, until Saturday morning when she'd kissed him, she'd never realized was so thick and at the same time so fine.

This interview was destined to be a total disaster. It would be a miracle if she escaped without revealing all the things their purely sexual arrangement didn't require he know. Especially the little sidebar fact that she was falling in love. She had to face it. Her heart didn't tumble to her stomach for just any man.

Without glancing his way again, she took her assigned seat, wishing for a hall pass or a doctor's excuse, anything to get out of this particular class. But once Jacob's assistant had measured the distance for the boom, and Ann had reassured Melanie with a last-minute pep talk and a pat on the knee, the interview got underway. After several deep breaths, Melanie calmed and put on the gIRL-gEAR face that was so much a part of who she was.

She breezed through the answers to the host's questions about the gIZMO gIRL and gOODIE gIRL lines, explaining her vision for meeting her customers' needs no matter their age or their income. Shared personal details of her early fascination with technical gadgetry, the computer lab as her home away from home and her resulting boot from the cheerleading squad brought a shared laugh.

And then Ann checked the notes in her lap and brought her gaze back to Melanie's face. "Tell us, Melanie. How has your extreme involvement in this very unique start-up impacted your relationships? Do you have siblings?"

Melanie shook her head even as her mind raced forward, seeking the answers she would want to give to the more difficult relationship questions sure to follow. She had to be careful, especially with Jacob in the room, that she gave away nothing of what she felt for him.

Instead, she would need to explain the difficulty inherent in taking on outside responsibilities when work demanded so much of her time. Work had to come first, and that did not make her a chicken.

This answer, however, was easy. "Actually, no. I'm an only child. And to answer your next question," she said as Ann smiled, "I was brought up by a very strong mother and equally strong grandmother."

"No male authority figures in your life?"

"No. And none needed," Melanie insisted. "Not with the models of female leadership I grew up with. My mother and her mother are the two women—no, the two *people*—who have most influenced my life. Because of them, I've never doubted that I can do anything I set my mind to."

Ann's smile was stage-perfect, but also appeared to

be sincere. "It sounds as if they were marvelous examples of independent thinking."

"Oh, yes. Without a doubt." Melanie nodded in enthusiastic agreement. "I owe all that I am to their unwavering support."

"All that you are?" Ann cocked her head to the side curiously. "But not all that you have?"

Melanie laughed. "Well, the legwork and late hours have all been mine."

"Late hours." Ann paused…one, two, three…and added, "How does your significant other deal with the pressures gIRL-gEAR imposes?"

"Honestly? Most of the pressure I impose on myself." Avoidance. Good honest tactic. And it worked, because the answer was honest, as well.

"A perfectionist?"

Melanie nodded. "And a workaholic."

"So, being reared by two women…two *unattached* women…" Ann tapped her pen on her notebook, increasing the drama as she thought. "Surely that influenced your thoughts on men. Whether or not you wanted one in your own life."

"Don't we all want men in our lives?" Evasiveness. An even better tactic. And obviously another good answer since she heard the laughter of her spying partners in the hall outside of her office.

Ann joined in. "I hear what sounds like agreement coming from the doorway. The recent marriage of Lauren Hollister, now Lauren Neville. How did that make you feel?"

*Careful, Mel.* She had no idea what the host was digging for, but she was not about to dump on her friends. "Thrilled, of course. I don't think I've ever seen Lauren so happy. Walking by her office requires sunglasses these days.'' Melanie sent a wink in the direction of her door. ''The glow is blinding.''

A loud protest sounded from outside in the hallway.

Ann continued undaunted. ''I understand several more of your partners have recently become involved with long-term significant others. Do you find yourself forced to shoulder more of the company load than your married or attached partners?''

''I'm not forced to do anything.'' Melanie gave a casual sort of shrug, even while her stomach began to burn. ''Sure, I work longer hours, but my lifestyle allows for that.''

An eyebrow lifted. ''Any resentment?''

Not really resentment, or so she didn't want to believe, but fear that her partners' shifting priorities were threatening the company. Okay. Resentment. And guilt for admitting to the feeling—even if the admission was only to herself. ''What would I resent? This is a partnership. We each have our strengths. We each have additional outside obligations. But one thing never changes. The fact that we are always here for one another. No matter what may be going on in our lives.''

''You're happily married to your job, then.''

''At the moment?'' Unable to stop herself, Melanie glanced at Jacob—or rather at the camera lens. The two were inseparable. A perfect couple. ''Yes. Very happily,'' she answered, summoning a bright smile for added emphasis. Though for the life of her she didn't know who she was trying to convince more.

Jacob…or herself?

# *12*

MELANIE STUDIED THE NOTES on her legal pad on her way down the office hallway later that afternoon. She scowled at the list; half of the gIZMO gIRL possibilities no longer made any sense. The other half...well, she couldn't even remember what most of them were.

Her decision-making deadline was drawing near. Lauren needed graphics for the site. And the new print team was waiting for catalog copy. That was Macy's department, but Macy couldn't write anything when she didn't have content from which to work.

At this rate, Melanie might as well add every single product to her line since she seemed incapable of choosing the ones most likely to start a buzz among site visitors or to fulfill shoppers' needs.

Oh, yeah. Her input was really going to have a big impact on the gIRL-gEAR bottom line. All her claims of being the someone needed to keep the company solvent in these days of e-tail ups and downs were nothing but hooey.

She couldn't even decide between leopard-spotted and camouflage-patterned cell phone covers.

What she ought to do was have Macy add a poll to the site and let the target audience decide for her, since she was so incredibly indecisive. The one and only thing about which she was certain was her need to throttle Jacob Faulkner for being the cause of her insanity.

Life and work would both be a whole lot easier if she didn't love him as much as she did. Because she had no idea what to do about it.

A shuffle of papers from the conference room caught Melanie's already distracted attention. She glanced in that direction, hesitated, tapping the eraser end of her pencil to her tablet while deciding whether or not to keep walking or to stop and go in.

Rennie Faulkner sat at one end of the long table, a sheaf of papers in her lap, her gaze focused out the window that faced nothing but the building's back parking lot and a strip of Kirby Drive. Her feet alternated left to right, drumming out a nervous rhythm on the thick purple carpet.

*Takes one crazy woman to know another,* Melanie mused, wondering what thoughts were keeping the other woman from her work. Wondering if Rennie was having as much trouble concentrating for a reason equally as aggravating as Melanie's.

Men. Who needed them?

Holding her legal pad tight to her chest, Melanie made her decision and entered the room. "They still haven't found you office space, I see."

Startled, Rennie pressed a hand to her heart, then waved off Melanie's concern and smiled. "I have an office at school. But since I'm also the visiting counselor at two other campuses, I'm used to working on my lap. I don't expect an entire office for the little bit of time that I'm here."

"Well, feel free to borrow mine whenever I'm not around." It was the least she could offer since, if circumstances hadn't been what they were, the other woman might have one day been her sister-in-law.

Melanie sighed inwardly. She just needed to get over it. "What about a computer? Maybe I should talk to Sydney about getting you a notebook PC?"

"I have one. I just haven't yet decided on a game plan for scheduling the counseling sessions." Rennie tossed the papers in her lap onto the stack already scattered across the table. "And thanks for the offer of the office. But as you can see—" she nodded toward the mess she'd made "—I'm not exactly the neatest freak around."

Now, that was interesting. Every time Melanie had seen the other woman, Rennie had been the epitome of put together, in her long skirts, coordinating cardigans and flats. So seeing her work space disheveled gave Melanie pause. She'd never seen Rennie at home, but it was still hard to imagine this to be the usual state of affairs.

Pulling out the closest chair, Melanie sat. "Hey, we all have our messy moments."

Rennie only rolled her eyes. "Thanks, but I've never seen so much as a pencil out of place in your office. Pardon my bluntness, but messy moments my ass."

Melanie grimaced and then grinned. She definitely liked Jacob's sister a lot. "Only one of my many flaws…as certain people enjoy reminding me more often than necessary. I'm trying to loosen up."

"Why?" Rennie asked with a shrug. "You are who you are. And there's not a thing wrong with having an organized office."

Maybe not…"Unless it's not about the office, but

more like a borderline compulsive disorder that spills over into every corner of your life.''

"Wow." Rennie shook her head, her smile obviously one of amusement. "Could either of us be more out of sorts?"

"Probably, but I'd really hate to be hanging out here if that were the case." Melanie nodded toward the stack of papers she recognized as questionnaires filled out by girls interested in the gUIDANCE gIRL program. "Is this turning out to be more work than you'd thought?"

"What? The counseling?" Rennie shook her head. "Not at all. No, my being out of sorts is…a horse of a different color. One I'm not sure of the best way to handle, as I'm dealing with my own conflicted emotions."

Hesitating for a moment, Melanie made an offer that she didn't think she'd ever before made to a woman she didn't know closely. "Do you want to talk about it? I'm not the best one to offer advice, but I do have a willing ear."

Rennie's mouth crooked in a grin that was uncannily similar to Jacob's. "Because psychologists need counseling, too?"

"Sure," Melanie said, feeling as if she'd just made a very good friend. "And this isn't exactly about physician healing thyself. Just woman to woman."

Her expression a sad sort of bewilderment, Rennie took a moment to consider. "As a woman, then, I guess it wouldn't surprise you to hear this is all over a man?"

Out of sorts didn't even begin to cover their shared man misery. Melanie sighed. "It happens to the best of us."

"You, too?" Rennie's tone was infused with a curious sense of hope.

And Melanie nodded.

"With Jacob?"

She nodded again.

Hope and bewilderment didn't stand a chance when Rennie finally decided to grin. "I can't believe it!"

"Is that a bad disbelief?" Because it was really hard to tell.

"How can you say that?" She tossed back her head and laughed. "It's wonderful. I'm beyond thrilled."

That made one of them. "Don't be too thrilled."

"Why not? This is the best news I've heard in forever. Jacob needs a strong woman in his life to be there for him. He's not an easy man to know."

"Well…" Melanie let the thought trail off, unsure how much of their arrangement to reveal to Jacob's sister. "It's not so much about knowing him, or being there for him."

"Well what?" The other woman frowned. "He doesn't know how you feel?"

Making love. Sharing that kiss. And then her really lame declaration of being happily married to her job. Yeah, he probably knew. "It's not that. We're both too involved with our careers to be involved with each other. As much as it sucks, and it does, neither one of us is in a position to be in a relationship."

Rennie snorted. "Try being in a position with three hundred miles between."

Three-hundred miles. Houston to…San Antonio? "Aiden Zuniga?"

"Good grief, woman. Are you psychic?"

Melanie chuckled. "I remember seeing how cozy the two of you were at Chloe's cookout."

Slumping back in the chair, Rennie closed her eyes and rolled her head back and forth on the headrest. "I should've walked away that day when he told me where he lived. I knew better. I *knew* better. But I told him I'd meet him for coffee and he kissed me and… God. My mind is taking a beating from my body and my heart."

"Exactly."

"After the way I grew up, I swore never to become involved with a man who wouldn't be home with me every night. Just like Jacob swore to never become obsessed with his career. And look at us now. What a pair." Her head lolled to one side; she opened her eyes and looked at Melanie. "So? You and me. What do we do?"

"You're asking the wrong woman." Melanie answered with a laugh of her own. "I'm useless."

"I guess this time *is* about the physician healing herself."

"I'd say so." Melanie pondered. "But once you're done? Feel free to send the healing vibes my direction. Or if that doesn't work, medication."

RENATA MADE HER WAY down the second floor hallway of the new loft complex built in an old-time gothic style. Her fingers closed around the door key she held, her grip tightening until the teeth bit sharply into her palm.

Even then she didn't let go. She wasn't afraid of losing it; she just needed to know it was still there. That she hadn't imagined Aiden had sent it. She was having a hard enough time believing the note he'd sent along.

He'd rented a place in town, he'd said. And he

planned to spend his weekends here. At least the weekends he could get away. Weekdays, too, when possible. He still worked the horses, yes. But much of his involvement in the ranch had taken an administrative slant.

That didn't make him particularly happy; give him a corral over a desk any day. But such was the nature of the business these days. And paperwork and phone calls could be handled in Houston, as well as from San Antonio. FedEx and faxes and DSL hadn't been invented for nothing.

She still couldn't believe he'd done all this to be with her, with no guarantee of any sort of return. That was the other thing his note had said. He wanted to be with her, to spend all the time he could with her. Even if she was doing no more than lying on the sofa watching the news while he worked in the spare bedroom office.

How could she say no? How could she say yes?

How could she say anything at all until she knew the truth?

She had to know if he was being honest. If he truly wanted to get to know her, to spend time in her company, to do no more than share as much of herself as she was willing to give…. Oh, but life was unfair, offering her everything she'd ever wanted in a man she couldn't have on her terms.

She finally spotted the doorway alcove with the smiling gargoyle above holding a sign carved with a gilded 206. Aiden's home away from home. The threshold into the rest of her life. Or the biggest mistake she'd ever made.

She slid the key into the lock and turned it smoothly; the door opened without a single squeak from a single hinge. The smells of fresh air and sun-shine spilled through the crack as she opened the door and she knew. Oh, yes, she knew.

He was here.

He was the one, in fact, stretched out on the egg-shell leather sofa watching the evening news. Pillows colored like toast and lemon and midnight-black sup-ported his head at one end. His heels were propped on the curve of the opposite arm.

And, actually, now that she looked closer, she saw that he wasn't watching the evening news at all but sleeping straight through. She stepped into the high-ceilinged living room and quietly closed the door. The dead bolt wasn't as cooperative; the click sounded like a pistol shot.

Aiden's head whipped around.

"I'm sorry," she said, the key again clutched hard in her hand. "I didn't know the lock would make that much noise."

He propped himself up on one elbow, dragged a hand down his face to push sleep away. "It's still new. I've thought about digging an old one out of the barn at the ranch and switching them."

"I'm sure it will break in." Which led to the ques-tion…if she didn't come by very often, would he con-tinue to keep this place? And how would she ever know if she wanted him to without obligation being a factor? She didn't want to feel that she owed him any-thing at all. "With enough use."

"I hope so." He sat all the way up, swinging his feet to the hardwood floor. "It's nice to see you using it."

"To tell you the truth," she began, sounding more nervous than she liked. "If I'd known you were here

I might not have come. I thought I'd take a quick tour before you caught me.'' Oh, why did he have to look at her like that? As if he'd been waiting all of his life for her to walk through the door?

He reached for the boots he'd obviously kicked beneath the glass-and-brushed-chrome coffee table.

''What are you doing?'' she squeaked.

He put one foot into one boot and gave a strong tug. ''Leaving. I don't want to put you off from your tour.''

She moved farther into the room, closer to the sofa and his sparkling blue eyes. ''Don't be silly. We're both here. You can show me around.''

He hesitated for a long moment, looking down at the other boot held in his hands. His knees were spread wide as he leaned forward, and the tails of his white chambray shirt hung loose down his back.

She realized too late that his shirt was unbuttoned. If she'd noticed while he'd been sleeping, she could've done her ogling unawares. But then he dropped the second boot to the floor, pulled off the first and pushed up to his feet.

And now that he was standing not three yards away, she was faced with an amazing expanse of bare chest and belly, muscles and smooth skin and a light dusting of hair. His silver belt buckle rode low on his abs, and Renata swallowed hard.

''Are you sure?'' he asked, and she couldn't even remember what she'd said until he added, ''I don't mind leaving.''

Oh, no. If he left now she wasn't sure she could stand it. ''No. Stay. It's your place, for goodness sake.''

"Well, then." He gestured with the sweep of one arm. "This is the living room."

She laughed, returning the key to her wallet as she did. "So I see," she said, and came even closer, setting her purse in the corner of the sofa because it was a believable reason to move. From here she could sense his heat. And she rubbed her palms up and down both arms as if soaking him in.

"Cold?" he asked. "I can adjust the thermostat."

"No. I'm fine." She glanced around the room. Even with the cool glass-and-chrome accent pieces, the space glowed with a creamy warmth that the air-conditioning couldn't chill. "I like the ambience. And the furnishings." She stepped around behind the sofa, putting the piece of furniture between them. "Your decorator did a great job."

Aiden scrubbed a hand through his hair before moving both to his hips. The tails of his shirt flared out behind him. And he tumbled Renata's heart with his carefree grin. "How do you know this look wasn't my idea?"

"Oh, I don't know." She ran fingertips along the curved back of the very expensive sofa. "You just don't look like the eggshell type."

"Eggshell?"

"The color of your sofa."

"Hmm." He frowned. "I thought it was cremello."

"Cremello?"

"A double-diluted palomino." He shrugged, his mouth crooked into a self-effacing smile. "Horse stuff."

He was so easy to look at, standing there with his shoulders slightly hunched and his fingers now tucked into the pockets of his jeans. And then there was his bare chest, which she was dying to get her hands on.

Oh, but this was not going well. She squeezed the sofa's padded back. "In the city, you'd call this eggshell. Though cremello does paint a nice…creamy picture."

"But a paint is a horse of another color."

"Very funny," she said, enjoying him way too much for her own good. She turned away, headed for the dining area and the kitchen set off from the main room by an island stove and floor tiles the color of old schoolhouse brick. "Do you cook?"

"Are you hungry?"

She glanced back to see him still standing where she'd left him. "It's getting close to dinnertime, isn't it?"

"If I fix something, you'll stay?"

He sounded so hopeful, timid almost, when nothing she'd learned about him was timid at all. He'd kissed her in the middle of Barnes & Noble, and that was about as bold as anything she'd known a man to publicly do. But he was uncertain about her, and that made her smile. "Sure. As long as you let me help."

"I'll cook. You're the guest."

"No." She turned and faced him fully. "I don't want to be treated as a guest. That's not why I'm here." She paused for a moment, realizing whatever she said next would determine the rest of the evening. But she had to be sure.

She had to be sure. "I didn't think that was the reason you sent me the key. I didn't think you wanted to spend time with me as your guest."

"What did you think?"

"That you went to a lot of trouble with no guaranteed return."

"You're here. That's all I wanted."

"Is it?"

"You know, Renata, you shouldn't bait me if you're not ready to have me bite."

When he put it like that, well, it sounded like exactly what she wanted. "This is tough for me, Aiden. I've enjoyed seeing you these last few weeks. I can't remember when I've ever been in a situation where things have been so perfect."

"But they're not."

She shook her head. "No. They're not."

"And that's the difference between you and me. Because I think they're about as perfect as they can get."

"How can you say that?" She crossed her arms tightly over her chest. "We live three hours apart. What's so perfect about being unable to see the one person you're most desperate to be with but can't?"

Aiden's expression grew dark, his eyes flat. "I'm not willing to never see you at all just because I can't see you every day." He paused. "Renata?"

"Yes?"

"Are you desperate to be with me?" he asked in a smoky velvet tone that had her crumbling inside.

She looked at him standing there, patiently waiting for her to make this call. He'd gone to such extreme lengths to be here, to give them this chance. A chance she was terrified to take.

A chance she wanted more than anything.

"*Desperate* is such a strong word. Implying there's no other choice, no other option." She hugged herself even tighter, wishing his arms were the ones twined around her. "I know it was my word, but I hate feeling that I've gone back on every promise I made myself about having a long-distance relationship."

He held his arms out to the side, a gesture that offered her all that he could. "I'm as close as I can get, Renata. I'll always be who I am, and there's not a lot of room in town to raise horses."

She couldn't help her sad grin. "I know."

"But I'm here now, baby. And there's nothing but a sofa between us."

*If only that's all there was,* she thought miserably, watching him as he watched her and as his decision was made. His hesitation was brief and seemed to be more a case of uncertainty about her reaction than anything. Because when he finally came around the end of the sofa, she saw nothing in his gait or expression but a man's determination.

And that stirred her soul beyond belief.

"Is this better?" he asked, moving to stand directly in front of her.

She shook her head. She nodded. She didn't know if having him this near did indeed make things better, or only made them that much worse. Putting what she wanted within her reach, as it were. A distance so easily closed, so easily widened.

"Renata?" His voice was firm, demanding even.

"I don't know." But, oh, she loved hearing him say her name. "This is so hard for me, Aiden."

She'd been standing with her arms still wrapped tightly around her middle, and when Aiden moved in to complete the circle, she laid her forehead in the center of his chest. His hands were hugely comforting as they kneaded the tension from her back, hugely arousing as she imagined them providing another sort of relief. Her thighs and abs flexed in an automatic response.

She still didn't know; she didn't know. But this time when she shook her head, swirls of his chest hair tickled her nose. And that was it. He was warm and he was here for her and he was the most solid wonderful thing she'd known in her life.

She kissed him, parting her lips there over his sternum and slipping her hands beneath his open shirt and around to his back, where straps of muscle bunched beneath her touch. When her tongue darted out to taste his skin, he groaned. The sound's vibration tickled her mouth and the thought of never knowing this man was too much to bear.

With a sigh, she made her decision, the right decision, the only decision she could possibly make, then pulled away and looked up into his eyes. "Are you going to give me the rest of the tour?"

An eyebrow flared upward. "Did you want to eat first?"

Oh, no. Her hunger would not be satisfied in the kitchen. "I'd rather you show me the bedroom."

For a moment he said nothing. Even his hands on her back grew still. And then his eyes seemed to darken, to grow hot and heavy-lidded. His desire was impossible to hide and obviously impossible to bank. She wondered if she would ever be able to live up to his expectations.

"Are you sure?" he finally asked, in a voice so gentle, a taming voice, a calming voice, that all she could think of were wild horses, and the way her body strained at the confines of clothing and propriety instead of corral fencing and bridles and bits.

She nodded, wanting to run free. "More sure than I've been about anything in a very long time."

He took her hand then, his hold firm but not frightening, insistent but not cruel, and she followed him into the loft's bedroom area, separated from the living space by a bathroom enclosure of bamboo and glass.

The bed was large, but welcoming rather than spacious and cold. With the sun setting on the building's far side and the shades pulled down over the windows, the only light in the room came from the far end of the loft.

It was enough, though, for Renata to see what she needed to see, the only thing she needed to see. Aiden. He guided her to one side of the bed, a hand at the small of her back and the other still holding hers. When he stopped and stared down at her as if she was the only thing he wanted to see, his pulse beat wildly in the hollow of his throat.

She wanted so much to kiss him, but instead she placed three fingertips there to check the beat of his heart. Her own thudded in a matching rhythm and she smiled. "Just making sure I'm not the only one here with a runaway pulse."

His hands went to her waist and he tugged her into his body. "Your pulse I can deal with. As long as the rest of you stays right here."

"I'm not going anywhere." She moved her fingertips to his lips, remembering the bookstore kisses, one soft and tender, one demanding and bold. She loved them both and didn't know which she wanted. "At least not far."

"Only as far as the bed," he said, before catching the tip of her index finger with his teeth, sucking the plump pad of flesh into his mouth and soothing it with his tongue.

She thought the pleasure would cause her to die. Her body flamed, there from the end of her finger to the tips of her breasts and down to the core of her sex buried deep between her legs. Arousal was a powerful thing; the potential for raw and savage beauty equaled by nothing else.

Pulling her finger away from his lips, she used both hands to push his shirt from his shoulders, completely baring the upper half of his body, with which he'd teased her since she'd walked in to find him asleep. He was a feast, and she wasn't sure where to start.

So she started where she could best reach, the center of his chest. Holding his arms captured in his shirt-sleeves at the wrists, she returned her lips to his body. This time, however, she allowed her exploration to drift until she found his nipple hidden in a swirl of soft brown hair.

Dragging the flat of her tongue over the tip, she pressed down into the resilient flesh surrounding the sensitive disk. Aiden groaned and pushed his body against her, asking for more of the same. *Oh, gladly,* she thought, moving to the other, knowing as she did that her strength was no match for his.

He had the ability to free himself from her hold at his wrists on a whim. She wondered how long he'd wait, how strong his willpower might be, how badly he actually wanted her, and she increased the pressure of her mouth, wanting to take him to that brink.

His pulse beat in his wrists held in the incomplete circle of her fingers. It wasn't that her hands were tiny; it was just that his were the size a man's hands needed to be. She couldn't wait to feel them on her body. She longed for the pleasure of his touch.

When she instructed him, "Don't move," he uttered his agreement with a rough sound that wasn't a word but a growl. She released him, moved her hands to his torso, where she placed her palms flat on his abs and trailed a line of kisses from his breastbone to the button fly of his jeans.

Once there, she went to work on his belt buckle with nimble fingers, backing up to sit on the edge of the bed, giving herself a better position and a much better view. His erection pressed fully, impressively along the ridge of his jeans, and she wasn't sure how long she was going to be able to wait to take him into her body.

But neither did she want his help, and she pushed his hands away when he impatiently tried to offer. "I want to do this."

"You're taking too damn long," he muttered.

"Careful, cowboy, or I'll take a whole lot longer." She loved the freedom she'd finally given herself to tease him mercilessly.

"Give me one thing at least."

"Maybe."

"If you're not going to let me get my hands on you, at least let me lose the shirt."

Her hands hovering at his fly, she pretended to consider. "Okay. But no touching. I've wanted this for too long to rush it."

He had one arm out and then the other and had tossed his shirt to the floor before he said, "I'm not sure what you're planning down there, but there's a good chance I'll be the one rushing here if you're not careful."

"Oh, I plan to be very careful," she said.

As if she had a clue what she was talking about! As hard as he was, she was correspondingly wet. Careful was barely a consideration. All that mattered was getting him out of his jeans so she could see him and taste him, so she could take him into her mouth and learn what he liked.

A very practical part of her wanted to get this fumbling first time out of the way so they could linger through a second. But she wasn't here to be practical. And she was going to hang on to the fantasy of a perfect first time as long as she possibly could.

Because for some reason, a reason she'd yet to examine too closely, this particular first time meant more than had any before.

She finished with his belt buckle and went to work on the row of copper buttons. Each movement of her hands brought a low moan to his mouth. One button, then two, and the waistband of his cotton boxers came into view. With the third button freed, his boxers took on a new dimension, a full dimension, and at the fourth button, then the fifth, she found herself in awe.

That awe refused to wait any longer. Seeing his bare belly, his abs so tight, rippled, the dusting of light brown hair, wasn't enough. She wanted more. And so she carefully, very carefully, tugged both jeans and shorts down his thighs. His beautiful erection sprang free.

Aiden kicked out of the rest of his clothing while she took him in her hand. He was so incredibly warm, hot even. So solid and so firm. The male body inspired such feelings of wonder and amazement and, in her, a truly intense need to love. She'd never been able to separate sex from emotional involvement, which made this encounter all the more frightening.

For the first time in her life she was going to sleep with a man before she'd made an emotional commitment. She smiled. Who was she trying to convince? She and Aiden might not have spoken of a future, but she wouldn't have come here if her heart hadn't been involved. And she knew by the way he wanted her that, if he wasn't there yet, he was close.

She took him in her hands, feeling the skin of his penis, so soft even stretched to such lengths as it was. She moved one hand to cup his balls, held his shaft in the other. With the heel of her palm pressed to the base rigid with veins, she slid her thumb along the underside to the crevice of the head.

And then she leaned forward and wrapped her lips around him, sucking him into her mouth until the vibrations from his groan tickled her tongue. Inwardly, she smiled, loving that she so easily drew him into that response as much as she loved his taste and his feel.

So, when he broke his promise not to touch, she found no reason to argue. His hands went to her shoulders where he pushed his fingers beneath her cardigan to the straps of her silk camisole. His frustration wasn't long in coming; he wanted her out of her clothes and couldn't get to her, considering the way she was sitting.

As much as she hated to do so, she released him and got to her feet, kicking out of her flats as she stood. He was so much taller than she was, his chest so broad, his legs so long, the way a man's should be. And, like a man, he didn't argue when she went to work on the more intricate fastenings holding her clothing together.

Her skirt dropped to her ankles and her cardigan followed, and soon she stood in nothing but her camisole and lacy bikinis. But when she reached for the hem to pull off her top, Aiden stopped her.

"My turn," he said, trading places. He sat on the edge of the bed and pulled her between his spread legs.

Her hands went to his shoulders, her gaze to his thick penis jutting upward so urgently. When he made no move to speak or to say another word, she returned her gaze to his face.

His eyes were so solemn and his expression intense with so much of what he seemed desperate to say. "Do you know how beautiful you are?"

She shook her head; her hair tumbled around her shoulders. "Not half as beautiful as you."

His laugh was a scoff. "I'm scraped and scarred and held together by pins in one ankle and a rod in one hip. Hardly much to look at."

"Beauty *is* in the eye of the beholder, you know," she said, and slid her hands from his shoulders to cup his face. If he was scraped and scarred, she'd never even noticed. All she cared about seeing was his soul in his eyes.

He closed his eyes then, moved his hands from her waist up her rib cage and brushed his thumbs over her nipples, which were straining beneath the silk. And then one thumb was gone and, in its placed, his tongue. He lapped and suckled and drew her into his mouth, silk camisole and all.

Sensation descended, as if a line ran from his mouth to the core of her sex, as if his lips tugged there between her legs at the same time. She wiggled because she couldn't help it. And he moved his hands to her back, slid them down to her bottom and into her panties—panties that quickly found their way to the floor.

She whimpered, wanting his touch, wanting him to finish stripping her. But he simply moved to her other nipple, leaving the cool air to blow on the wet silk covering the one he'd so thoroughly aroused. This time her whimper came with a shiver, and the shiver only worsened when Aiden's hands made their way up the backs of her thighs.

He reached the cleft of her bottom and urged her legs apart. She clenched her belly and opened, and he slipped his fingers between, seeking her moisture and growling in approval at the dampness he found. Dampness, ha! She was so incredibly wet and so incredibly ready, and she wanted out of the rest of her clothing now.

"Please, Aiden," she begged, her hands moving to the camisole's hem. "Let me get this off."

With his tongue still circling her nipple, he looked up at her with a wild sense of discovery in his eyes. And looking down at him there, his mouth still on her breast, was almost more than she could take. She shoved him away and whipped off her top.

Before she even had a chance to look at him again, he'd grabbed her up by the waist and tossed her none too gently to the bed.

She bounced, and scrambled to the center, and barely a second passed before he'd covered her body with his. Her legs parted automatically; her arms went around his neck, and without asking for permission she brought his mouth to hers. His tongue slid over hers as he rolled on a condom and entered her. When she gasped, he swallowed her cry.

He moved his hands to cradle her head, and loved her with his beautiful mouth and body. She surged upward to meet each of his smooth, easy strokes, clutching him tightly, fearing to let him go and never again know such pleasure. Her body glowed with a heat that turned her inside out.

She wasn't going to be able to wait. As much as she wanted to, as bitterly as she fought to hold off her completion, she failed. But the success that followed was worth letting herself go. She pulled her mouth free from Aiden's and cried out, her arms around his back holding him pressed to her.

She wanted him there, needed him there, his solid strength grounding her as she shuddered through her release. He waited until she was done, kept up the rhythm she needed until she was splintered and exhausted and spent.

Only then did he drive himself downward with furious strokes, taking her apart a second shattering time as his orgasm ripped through his body. He continued to thrust, and she kept her legs wrapped around the backs of his thighs, her hands pressed there to the sensitive small of his back.

When he finished, when he slowed and shuddered, when he sighed and finally collapsed, only then did she let him go, moving her hands up and down his back in a soothing, loving caress. She whispered into his ear words that made no sense, that were sounds more than decipherable, intelligible avowals of what this moment meant.

In a language of her own making, she told him all the things that would come with time.

For now, however, this was enough.

# *13*

SITTING IN HER OFFICE late that evening, Melanie turned her chair to face the windows, and ignored the work on her desk. Except for the tech guys who always pulled strange hours, the place was empty. Her partners had long since gone home to their men.

Even Kinsey, another remaining holdout in the permanent mating game, was out to dinner and a movie with Doug Storey, Anton Neville's business partner. Melanie didn't know about Poe; the other woman's private life was still an enigma.

Melanie's wasn't much better because...oh, wait. She didn't have one. She had work and she had sex and she had exercise and she had sex. She had a man, one she could probably even go home to if she wanted, but she'd be going home to him solely for sex.

She just didn't have the sort of *thing* going on with Jacob that Chloe did with Eric, or Sydney did with Ray, Macy with Leo, Lauren with Anton, ad nauseum.

*And whose fault was that?* Melanie thought, twirling her pencil between her forefingers and thumbs.

Not that such a relationship was what she wanted. After all, she was the one so very happily married to her career.

She was also the one coming to realize that none of her worries over where the company was headed mattered to anyone else involved. Her partners were of the "winds of change" attitude, bending and blowing in the breeze.

Melanie was concerned about the imminent break when the storms got too strong—a situation all too common in the e-tail market. Why was she the only one able to see that? gIRL-gEAR was not an indestructible force.

What the company was, however, was the investment into which she'd poured her entire life since that senior year at the University of Texas when the partnership inspiration had struck on a cold November night in a new Austin Starbucks.

Suddenly she was in a very bad mood.

Feeling betrayed.

Feeling resentful.

Feeling as if she was actually the one drifting while the others had dropped anchor in a port foreign to her, a port secure enough that none of them ever again had to worry about swimming in open shark-infested man-waters.

Fighting a sudden sting of tears, Melanie stared at the traffic sweating along on the Southwest Freeway in the heat and humidity that lingered at day's end. She felt raw and exposed, but, unlike the earlier interview process, this disclosure of emotion was private, one she'd never thought she would make even to herself.

All this time she'd so proudly proclaimed her independence, the complete fulfillment she found through her work, when the brutal truth, the unvarnished reality, was that she wanted exactly what her partners had.

God, but she wanted what they had.

A reason to go home at the end of the day. To be

wanted, cherished, supported, encouraged. To have a best friend who was also her lover. As much as she longed to be the independent woman she'd been brought up to be, she wanted even more to simply be loved.

She sniffled and blinked, and then she got mad—at her partners and at Jacob and at herself and, oh, too many other things to list. Fine. She'd just call up *her* man and invite him over for a night of mindless oblivion. That was exactly what she needed, to sex her way into a better mood.

Lately, though Jacob had been as inspired and inventive as ever, she'd sensed a change in him when they were in bed. The last two nights he'd seemed especially distracted, as if his body was willing but he had too much on his mind.

The downside of a being workaholic. And the very reason a long, hot night together was just what Dr. Melanie ordered for the both of them.

She started to reach for her phone, then remembered the URL he'd sent her the day she'd stripped for him in her office, the link broadcasting the feed from the Webcam in his office. She pulled up the e-mail with the link to the page and clicked, tapping her fingers on her mouse as she waited.

If he was there—and no doubt he was—she'd send a text message to his cell phone and dare him to play the male stripper for her. It was about time turnabout turned into fair play. The stripping around here had not exactly been of the equal opportunity sort.

Yes! There he was! Sitting in front of his desk in one of the two visitors' chairs, another man in the one at his side. Hmm. There went the stripping fantasy. Her excitement quickly became resignation. As adventurous as he was, performing for a live male audience would be drifting into territory better left uncharted.

Both men sat forward in the chairs, Jacob with his elbow propped on the front edge of his desk, their attention riveted to the television sitting on the office's corner credenza. The Webcam's fixed angle allowed her to catch only flashes of movement and color—until Jacob's visitor sat back and out of the way of the screen.

They were looking at a scene shot in the gIRL-gEAR office. There was no way to mistake that deep purple office decor. It seemed Jacob was sharing documentary footage he'd shot. Asking for input, perhaps? A second professional opinion? She leaned toward her monitor and squinted, adjusting her glasses as if one or the other of the actions might help clarify her voyeuristic curiosity.

Jacob was gesturing toward the television where—finally!—Melanie caught a glimpse of Chloe in her candy-heart pink office, sitting at her desk with her makeup mirror out and her train case of cosmetics emptied out onto her blotter.

Hmm. Melanie knew that her partner dolled herself up every night before heading off to meet Eric. And…now that she thought further, Melanie seemed to remember complaining about that very thing to Jacob. A funny feeling had her shifting around in her chair.

She propped her elbow on her desktop, leaned her chin into the palm of her fist and frowned as she watched Jacob and the other man exchange words before he fast-forwarded through that section of tape to another. In this scene, Lauren lounged in her desk chair, doodling on her desk blotter while chatting.

An intimate, very unprofessional conversation if her drowsy lids and half smile were any indication. Meanwhile, lights on her phone flashed unnoticed and unattended. Another complaint made in confidence to Jacob…

Melanie felt as if she'd been hit with a stun gun. She could not believe this was happening. This time the burn of tears was anger-driven, anger over Jacob's betrayal and at her own naiveté. He'd told her the documentary was his best work ever, that this was the project guaranteed to bring fulfillment of his ambition.

Right now she was wishing her original character assassination of Jacob as a lazy bum had been dead-on. She didn't want him to have anything resembling ambition. Not if this was the result.

He might benefit from what she was seeing, from exposing provocative office scenarios sure to spark questions and prurient interest, but this documentary would never take the company to a higher level. One that would reassure clients and an industry controlled by men.

It would totally devastate their image.

Especially the next scene, of Sydney in the conference room studying quotes from wedding caterers, honeymoon resorts and bridal magazines. If viewers realized that even gIRL-gEAR's CEO rarely had a head for business anymore… Melanie couldn't begin to fathom the imminent damage to their example as pioneering entrepreneurs.

She pressed her forehead into the X of her arms crossed on her desk. A strangled moan originated in the depths of her anguished heart. This couldn't happen. Wouldn't happen. She had to make certain no one ever saw this footage. The partners were scheduled to visit the Avatare screening room as a group tomorrow. Jacob was going to show them a portion of the completed project.

Melanie wondered if that was the reason he and his buddy were sharing this little preview party, getting a good laugh out of the partners gullibility and preparing defenses against certain shock and accusations of betrayal.

She'd trusted him with confidences and concerns never before entrusted to a man, yet he was going to reduce everything they'd shared down to a career move that would leave her and her best friends if not ruined, then revealed by a cruel spotlight. Was this what career obsession did to a man?

Or to a woman?

The thought left her reeling. She never would've believed this possible of Jacob if she hadn't seen it with her own eyes. She'd fallen in love with his artistic integrity, his sense of honesty in his work. He never compromised, making sure the work he did was real and faithful to the truth. He didn't use or manipulate people for his own gain.

Or so she'd thought until now....

*You were right, Mama. I won't make the same mistake again.* So much for honor and integrity. Sniffling, she sat back up, then pushed herself out of her chair to pace. She had to think of a solution and fast. Her personal feelings she would deal with later.

She would not stand back and let Jacob destroy her friends. Before anyone else got a look at what she'd just seen, she and Jacob Faulkner needed to have a little talk.

JACOB SAT IN FRONT of the editing equipment in the Avatare studio and wondered how in the world he was going to deal with this fight between his heart and his head. Dealing with his dick was so much easier. Then again, dicks had a history of getting men and governments into a whole lot of trouble.

This was the very reason he found it so much easier to do his work on film. He could express himself precisely, exactly, and not have to figure out if he was making his point, if he'd screwed up, if he'd hurt feelings, if he'd forgotten to say something he should have. His heart and his head got along so much better that way.

Thing was, he'd become so intent on getting his vision perfected that he'd totally overlooked the need he really did have for including personal relationships in his life. Instead, he'd fallen victim to the very single-minded career obsession he'd sworn to steer clear of.

Hard not to when opportunities such as the one offered by Equity Beat were the result of his dedication.

He had no idea yet what he was going to say should they offer him a place on their production team. He didn't want to borrow that trouble since he'd yet to meet with them. It was easier to think they might not want him for more than contract assignments, or that they might not want him at all.

That way he didn't have to wonder what he was going to do without having Melanie in his life.

Ask him a month ago, and he'd have never thought it possible to reach an even higher level of excellence in his work. But he had, claiming on more than one occasion that it was the documentary making it happen.

*Wrong-o, buddy.*

It had happened because of Melanie Craine—not the same thing at all.

This wasn't about Melanie as vice president of whatever kooky divisions she headed up. This was about Melanie as the woman who'd treated him as if he didn't have any potential. He'd felt compelled to prove her wrong, and in doing so had opened a window his career's forward motion had soundly closed at his back.

Never before had he captured such subtle nuances, such provocative images. And here he'd always thought a woman would hinder him and hold him down. The very opposite had happened. His focus hadn't narrowed, his world hadn't been reduced to limited choices.

It was as if she had opened his eyes to all that he could do, all that he could be. Then she'd fed his confidence by respecting what she'd expected of him all along.

And it wasn't about what they did in bed. Sure, that was part of it. But it was about her incredible commitment and strength of purpose. Watching her at work, seeing how she calmed Kinsey's panic over a vendor going belly-up, seeing the way she talked Chloe out of throttling more than a few of the girls who'd signed up for the new mentoring deal, inspired him to live up to the same standards for himself.

Humanity. She had it in spades. Hell, she'd even tucked Renata under her wing—as if his sister needed nurturing. He stopped, thought. What if she did, and had all this time? Maybe he'd never seen what Melanie's brilliant female intuition allowed her to see.

"Hey, Faulkner," Harry called from the editing room doorway. "Your girlfriends are here."

"Be right there." The documentary was nowhere near being finished, but Sydney Ford had asked if she and her partners could see an early cut. Jacob didn't mind, since gauging their reactions would give him a better feel for how the project was coming together.

He shut down his work in progress and turned toward the door, stopping dead in his tracks when he looked up to see Melanie standing there. *Get a grip.* It's not as if she'd had her ear to a glass pressed to his head, listening to his thoughts.

"Hey, sweetheart." He grinned because his heart made him do it. "Had to get a few minutes alone with me before the big show?"

She didn't stay a word, just stood in the shadowed doorway wearing black pumps, black pants and a sleeveless black top that came all the way to her hips. Her glasses were black, her jewelry onyx. Even her mood was dark.

Jacob walked toward her. Once in the hallway, he turned out the light, intending to lock the door behind him. But Melanie had other plans. She placed her hand in the center of his chest and pushed him back into the editing room, closing the door once they were both inside the space, now lit only by colored electronic lights beaming off various machines.

"I have something I need to say to you."

And she didn't sound as if it was something he was going to enjoy having her say. She was practically spitting, like a black cat with its hackles up. As much as he loved seeing her in red, he'd be hard-pressed to deny she did amazing things to all-black.

He stepped toward her; she stepped back. He continued, as did she until she had no farther to go. He, on the other hand, wasn't finished, and wouldn't be until his body was pressed into hers. And he was just about there, just about ready to lean into her from knees to cheeks, when she put up a halting hand between them.

"I said I have something to say to you, not that I've come here for sex. This may be hard for you to believe, but I really do have a mind for something other than getting you into bed."

In the dimly surreal light, he watched as she pressed her lips together in that way she did when she wasn't sure what he was thinking. He didn't want her to know. Not right now. Mostly because he wasn't sure where she was coming from, and that meant he didn't know how to react.

So he leaned to one side instead of into her body, bracing his weight on the hand he placed above her shoulder, flat on the door. The movement brought him close enough to kiss her, to catch a hint of her subtly smoky perfume, to see her eyes hidden as they were behind the armor of her glasses.

He wanted to reach his fingers down and play with her wonderfully soft hair. But instead he brought his other hand up to touch her lips. "Can't say much of anything with your mouth all smashed up like that."

And she obviously wasn't going to say anything at all until he moved his hand away. So he did, only to have her turn her face from him, as well.

Clutching her purse tightly in front of her, she stared toward the editing console. "I don't want you showing the video tonight. I don't want my friends hurt."

He frowned. "Mel, I think they all know it's not a finished project. Knowledge being power, and all that, I'm pretty sure no one is going to get hurt by seeing what's been done."

"I've seen what's been done." Still, she didn't look at him. "And I beg to differ."

"Wait a minute." He shook his head, feeling as if he needed to shake off some sort of fog. "What are you talking about? When did you see any of the footage? Do you mean what you saw on the DVD I brought to the cookout?"

Her head whipped back in his direction so fast he marveled they both didn't suffer from whiplash. "No. I mean what I saw last night."

"Last night?" When would she have seen anything last night? Where had he been last night? He thought, thought, remembered. He and Asa in the office, working through the kinks that had to be cut. The office was the only place he'd run the tape. How had Melanie…

"The Webcam." He slammed his hand against the door.

Melanie jumped. "It wasn't a perfect screening, but I saw enough to know I'm not going to let you show that garbage to my friends."

Jacob shoved away from the door and headed for the windows on the opposite wall—as far away from Melanie as he could get. It wasn't garbage. Goddammit, it wasn't garbage. What she'd seen were outtakes he wasn't going to use. He'd run the lot of them by Asa first, making sure the other man shared his intuition.

But none of it was garbage. It was an honest look at the hardest working, sexiest bunch of women he'd even had the pleasure to know. And the fact that they blew off steam the way they did and with the men they loved, made him jealous as hell of their partners.

He'd been thinking he wanted the same with Melanie, but if she didn't trust him…

This time he slammed his hand against the supporting column. How the hell could she think that what she'd seen was what he intended to show today? Even knowing the documentary was far from being finished, she couldn't possibly believe what she'd seen would be anything he'd include in the final product.

So much for respect and humanity. His heart twisting, he hung his head and sighed. Headlights cut through the gaps in the miniblinds, sharply slicing his black T-shirt and his hand at his hip into what might as well be prison stripes.

Finally, he turned around and faced her across the immense expanse of the average-size room. "I'm not going to show garbage to anyone."

"This isn't your call to make," she said priggishly.

"Yeah, it is. It's my show. My call."

"Wrong, Faulkner. I may have been out of line the day of Lauren's wedding, getting in your face and not letting you do your job. But this isn't a wedding." She paused; he could hear her pull in a huge breath. "This is about my best friends and their reputations. It has nothing to do with me being a control freak or your artistic integrity. This is about you being wrong. And about me being right."

"No, sweetheart. It has to do with a lot more than that." He started his long walk across the room, wondering if she had any idea how absolutely furious he was. "It has to do with trust."

"Trust?"

"Trust." He drew even closer, one step, another, watching the widening white of her eyes. "I could tell you that I'm not going to show you and your friends

the footage you saw me going over with Asa. But I'm
not going to tell you anything except that it's time for
you to get your sweet little butt into the screening
room. The show is about to go on.''

WHEN SHE WALKED INTO her living room at the ridiculously late-for-her weeknight hour of 1:00 a.m., Melanie kicked off her shoes, sending them flying in the
direction of her entryway table. Her keys and tote followed. She'd never been the party-girl type, needing
instead a decent seven hours of sleep to recharge for
the following day.

But tonight she just hadn't been able to face going
home alone. Not after her confrontation with Jacob
and the exorbitant amount of emotion involved. So
she'd gone out with her girlfriends, who all wanted to
celebrate, each of them drinking way too much while
at Paddington's Ford. Nolan Ford had actually been in
the bar, and had picked up the tab after hearing Sydney rave about the documentary success.

Melanie hadn't raved at all. She'd wanted to crawl
under the table and die.

Success hardly covered the excellence of what Jacob had shown. And she'd had to sit there in the bar
and listen to each of her partners wax enthusiastic
while the voices she heard in her head were those of
her and Jacob arguing. No. Not arguing. She had accused, and Jacob had neither defended nor denied.
He'd simply told her to mind her own business.

She'd thought that was what she'd been doing.
Minding the business of gIRL-gEAR. But from first
frame to last, his documentary proved that she'd had
no need. That she'd been borrowing trouble instead of

giving Jacob the only thing he'd ever asked her to give.

Trust. The stuff on which true relationships were built, of which she'd shown a pitiable lack. She'd reacted on what she had seen rather than on what she should've known. Jacob's integrity would never have allowed him to cast his subjects in such a cruel light.

Instead of the bimbos she thought she would witness on screen, she'd seen Jacob's portrayal of the partners as competent businesswomen who were also unabashedly female. Yes, Sydney sat at the conference room table poring over bridal magazines, but it was all part of a clip showing a gIRL-gEAR feature on weddings.

Yes, Lauren doodled while chatting on the phone, but the doodles were graphic design ideas for new Web site pages. Yes, Chloe dug into pots of lip color and eye shadow like a little girl at her mother's dressing table, but on the other side of her desk sat a group of girls from the mentoring program intent on learning makeup techniques.

Everything Melanie had seen via the Webcam had been the truth, yet she'd accused Jacob of putting together a lie. She'd shown him nothing resembling trust, believing her eyes instead of her heart, which knew him so much better. She'd sat there in the darkened minitheater, listening to her partners giggle and chuckle and laugh until they cried.

She'd cried along with them, but for reasons that had nothing to do with being tickled by seeing herself on the big screen. She'd cried for all she'd ruined because she'd lost sight of what mattered—believing in the man she'd come to love so very much. And she'd never had the chance to tell him. Not even when she'd told him goodbye.

She'd been the last one to walk out the door. It had been so hard to hold her head as high as she had, knowing what she was walking away from. Jacob had stood there in the hallway outside of the screening room. He hadn't said "I told you so" as she'd expected him to. He'd simply looked determined to let her stew, to figure things out for herself.

The one thing that had made her departure even more brutal was that he hadn't let her go until she'd taken the videotape he'd forced into her hand. Outtakes from the documentary that he'd put together just for her, he'd said, his voice quiet when she'd expected a storm.

The calm had nearly killed her, and she couldn't bear the thought of going home alone to her condo, which seemed so empty when he wasn't there. She'd gotten used to having him around. So instead, she'd gone back to the office, where she could've easily watched the tape in private. Except she hadn't been sure she wanted to see it.

Though the minute she'd arrived home, having exited the city bus on the corner where she lived, she'd shoved the tape into the VCR, she still wasn't sure she wanted to watch. Why subject herself to further torture, except that maybe seeing this final kiss-off would at least finish breaking her heart? She would much rather completely kill her emotions and rise up again from the ashes. A phoenix and all that.

Except she doubted any man would ever again make her fly.

Melanie sighed. So she'd fly on her own. And she'd do it by making gIRL-gEAR the best it could be.

Stronger and better than the documentary had depicted. Come tomorrow morning she'd be in the office kicking ass and taking names. No more man-mooning and lunch hour quickies. It was time for this ship to shape up.

She wondered if anyone would listen.

She wondered if she'd ever sounded so arrogant.

She wondered when she'd finally get it through her head that the changes to the company had done nothing but make it stronger—exactly what Jacob's work had so brilliantly revealed. gIRL-gEAR and the partners were exactly the sort of role models for young women they'd always strived to be.

And she had screwed everything up by being so ridiculously obsessive over work instead of trusting the man she loved.

Sitting in total darkness, she reached for the remote control on her side table and hit Play. No more than three minutes into the tape, she pulled her legs onto the sofa and hugged her knees to her chest. She tucked her chin down, as well, hoping if she curled up into a tight enough ball she could contain the threatening sobs.

If Jacob's outtakes were meant to teach her a lesson, it was a lesson in the ways that he loved her. The clips were of her doing the things that captured his attention, that caused him to do a double-take, that caught him by the throat and wouldn't let him go. And she knew this because he was telling her. There on the tape.

He talked about no other woman being able to turn black into his favorite color, about how when she finally let herself go and laughed as she'd never laughed before, he heard the music of her voice for days to follow. He talked about loving her eyes even behind her glasses, loving her body even underneath her clothes.

And then he talked about seeing her at work, about how her aspirations to be her very best gave him the push he'd been needing to make a difference. Finally, with tears trickling down her cheeks and her nose a runny mess and her heart aching so fiercely that she had trouble drawing one even breath, he talked about making her a permanent part of his future because he couldn't imagine a day without having her in his life.

The video came to an end and she hit Rewind and watched it again. The third time she stopped it in the middle, shutting off both the VCR and the TV because she couldn't take another second of the miserable feeling that she'd messed up in ways she'd never be able to fix.

She let the darkness consume her, let herself grieve, because it had to be done. Going back to work tomorrow seemed an impossible feat. She couldn't imagine not having Jacob in the office, appearing out of nowhere as if he knew she'd been thinking about him.

Her head lolled back against the sofa cushions and she closed her eyes and breathed. God, was there any way to fix what had gone so horribly wrong? The silence of the condo wrapped around her coldly; she shivered and pulled her nana's afghan from the corner of the sofa around her shoulders, deciding this was where she was going to sleep. Moving required more strength than she'd ever have again.

Seconds later, her mind drifting, she heard the music begin to play. Her file of dance numbers, the one she'd stripped to that first time for Jacob, the one they'd made love to that amazing afternoon in his loft. Her heart raced when she finally realized the sound wasn't in her head but coming from the back of her condo.

With the afghan still around her shoulders, she made her way silently down the hall, treading softly in stocking feet. The rear was as dark as the front, the only lights shining those of clock LCD displays and bathroom night-lights and the PC monitor in her workout room.

She found Jacob there in the oddly lit darkness, sitting on the floor with his back to the pole, his legs pulled up, his wrists draped over his knees. His dark eyes flashed hotly when she moved into the doorway, as if he'd been waiting for her a very long time.

"What are you doing here?" She didn't care how he'd got in; he knew exactly where she kept her emergency key. "How long have you been here?"

"Which question do you want me to answer first?" he asked, his voice low and throaty, a gruff sort of bark that made her wary of his bite.

There was only one question to which she truly needed an answer. She wrapped the afghan tighter as she moved into the room. "Why the tape? Why didn't you tell me that what I'd seen was all wrong? Why did you let me think what I was thinking about you?"

The corner of his mouth lifted. "That's three questions."

"I can't count." She came even closer, feeling stirrings of hope she'd never expected to feel. Tentative feelings, but tentative was better than nothing when minutes ago what she'd felt had been despair. When his silence continued, she offered, "I can narrow them down to one."

He shook his head. "What were you thinking about me?"

"Thinking about you?"

He nodded, keeping eye contact while pushing himself up to his feet. The music continued to thrum in low sultry tones. Jacob's voice remained low, as well. "You asked why I'd let you think what you were thinking. I want to know what it was."

Honesty and trust and nothing else. Minutes ago she'd given up hope. But now...now... She shook her head.

Even if his eyes hinted that this might turn out the way she wanted, she couldn't prevaricate her way there. "I wasn't thinking. Not thinking straight, anyway. If I had been, I would've known you weren't capable of what I thought you were doing."

"Which was?"

"Putting a sensationalistic spin on the show." It took her a moment to gather the rest of her thoughts, a moment during which Jacob came toward her, his steps on the wooden floor thudding louder in her ears than the music's hard beat. "Using gIRL-gEAR as the means to an end—no matter the means. And no matter what might have well been the end of us."

At first he appeared sad, sad enough that her heart began to race furiously. Surely this wasn't going to be the end. He wouldn't have come here and waited for her if that was all he wanted. He was too smart and he knew her too well not to have guessed where her outburst had come from.

Except she was still having trouble accepting the conclusion to which she'd jumped when she stopped to consider all she knew about him. She hadn't stopped to consider anything except what on the surface had appeared to be a threat. That was *her* single-minded career tunnel vision at work, and she'd been so amazingly stupid.

Now, however, as she looked at him, as she saw that smile she'd come to love and the lights in his dark espresso eyes, now she saw an acceptance, as if he understood where she'd been coming from and shared rather than cast any blame.

"And why would you think that?" he asked.

She looked down at her toes, which peeked out from beneath the trailing afghan. "Because you've said more than one time how important this project is to your career."

"But you know better than that, don't you?" He took hold of the crocheted coverlet where she held it together. "Which is why my career isn't the real reason."

She looked up again, hardly able to see him clearly through the tears in her eyes. "It's always been about the company for me. I thought if I didn't have gIRLgEAR, I wouldn't have anything."

"Some things we have to figure out for ourselves."

"And what have you figured out?" she whispered, surprised she was able to get that much out.

"C'mere." He wrapped his arms around her, afghan and all.

She leaned her forehead against his chest, pulling in a sob that refused to stay contained.

He held her tighter. "It killed me to think you thought what you did—"

"Shh." She pressed her fingers to his lips. "I was stupid, putting the company first the way I've done for so many years instead of listening to my heart." She slid her hand around to cup his cheek, loving the prickly feel of his whiskers on her wrist. "I should've used my heart."

He turned his head, kissed her palm. "It's hard to use something that's been pretty much a nuisance for most of your life. At least it's been hard for me."

She touched the center of his chest where his heart was beating as madly as hers. "This heart?"

He gave a humorous snort and pulled her even closer. "Yeah. That one. It's all yours, Melanie. All yours."

"Oh, Jacob." He was giving her his heart. And all she could do was nuzzle her face into the soft skin there at the base of his throat. He smelled wonderful, sweet and warm like the man she knew better than anyone, her best friend and her lover, and she would never let him go. "I love you, too."

"So?" he asked gingerly, shifting his weight from one foot to the other. "What do we do now?"

She absolutely adored his nervousness. "You know what I'd love to do—and I know this is going to scare the crap out of you."

"What's that?"

"Talk." She looked up, again holding his face. She would never get enough of looking at him. She'd had no idea she could actually be this happy. "Without any interruptions for days on end if we want. There's so much I want to know about you."

"I think you know most of what's important. I love you."

"Oh, Jacob, I love you, too." And she kissed him. "Still…how about a weekend at a quiet bed-and-breakfast? I happen to have one paid in full that I've never used."

He took a moment to consider, then teasingly said,

"As long as room service will deliver the breakfast, because I plan to take full advantage of the bed."

"Well, as long as you take full advantage of me, then you've got yourself a deal."

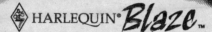

**HARLEQUIN® *Blaze*™**

"(NO STRINGS ATTACHED) battle of the sexes will delight, tantalize and entertain with Kent's indomitable style. Delicious! Very highly recommended."
—*Wordweaving.com*

"(ALL TIED UP) is hot, sexy and still manages to involve the reader emotionally—a winning combination."
—*AllAboutRomance.com*

"With electrifying tension, creative scenes and...seductive characters, Alison Kent delivers a knockout read."
—*Romantic Times* Book Club

Find out why everybody's talking about Blaze author Alison Kent and check out the latest books in her gIRL-gEAR miniseries!

## #99 STRIPTEASE
August 2003

## #107 WICKED GAMES
October 2003

## #115 INDISCREET
December 2003

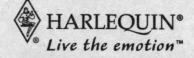

**HARLEQUIN®**
*Live the emotion*™

# Is your man too good to be true?

### Hot, gorgeous AND romantic?
### If so, he could be a Harlequin® Blaze™ series cover model!

Our grand-prize winners will receive a trip for two to New York City to shoot the cover of a Blaze novel, and will stay at the luxurious Plaza Hotel.

Plus, they'll receive $500 U.S. spending money!

The runner-up winners will receive $200 U.S. to spend on a romantic dinner for two.

### It's easy to enter!

In 100 words or less, tell us what makes your boyfriend or spouse a true romantic and the perfect candidate for the cover of a Blaze novel, and include in your submission two photos of this potential cover model.

All entries must include the written submission of the contest entrant, two photographs of the model candidate and the Official Entry Form and Publicity Release forms completed in full and signed by both the model candidate and the contest entrant. Harlequin, along with the experts at Elite Model Management, will select a winner.

For photo and complete Contest details, please refer to the Official Rules on the next page. All entries will become the property of Harlequin Enterprises Ltd. and are not returnable.

**Please visit www.blazecovermodel.com to download a copy of the Official Entry Form and Publicity Release Form or send a request to one of the addresses below.**

Please mail your entry to: **Harlequin Blaze Cover Model Search**

| In U.S.A. | In Canada |
|---|---|
| P.O. Box 9069 | P.O. Box 637 |
| Buffalo, NY | Fort Erie, ON |
| 14269-9069 | L2A 5X3 |

No purchase necessary. Contest open to Canadian and U.S. residents who are 18 and over.
Void where prohibited. Contest closes September 30, 2003.

◆ HARLEQUIN® *Blaze*™

HBCVRMODEL1

# HARLEQUIN BLAZE COVER MODEL SEARCH CONTEST 3569 OFFICIAL RULES
## NO PURCHASE NECESSARY TO ENTER

1. To enter, submit two (2) 4" x 6" photographs of a boyfriend or spouse (who must be 18 years of age or older) taken no later than three (3) months from the time of entry: a close-up, waist up, shirtless photograph; and a fully clothed, full-length photograph, then, tell us, in 100 words or fewer, why he should be a Harlequin Blaze cover model and how he is romantic. Your complete "entry" must include: (i) your essay, (ii) the Official Entry Form and Publicity Release Form printed below completed and signed by you (as "Entrant"), (iii) the photographs (with your hand-written name, address and phone number, and your model's name, address and phone number on the back of each photograph), and (iv) the Publicity Release Form and Photograph Representation Form printed below completed and signed by your model (as "Model"), and should be sent via first-class mail to either: Harlequin Blaze Cover Model Search Contest 3569, P.O. Box 9069, Buffalo, NY, 14269-9069, or Harlequin Blaze Cover Model Search Contest 3569, P.O. Box 637, Fort Erie, Ontario L2A 5X3. All submissions must be in English and be received no later than September 30, 2003. Limit: one entry per person, household or organization. **Purchase or acceptance of a product offer does not improve your chances of winning.** All entry requirements must be strictly adhered to for eligibility and to ensure fairness among entries.

2. Ten (10) Finalist submissions (photographs and essays) will be selected by a panel of judges consisting of members of the Harlequin editorial, marketing and public relations staff, as well as a representative from Elite Model Management (Toronto) Inc., based on the following criteria:

Aptness/Appropriateness of submitted photographs for a Harlequin Blaze cover—70%
Originality of Essay—20%
Sincerity of Essay—10%

In the event of a tie, duplicate finalists will be selected. The photographs submitted by finalists will be posted on the Harlequin website no later than November 15, 2003 (at www.blazecovermodel.com), and viewers may vote, in rank order, on their favorite(s) to assist in the panel of judges' final determination of the Grand Prize and Runner-up winning entries based on the above judging criteria. All decisions of the judges are final.

3. All entries become the property of Harlequin Enterprises Ltd. and none will be returned. Any entry may be used for future promotional purposes. Elite Model Management (Toronto) Inc. and/or its partners, subsidiaries and affiliates operating as "Elite Model Management" will have access to all entries including all personal information and may contact any Entrant and/or Model in its sole discretion for its own business purposes. Harlequin and Elite Model Management (Toronto) Inc. are separate entities with no legal association or partnership whatsoever having no power to bind or obligate the other or create any expressed or implied obligation or responsibility on behalf of the other, such that Harlequin shall not be responsible in any way for any acts or omissions of Elite Model Management (Toronto) Inc. or its partners, subsidiaries and affiliates in connection with the Contest or otherwise and Elite Model Management shall not be responsible in any way for any acts or omissions of Harlequin or its partners, subsidiaries and affiliates in connection with the contest or otherwise.

4. All Entrants and Models must be residents of the U.S. or Canada, be 18 years of age or older, and have no prior criminal convictions. The contest is not open to any Model that is a professional model and/or actor in any capacity at the time of the entry. Contest void wherever prohibited by law; all applicable laws and regulations apply. Any litigation within the Province of Quebec regarding the conduct or organization of a publicity contest may be submitted to the Régie des alcools, des courses et des jeux for a ruling, and any litigation regarding the awarding of a prize may be submitted to the Régie only for the purpose of helping the parties reach a settlement. Employees and immediate family members of Harlequin Enterprises Ltd., D.L. Blair, Inc., Elite Model Management (Toronto) Inc. and their parents, affiliates, subsidiaries and all other agencies, entities and persons connected with the use, marketing or conduct of this Contest are not eligible to enter. Acceptance of any prize offered constitutes permission to use Entrants' and Models' names, essay submissions, photographs or other likenesses for the purposes of advertising, trade, publication and promotion on behalf of Harlequin Enterprises Ltd., its parent, affiliates, subsidiaries, assigns and other authorized entities involved in the judging and promotion of the contest without further compensation to any Entrant or Model, unless prohibited by law.

5. Finalists will be determined no later than October 30, 2003. Prize Winners will be determined no later than January 31, 2004. Grand Prize Winners (consisting of winning Entrant and Model) will be required to sign and return Affidavit of Eligibility/Release of Liability and Model Release forms within thirty (30) days of notification. Non-compliance with this requirement and within the specified time period will result in disqualification and an alternate will be selected. Any prize notification returned as undeliverable will result in the awarding of the prize to an alternate set of winners. All travelers (or parent/legal guardian of a minor) must execute the Affidavit of Eligibility/Release of Liability prior to ticketing and must possess required travel documents (e.g. valid photo ID) where applicable. Travel dates specified by Sponsor but no later than May 30, 2004.

6. Prizes: One (1) Grand Prize—the opportunity for the Model to appear on the cover of a paperback book from the Harlequin Blaze series, and a 3 day/2 night trip for two (Entrant and Model) to New York, NY for the photo shoot of Model which includes round-trip coach air transportation from the commercial airport nearest the winning Entrant's home to New York, NY, (or, in lieu of air transportation, $100 cash payable to Entrant and Model, if the winning Entrant's home is within 250 miles of New York, NY), hotel accommodations (double occupancy) at the Plaza Hotel and $500 cash spending money payable to Entrant and Model, (approximate prize value: $8,000), and one (1) Runner-up Prize of $200 cash payable to Entrant and Model for a romantic dinner for two (approximate prize value: $200). Prizes are valued in U.S. currency. Prizes consist of only those items listed as part of the prize. No substitution of prize(s) permitted by winners. All prizes are awarded jointly to the Entrant and Model of the winning entries, and are not severable - prizes and obligations may not be assigned or transferred. Any change to the Entrant and/or Model of the winning entries will result in disqualification and an alternate will be selected. Taxes on prize are the sole responsibility of winners. Any and all expenses and/or items not specifically described as part of the prize are the sole responsibility of winners. Harlequin Enterprises Ltd. and D.L. Blair, Inc., their parents, affiliates, and subsidiaries are not responsible for errors in printing of Contest entries and/or game pieces. No responsibility is assumed for lost, stolen, late, illegible, incomplete, inaccurate, non-delivered, postage due or misdirected mail or entries. In the event of printing or other errors which may result in unintended prize values or duplication of prizes, all affected game pieces or entries shall be null and void.

7. Winners will be notified by mail. For winners' list (available after March 31, 2004), send a self-addressed, stamped envelope to: Harlequin Blaze Cover Model Search Contest 3569 Winners, P.O. Box 4200, Blair, NE 68009-4200, or refer to the Harlequin website (at www.blazecovermodel.com).

Contest sponsored by Harlequin Enterprises Ltd., P.O. Box 9042, Buffalo, NY 14269-9042.

HBCVRMODEL2

# eHARLEQUIN.com

The eHarlequin.com online community is *the* place to share opinions, thoughts and feelings!

- Joining the community is easy, fun and **FREE!**

- Connect with **other romance fans** on our message boards.

- Meet your **favorite authors** without leaving home!

- **Share opinions** on books, movies, celebrities…and *more!*

### Here's what our members say:

"I love the friendly and helpful atmosphere filled with support and humor."
—Texanna (eHarlequin.com member)

"Is this the place for me, or what? There is nothing I love more than 'talking' books, especially with fellow readers who are reading the same ones I am."
—Jo Ann (eHarlequin.com member)

**Join today by visiting**
**www.eHarlequin.com!**

INTCOMM